Fred's heart leaped when she saw that the person coming through the door was in fact a person, one hundred percent human-looking, and not some kind of hellbeast.

The first thing he did after he'd closed the door behind himself, before he even looked her way, was to sniff the air.

So maybe not so human after all? Fred wondered.

"Blood," he said, his voice calm and even. Fred would have thought it was a pleasant voice, under other circumstances. "Cut yourself." It wasn't a question.

Now he looked at Fred. She'd tucked the hinge pin into the waistband of her skirt, but the rest of her mess was in plain sight. She held up her bloody arm. "A little, yes," she said. "I don't suppose you have a bandage on you? Or maybe an emergency room doctor?

"You won't need one," the man said.

Angel™

City Of
Not Forgotten
Redemption
Close to the Ground
Shakedown
Hollywood Noir
Avatar
Soul Trade
Bruja
The Summoned
Haunted
Image
Stranger to the Sun
Vengeance
Angel: The Casefiles, Vol. 1—The Official Companion
Endangered Species
Angel: The Longest Night, Vol. 1
Impressions
Fearless
Sanctuary

Buffy/Angel Crossovers:

Unseen #1: The Burning
Unseen #2: Door to Alternity
Unseen #3: Long Way Home
Monster Island

Available from Simon Pulse and Pocket Books

The Essential Angel Posterbook

Available from Pocket Books

ANGEL™

sanctuary

Jeff Mariotte

An original novel based on the television series
created by Joss Whedon & David Greenwalt

SIMON PULSE

New York   London   Toronto   Sydney   Singapore

This one is for Andy, who looks so good in green.

Historian's note: This story takes place during the third season of Angel, before the episode "This Old Gang of Mine."

First Simon Pulse edition April 2003
Text copyright © 2003 Twentieth Century Fox Film Corporation.
All Rights Reserved.

SIMON PULSE
An imprint of Simon & Schuster
Children's Publishing Division
1230 Avenue of the Americas
New York, NY 10020

The text of this book was set in New Caledonia.

Printed in the United States of America
10 9 8 7 6 5 4 3 2 1

Library of Congress Control Number 2002117779
ISBN 0-689-85664-4

Thanks to Lisa Clancy and Lisa Gribbin of Simon & Schuster, Debbie Olshan at Fox, the gang at Mutant Enemy, and the cast of *Angel*. Also big props to Tara, Howard, Ryan, Maryelizabeth, Holly, and Dave. They keep me safe.

CHAPTER ONE

"Do you ever get that all-dressed-up-no particular-place-to-go feeling, cats and kittens? I know I used to, but that's why I opened Caritas. Now I can just roll out of bed, don my finest duds, *et voilà*, someplace to be, to see and be seen, a sanctuary for the spirit, a haven for the hideous. Outside it's a dark world and getting darker, but in here it's all bright lights and big dreams. And speaking of big, our first performer tonight is Mif'tal, a Nemchuk, as big as Moby Dick but with a heart to match. Mif'tal's a pussycat, people, and he's here to thrill with his rendition of 'Like a Virgin.'" Lorne paused for a moment, ticking his red eyes to the right to watch the behemoth shamble onto the elevated stage, and then leaned into the microphone, speaking sotto voce. "But don't get the wrong idea, folks. Mif'tal's married, and it's just a song."

He surrendered the stage, and the Nemchuk took the mike in one enormous, clawed hand, beginning to sway as the music swelled from the speakers. Mif'tal wasn't quite as big as the Host had implied, but he was massive and muscular, with sharp-edged fins protruding above each eye like a fifties-era Buick, and a mouth that seemed overstuffed with multiple rows of tiny, daggerlike teeth. His skin was green, but lighter than Lorne's, almost the color of mint ice cream. When he sang, his voice was raspy, but he carried a tune well. Angel watched Lorne flash a smile at Mif'tal's mate, sitting stage side at one of the small tables, and then work his way through the room to the table where the Angel Investigations gang waited.

"I'm so glad you folks could make it tonight," Lorne said when he reached them, his smile wide and welcoming. Lorne—more formally, Angel knew, Krevlornswath of the Deathwok Clan, late of a dimension called Pylea—was decked out in a typically colorful ensemble. An open-necked yellow shirt set off his dark green skin and red lips, eyes, and horns well, accentuating the blond highlights in his hair. His Italian silk suit was royal blue and just shiny enough to fairly glow when the spotlight was on him—which was often; Lorne seemed to have been born to the spotlight.

"We wouldn't have missed it for the world,"

Cordelia Chase said brightly. She rose to give Lorne a hug, which he accepted with open arms. "After all, it's your party, right?"

"*Absolument*," Lorne replied. He released Cordy and spread his arms wide again. "Whatever you darlings want tonight is on the house. After all, what's a little profit margin between friends? It's the least I can do to repay you all for what you did in Pylea."

Angel nodded. He, Lorne, Wesley Wyndam-Pryce, and Charles Gunn had followed Cordelia to the Host's home dimension when she had accidentally passed through a portal between their worlds. By the time they'd arrived, Cordy had been made a princess, but one who was subject to the whims of the priests who really controlled the dimension. Working with local rebels, though, they managed to overthrow the priests, destroy the Slave-killer console with which the priests ruled, and install a mighty warrior called the Groosalugg on the throne. Returning to their own dimension, they had brought with them a young human named Winifred Burkle, who had been sucked through a portal years before and had spent much of her five years there in a cave, hiding from the Pylean rulers.

Lorne had promised them a party at Caritas, his karaoke bar-slash-demon sanctuary, as a small token of his appreciation for having freed his world from the scourge of slavery. He preferred

Los Angeles to Pylea—there was no music in Pylea, for one thing, and he was looked on as a bit of a social pariah there—but he was nevertheless grateful for what they'd done.

Now, moving around the table, he extended his arms to Fred. She looked away, still shy about contact with others after her years alone in the cave, but she wrapped her thin arms around him and squeezed the demon tightly. When she sat down again, Angel noticed that her cheeks were crimsoning but her beaming smile was genuine.

He watched Lorne work the table, clasping hands with Gunn, shaking Wesley's in a more traditional fashion, as befitted the occasionally stuffy British ex-Watcher, and felt enveloped in a rare cloud of peace and comfort. As a unique individual, a vampire with a soul, Angel was never fully at home in the world of light or darkness. He couldn't walk in the sun with humans, but it had become his calling to do battle against others of his kind: vampires, demons, and night creatures who preyed upon humans. Most of the people whose lives he saved remained ignorant of the threat that waited for them in the dark hours. So Angel was a stranger to both, caught between two worlds with a foot in each, and only really at rest with the people seated around this table, his surrogate family. And, of course, here at Caritas, where all demons were accepted and the rules, strictly observed, prohibited any kind of combat between them.

Caritas had been trashed by their reentry from Pylea in Angel's GTX—the portal had deposited the car right in the middle of the club—but Lorne had rebuilt it, better and brighter than before. Arches behind the bar held glass shelves containing fluids of every description, including many that humans never sampled. Carefully placed spotlights reflected off the tabletops so rainbow-hued beverages seemed to glow from within. The Host was justifiably proud of his renovation, and the party tonight had been intended to show it off, Angel suspected, as much as to express his appreciation for the group's efforts.

Finally Lorne stopped in front of Angel, who rose from his seat to embrace the green-skinned Pylean. "The place looks great," Angel said sincerely. "Really."

"Thanks, sugar buns," Lorne replied. Angel had learned long ago not to make anything of the Host's somewhat over-the-top endearments. "I couldn't have done it without—well, you know, without your driving your car through and wrecking it in the first place," Lorne continued. "But the end result is definitely worth it, I think."

"Yeah," Angel agreed. The club really did look spectacular. He glanced toward the stage, where Mif'tal was wrapping up his Madonna song. "You going to read him?"

Lorne was an anagogic demon—he could read the auras of anyone who sang in his presence. But he shook his head. "Mif'tal knows his path. He just comes to sing."

The crowd broke into applause as the Nemchuk ended the song and took a deep bow.

"You're on again."

"I'm always on, Angel," Lorne said. His usual smile vanished, and he was serious for a moment, staring into Angel's eyes. "You did me a solid, Jackson. Anything I can do for you, anytime, you know all you have to do is say the word, right?"

"I know," Angel said, certain the demon would live up to that promise. "I appreciate it."

Lorne turned on the smile again, neon-brilliant. "Duty calls." He started back toward the stage. "But you're off-duty tonight," he tossed back over his shoulder. "Relax, drink up, enjoy the show."

The room burst into honest applause when the Nemchuk finished his number, and as Lorne took the microphone from the demon's sharp-clawed hand the spotlight settled on him. He opened his mouth to speak, but in the hushed moment before he could get a word out, a muffled boom sounded from outside the club. Lorne's smile vanished.

Bedlam reigned.

"What's that?" someone shouted. Other voices joined in, creating a chaotic chorus. Demons leaped to their feet, rushing toward the exit.

"We're under attack!"

"An explosion!"

"A bomb!"

Angel didn't think it was an attack—the doors to Caritas weren't kept locked during business hours, so if anyone did have it in mind to attack the place, they wouldn't tip their hand by exploding a bomb outside. But it did sound like an explosion of some kind. Angel had had enough experience with those—one had very nearly taken Wesley's life, and another ally, Doyle, had been lost to a bomb's blast—to be nervous about the demons dashing outside without knowing what might await them. He tried to shout over the din, but his warnings went unheard.

Unable to prevent the club-goers from running outside, Angel decided the next best thing was to join them. He shoved his way through the throng—demons of every shape, size, and description, in varying stages of panic or curiosity, all pushing toward the single exit. But even among these creatures, Angel's reputation was well known, and they let the vampire pass.

Outside, the world was fiery pandemonium.

The building directly across the street from Caritas was engulfed in flames. Fire gouted from unglassed windows, and thick dark smoke roiled up into the nighttime sky. Chunks of steel and concrete littered the street, some still smoldering or red-hot. Car alarms blared. Sirens screamed in the distance, already converging on the spot.

The demons stood transfixed by the sight. Normally their innate caution would have kept them inside, safe from the possibility of being observed by humankind. But whether it was curiosity or concern or sheer weight of numbers, they stood watching the fire with seemingly no regard to their own security. Angel watched as Lorne moved quietly among them, urging them back inside. Out here, faces raised to the fire, eyes wide, flames washing them all in warm yellow light, their individual colors faded and they all looked like they might be members of the same tribe.

"What's over there?" he demanded when the Pylean came near.

Lorne shrugged. "The monstrosity is still under construction. Has been for a long time, but it's been stalled out for a few months now. I think the developer ran out of money. You want my guess, it's probably an arson job, to collect insurance money since he can't afford to finish the building and lease the space out. Either that or some architecture lover on a rampage."

"I take it you're not a fan," Angel observed.

"It's an eyesore. If I'd thought of burning it down myself, I'd have done it long ago. Well, that and if I didn't have a morbid fear of prison."

The sirens were coming closer, and Lorne's

urgency to get his guests back inside increased. "Let's go, everyone!" he called anxiously. "Off the street, people. We're going to have company in a minute. Lots of it. And not the kind we want to party with."

As he turned back to Angel, a squeal of tires sounded at the corner. "You've gotta help me herd them inside, big guy," he insisted. "It's not so much that they've never seen fire—it's that some of them love it so much, they hate to leave it behind."

Angel glanced away from Lorne and down the street, toward the corner where he'd heard the vehicle coming. There were no flashing lights, though, which was strange—if it had been a fire truck, he'd expect lights and sirens, not just screeching tires. But he saw no fire truck, just a dark car roaring down the middle of the street toward them, windows rolled down and bristling with what looked like narrow steel pipes.

"Everybody down!" Angel shouted. He shoved the nearest demons to the ground and hurled himself on top of Cordelia and Wes, driving them down. Others, seeing for themselves what Angel had spotted, flattened. Screams sounded in a variety of voices, human and otherwise, but then all voices were drowned out by the staccato bursts of gunfire from the car as it raced past. In the flashes of light from their weapons' muzzles, Angel could see that the shooters were demon, not human. Their skin had a bluish cast to it, he thought, and had a texture different from normal human skin—*maybe bumpier, or with low ridges or small horns.*

He was on his feet as soon as the gunfire stopped, ready to race off after the car. "Everyone okay?" he asked before he went. "Is anyone hit?"

A chorus of negatives greeted him. In spite of the density of possible victims, there seemed to be no injuries, so maybe the intent was just to frighten them, not kill anyone. Demons and humans alike found their footing and dusted themselves off. Angel was taking a last look around before going in search of the car when he heard Gunn's voice, trembling with near-panic. "Anybody seen Fred?" he asked. "She's gone. Angel, Fred's gone!"

"No, she can't be," Wesley replied calmly. *The voice of reason,* Angel thought. *Good old Wes.* "She's just gone inside or something, I'm sure of it. Let's just check."

"No, man, I'm tellin' you, she was right here. Before that car came down, I saw her, back near the door. I was gonna go get her. When I got up, she was gone."

"Are you sure?" Cordelia asked him. Her hand trembled a little as she made a flat-palmed gesture to indicate Fred's approximate height. "She's little, right? Maybe she's, you know, standing behind one of those big demons or something." Her tone didn't sound as certain as her words, though. "Fred!" she shouted anxiously. "Oh, Fred!"

"I looked inside," Gunn said defiantly. "And checked with the bartender. He hasn't seen her either."

"Fred!" Wesley started calling, and Gunn joined in. Angel didn't bother adding his voice to the choir, but went back down the stairs and looked around the still largely empty club for himself, just in case. She was small, and had a knack for squeezing herself into tight places. But she wasn't there. When he came back out, demons streamed in past him. Firefighters really were starting to arrive now, and the demons were finally heading inside, where they'd stay until the coast was clear enough for them to make their way back to their homes.

Lorne touched Angel's arm. "Look, Angel, I know she's a friend of yours—I love her to bits too. But Fred is a bit on the . . . well, solitary side. She may not exactly be a hermit anymore, but she's not Miss Congeniality, either. Do you suppose she might have just wandered away someplace while we weren't looking?"

Angel shook his head. He'd already thought of the possibility, and dismissed it. "She wouldn't. Especially with the gunfire. She might find a hiding place and stay in it, but not if she'd heard us calling her. She'd come out for us. And her purse is still on the table. Not that she has much to carry in it, but she likes it."

"You're right," Lorne agreed. "Which is almost too bad, because it doesn't really leave a lot of other options."

"Meaning what?"

"Meaning, if she didn't go anyplace of her own free will and she's not here, there aren't a lot of choices left. Either somebody booked her a return ticket to Pylea, or she's been kidnapped."

Gunn, Wesley, and Cordelia were the only ones left on the sidewalk with Angel and Lorne now. Fire trucks and emergency vehicles choked the street. Police officers watched as firefighters hooked hoses to a hydrant and began to play powerful jets of water across the burning building. A couple of them glanced toward Caritas.

"Get back inside with your guests, Lorne," Angel warned, blocking the Host from anyone's view. "You don't want to be seen out here."

"Yeah, okay. I'll try to find out if any of them saw anything. If Fred was snatched, someone would have noticed, right? Nobody gets out until I find out everything they saw."

Angel nodded, distracted, and Lorne disappeared down the stairs. Gunn, Cordy, and Wes looked stricken. "We've gotta find her, man," Gunn said, his voice tight with rage.

"We will, Gunn," Wesley assured him. "She can't have gone far. Remember, this is what we do."

"And we're good at it," Cordelia added. "We almost always find who we're looking for. I meant to say always. Always always, twice for emphasis. Look at Angel, he's already got an idea."

It shows on my face? Angel wondered. *Whatever, she's right.* "It's just a hunch, but what if this is all part of a larger plot?" he suggested. "Either all of these events happened at once by pure coincidence—which is hard to believe. Or else the bomb was meant to draw us outside. The drive-by—look, if they really wanted to hit some of us, they could have, we were all just standing there in a big clump. That was meant to distract us while somebody grabbed Fred."

"You could be right," Gunn said. "Pretty elaborate, though. Who? And why? What do they want with her?"

"If we knew the answer to that, we'd know where to find her," Wesley offered.

"Then we'll find out," Angel declared. "And we don't let up until we have her back."

CHAPTER TWO

"Slight change of plans for the evening, folks," Lorne announced from the stage, speaking with uncharacteristic gravity. "A friend of mine is missing, and it's just possible that one of you saw something that will help us find her—even if it's not something you think is significant or important. So we're all going to stay put in here while I talk to each of you, one on one, okay? Don't think of it as a hardship, think of it as sparkling conversation with your charming and talented Host."

There were some groans from the audience, and Lorne could see at a glance that this wasn't going to be particularly popular.

"You can't go out the front door, anyway," he reminded them. "Not with all those firefighters and cops out there. So stay put, enjoy the music, and"—he hated to take it this far, but it was what airlines did when planes were stuck on the tarmac for too long, and maybe it would loosen some tongues—"and the free drinks!"

At this announcement, cheers outnumbered the groans. *That's more like it,* Lorne thought. *No difference between demons and humans in that respect. If it's free, they're in favor of it.* "So who's up first?" he asked, filling his voice with enthusiasm. "Who's got a song they're dying to sing? Who wants to excite our ears with their dulcet tones?"

A Brachen demon Lorne vaguely knew pushed his chair back from his table and rose. "I'll go," he offered with a wan half-smile. His name was Stark, Lorne remembered, and like all Brachens he had soft blue spikes jutting out from his flesh, pincushion-style. He was a mild sort, and seemed a bit hesitant to approach the stage.

"Excellent, Mr. Stark," Lorne said effusively. "Mr. Stark here has a terrific voice, gang—think Robert Goulet, only with even more personality. What are you going to sing for us tonight, Mr. Stark?"

"I thought I'd go for 'I Write the Songs,'" Stark replied.

Lorne clapped his hands together once. "Perfect," he said. "Look out, Barry Manilow. Who in fact *didn't* write that one, of course—Barry's megahit was penned by none other than L.A.'s own Beach Boy Bruce Johnston. So who said irony is dead? Cue it up, maestro!"

He surrendered the stage to Stark, who swayed uncertainly at the microphone as the first notes of the song began to play. Lorne didn't have any particular plan in mind beyond, as he'd said, talking to every single demon in the club tonight to see if they knew anything or had seen anything that could help locate Fred. He knew that, in human society, police detectives would have done the same thing. But human cops weren't likely to be called in on this case, and even if they were they'd get no cooperation from the clientele of Caritas. The peaceful coexistence of demons and humans was tenuous at best, no doubt aided by the fact that most humans didn't know that demons existed. If they did, the story would certainly be different. As it was, demons made most of the necessary concessions to live in a human-dominated world. If the humans knew what they shared the planet with, though, they'd likely spare no expense or effort to wipe out the demon population.

With no more developed plan than he had, Lorne decided to just start at the nearest table to the stage and work his way around the club table by table. As Stark began belting out the first chorus—*he really is good,* the Host thought, *once he gets past his initial intestinal butterflies*—Lorne pulled out a chair and sat down across the small table from a Skander demon. Before he spoke he watched

Stark for a moment, getting a sense of the Brachen's path. He reasoned that if anyone remaining in the club had been involved with Fred's disappearance, that might show up in a reading. But from Stark all he got was a sense of deep sadness relating to a romantic complication. If Stark had asked him for a reading he'd have to tell the demon that he should give up on the human woman he'd been courting, since it was clear that the relationship would only end in heartbreak for him if he pursued it.

Which didn't rule him out in any way—the trouble with Lorne's empathic power was that it couldn't predict with certain accuracy and it couldn't focus only on certain topics. He saw what he saw, but usually that was only a glimpse, the merest fraction, of someone's possible future. Never the whole picture.

Lorne turned away from the stage and faced the Skander demon. "Enjoying the show?" he asked by way of an opening.

The Skander barely glanced at him and grunted something that may have been an affirmative. Skanders weren't known as excessively skilled in the social graces—*kind of like Angel in that regard,* Lorne thought offhandedly.

"You heard about what happened?" Lorne prodded. "The girl disappearing? Angel's associate, Winifred?"

"Heard about it," the Skander answered plainly. "Everybody heard about it. Don't know anything, though."

Lorne looked at the Skander carefully, as if he could read the demon's aura even without the singing. The Skander's skin was a flat gray, like freshly poured cement, roadmapped with blue and purple veins. His face was broad and flat, with two glowing orange eyes set far apart under a heavy ridge of brow and a thick-lipped mouth filled with what seemed like hundreds of small, needle-pointed teeth. He had gone heavy on the cologne, which seemed odd considering the unpleasant physical form he took. Skanders could cast glamours, Lorne knew, changing how anyone perceived them, and he wondered why they would choose to walk around in what he believed to be their natural, but horrendously ugly, form. *Why not pick a more pleasing shape,* he thought, *like mine?*

Perhaps more significantly, Skanders were dimensional travelers, capable of opening—even creating, according to some scholars—hidden dimensional portals wherever they went. And it made sense that since Fred had been spirited away virtually behind everybody's backs, a dimensional portal would have been one way to do it. Lorne was determined to keep his suspicions to himself, though, and to try to approach each interview with an open mind. "You went outside, though," he said, "when the first big bang went off, right? Tell me what you saw with your own baby blues. Or oranges, as the case may be."

The Skander's voice sounded like rocks being run through a food processor. "I saw a building on fire. Then I came back in."

"Look, handsome," Lorne urged him. "We're all kind of in this together, you know. So you might as well be cooperative, because we're going to be here a long time if you hold back on me. What's your name, friend? You know mine."

"Quortloothtonsiv," the Skander told him, his voice expressionless. One of his meaty hands was wrapped around a martini glass, and he took a quick drink from it.

Lorne tossed him a smile. "Let's just go with Quort, okay? It'd take me all night just to learn that. So, backtracking, Quort. You went outside and there was a building on fire. What else?"

"Hurt my eyes." Quort touched the gray skin beneath his right eye with one sausagelike finger. The eye had an internal glow, as if some of the fire was trapped inside it. "They're sensitive to light."

"I'm sorry to hear that, brother," Lorne said with genuine sympathy. It happened to a lot of the demonic races—they spent most of their time in the dark, trying to remain unnoticed by the human world, until bright light became painful to see. "Go on."

The Skander sighed, as if realizing that the Host

19

wasn't going to leave him in peace until he elaborated on his story. "I saw the fire and turned away," he said. "I was blinking and my eyes were watering from the light. Then I heard the car coming, and looked up again. I still wasn't seeing clearly, because of the fire, but I thought maybe they were Roshons, in the car."

"Roshons?" Lorne echoed. "Really?"

"Like I said, my vision was pretty blurry. But maybe."

Roshons were vicious, predatory flesh eaters, Lorne knew. They had no love at all for humans, except maybe as between-meal snacks. They even tended to keep away from places like Caritas, where demons who could get along with humankind were tolerated. Roshons preferred the company of their own kind, but Lorne had never heard of them attacking a mixed group of demons before. *It would have been more like them,* he thought, *to go out and stalk a single human, or even a small group of them, for the sport of it.* If they did pull off something like the night's drive-by shooting, there would have to be a profit element to it, as Roshons were basically gangsters of the demonic world.

"Why do you think that?"

"The shapes of their heads, mainly," Quort answered. "I mean, it could have been a bunch of baldheaded humans with strange growths on their heads and blue skin, but how likely is that?"

"Not very," Lorne agreed. "You're pretty sure about the blue skin? Because I was thinking green." He held out one of his hands and looked at it thoughtfully. "Although not as rich and pleasant a shade as my own, of course."

"I told you, I can't be sure of anything." There was an undercurrent of anger in the Skander's voice, probably in reaction to Lorne's insistent questioning. "You asked what I think I saw, so I'm telling you. You don't want to hear it, move on and bug somebody else."

"I'm not finished bugging you," Lorne said quickly, with a smile he hoped was ingratiating enough to calm the big guy down. "I just want to hear your story as well as you can tell it."

Quort nodded once, curtly, and toyed with his glass. Lorne noticed that he'd emptied it and snapped his fingers, pointing at the glass, for Luis the bartender to refill. "Okay, then. I thought maybe they were Roshons, but I wasn't sure. I saw the guns and I ducked."

"Can't blame you for that."

"Right. They opened fire—although if they'd really wanted to do some damage, doesn't it seem like there'd be dead demons all over the sidewalk? Big group like that, all standing close together, makes a pretty easy target, doesn't it?"

"Good point," Lorne said, surprised. Angel had

thought of that, but he was an experienced detective.

"Doesn't take much thinking to figure it out," Quort followed up. "They wanted to make some noise, scare some of us. They weren't really looking to kill."

"But why?" Lorne wondered. "Unless they're trying to tell me something about my business insurance. . . ."

"Create a distraction, is my guess. That's when the human disappeared, right?"

"Fred. Her name's Fred. Winifred Burkle, really," Lorne insisted. He didn't want anyone to lose sight of what was really at stake—Fred's safety, maybe her life. "She's a perfectly lovely young lady."

"She's a human. Far as I'm concerned, the fewer the better. And she's a friend of Angel's, right?"

"Well, yes," Lorne replied, feeling defensive now. "Of Angel's and of mine, now that you mention it. What about it?"

"Angel hates our kind. He's a demon-killing machine. I've heard he'll kill demons whenever he can, he doesn't care who or why or what they've done. I'm surprised you even let him in here, with all the blood on his hands."

"You were sitting in here with him earlier. Did he kill anyone then?"

"This is a safe zone—even *he* respects Caritas.

But if he caught any of us outside, you think he'd hesitate for a second?"

Lorne was astonished to see the conversation take this turn, though perhaps he shouldn't have been. He'd never felt at any risk from Angel. He knew the vampire better than that. But the rest of the demonic community didn't necessarily share his viewpoint or experience. "Of course Angel wouldn't hurt anyone without a reason," Lorne insisted. "He helps people—and sometimes demons—in trouble, but he doesn't go out hunting for demons just because he can. He only does what he has to in order to help those who can't fend for themselves."

The Skander twirled his empty glass around on the tabletop and waited while Luis brought him a fresh drink. Then he took a sip of that one. When the bartender was gone, he finally spoke. "I had a friend who knew a Prio Motu," he said. "This Prio was friends with a woman—helped her, protected her. Angel up and killed him for no reason at all."

Lorne remembered the incident, though it had happened around the time he and Angel had first become acquainted. "I heard about that," he said. "I also heard that Angel realized he'd made a mistake, felt just awful, and served as the human's champion in the Prio's place."

Quort *humphed.* "Maybe. I don't know about that. I just know that Angel's got a rep for killing our kind at every opportunity. One of his human friends gets herself in trouble, it's no skin off my nose."

Lorne barked out a sharp laugh. "You don't have a nose, Quort!"

The Skander just shrugged.

"So you don't want to help because you think Angel's a demon-killer?"

The words rushed out of Quort in an angry torrent: "I don't want to help because I didn't see anything helpful. I saw the car coming, but it was blurry. Then I was down on the ground like everybody else. When that was over, everybody was herding us back inside, and some humans were crying about somebody being missing. Well, big deal, you know? It's not like there aren't more than enough of them around already. What's one more?"

The casual way he said it chilled Lorne to the bone. Quort didn't care what happened to Fred, just because she was human and a friend of Angel's. But certainly there were humans who felt the same way about demons—and if more humans knew they existed, Lorne knew, that attitude would be even more prevalent.

He was a peace-loving sort, and he wished everyone else could feel the same. *Make love, not war,* that was his philosophy. *Life's too short for blind hatred. Even for an immortal, like Angel.*

"One more thing," Lorne said, trying hard to

keep a friendly tone in his voice. "Sing me a few bars."

The Skander looked unhappy at the idea. "Of what?"

"Whatever strikes your fancy," Lorne suggested. "It's a karaoke bar—you must know a song or two."

"I didn't come in for a reading, I came in for some drinks," Quort insisted.

"You got the drinks on the house," Lorne riposted. "The trade-off is that you sing. Nobody has to hear you but me."

Quort glanced left and right, as if checking to make sure he was unobserved. Then, softly, almost in a whisper, but with perfect pitch and surprising skill, he sang the first, ironically timeless lines of "As Time Goes By." Then he stopped, clamping his mouth shut with a definitive clacking of teeth. He was done.

"That's terrific," Lorne told him, thinking, *You must remember this*. Even the skeeziest demons have a sense of romance. "There's nothing like the classics."

As with the Brachen onstage, though, he didn't get anything helpful from the Skander demon. He saw a confusing mixture of images when Quort sang, and sensations running from glee to terror to humiliation. Nothing seemed to pertain to Fred, though, and if he was to give the Skander a thorough reading he'd have to sit through a much longer song than that brief snippet.

But it was looking pretty apparent that old Quort wasn't going to be much use in finding the poor girl. Lorne stood up and, without bothering to hide the sarcasm, said, "Thanks so much for all you've done. Enjoy the free drinks."

As he walked away, he could hear the Skander *humph*ing again.

CHAPTER THREE

Cordelia turned in a slow circle, trying to take in all of Fred's room at once. Her bed was neatly made, which was an improvement over the days when she had leaned her mattress against the wall and slept behind it. On top of a dresser were a hairbrush and a hand mirror and some cosmetics Cordy had given her but that she rarely used. She had thumbtacked a picture torn from a magazine to one wall: a bucolic Texas scene of bluebonnets in a meadow under a vast, cloudless sky. "Take a look at her room," Angel had said. "See if you can spot anything that would make her a target."

But Cordelia couldn't, unless maybe some of the complex equations she had written on the walls in Magic Marker meant more to someone else than they did to her. *Which is certainly possible, seeing as none of it means anything to me.*

Fred hadn't left the Hyperion Hotel much since they had brought her back to Earth, so she hadn't had a chance to acquire many personal belongings, or make many enemies. She'd spent most of her time huddled in this room, working out math problems on the walls, and maybe mooning over Angel a bit. She was a strange young woman—brilliant, Cordelia knew, but her years in Pylea had left her more than a little offbeat. She came across as scattered, even nuts, at first glance. But Cordy knew that initial appearance disguised a steel-trap mind and an enormous heart.

Cordy herself had been considered scattered, in her high school days, for that matter—by people of a generous nature. Less kind people called her other names. It was true that school hadn't been her highest priority. Popularity had been, with money and material things running a very close second, and then somehow she had gotten roped into the whole vampire-slaying gig with Buffy Summers, Willow Rosenberg, and Xander Harris, and little by little her priorities had shifted. She had grown a lot since then, she knew. She had become Angel's best friend, she believed, and his most important associate in Angel Investigations, helping connect him to the human world and aiding him in his fight against evil. She had taken on the vision power that tied him to the Powers That Be—*okay, unwillingly at first*, she thought, *but I really did have a chance to leave them behind, in Pylea, and I didn't take it.*

But with that position and those powers came a certain responsibility, and right now her responsibility was to the missing Fred, and standing here looking at an almost completely bare room, eyes glazing over at the complicated equations, wasn't going to help her locate their friend. She left the room and went downstairs to the hotel's office, anxious to get busy, to start making progress. Every minute Fred was missing, she might be in danger, and Cordelia didn't want anything to happen to her.

The other part of Angel's instructions made more sense to her. She booted up her computer and pulled up a rolling chair. Angel's version of how the night's events had progressed made sense to her: the explosion to lure everyone outside, the fire to keep them there, the drive-by to distract everyone while somebody grabbed Fred. Looking for a motive to snatch Fred seemed counterproductive—she'd been in a different dimension for five years, so it wasn't like there were lots of people, or demons, who even knew she existed. But the M.O., the multiple layers of distraction, might bear fruit. It was a complex scheme, but it had to have been hatched and executed on a tight schedule—hardly anyone outside of their immediate circle, and Lorne, had known they'd be at Caritas that night. Since she couldn't imagine that any of them had turned traitor, that meant someone must have been watching the club, waiting for the right opportunity, and then had put the plan into motion. And it had come off without a hitch. The most reasonable conclusion had to be that whoever had done this had pulled similar operations before. Cordelia would look through her demon databases to see if she could find any similar plots; if that failed, she'd then follow a back door that Willow had once helped her find into L.A.P.D. records, to see if she could identify any human criminals who had employed such a scheme. Finally, she'd look into demons who had the ability to materialize transdimensional gateways or to transport others telekinetically, because somebody had somehow snatched Fred right out from under their noses. It seemed like if they'd just carried her away physically, someone would have noticed.

In which case we'd better have Dr. Freud himself on hand when we get her back, because another unexpected portal jaunt would definitely throw Fred into the deep end of the pool without her water wings.

Cordy tapped her fingernails on the desktop waiting for the system to be ready. She was itching to get started. *The sooner we can figure out who might have taken her,* she thought, *the sooner Angel can go to wherever her kidnappers might hang out and start pummeling demon booty to get her back.*

• • •

Angel kicked in the door to the back room of Slater's Meats, a butcher shop off Appian Way in Santa Monica. *There are quieter ways of entering, but none that make the right kind of statement.* When the door flew back, jamb splintering under the pressure, the five demons sitting around a table playing cards leaped to their feet, two of them pulling guns.

No problem, Angel thought. *Stakes, maybe a problem. Guns, not at all.* He was in a hurry for results, and he wouldn't allow the inconvenience of a bullet wound or three to slow him down. Fred had been missing for thirty minutes at this point, and that was half an hour too long.

"Angel!" one of the demons shouted, pointing his gun with a shaking hand. Angel took two steps into the room and kicked again, upending the table. Cards fluttered into the air like backward snowflakes. The demon fired, but the table flew up into his arm, and his bullet thudded harmlessly into the ceiling. Another demon tried to slip around Angel and out the open door, but the vampire didn't want anyone leaving just yet. He snaked an arm around the demon's midsection and caught him, hurling him back into the room and knocking down two of the others at the same time. Continuing his advance, Angel grabbed the other gun and wrenched it from its wielder's claws, then used it as a club to smack the fifth demon in the forehead.

31

That one went down, bloodied, scalp torn open.

Angel dropped the gun to the floor, put his hands on his hips, and waited. In a moment, the room was quiet, five pairs of eyes on him. He waited for another couple of beats. Finally, someone spoke—the one who had fired on him, a short but stocky creature with shocking pink skin and a semi-human face, but with jowls that drooped lower than any basset hound's.

"We're just playing a friendly game of cards, Angel." The demon's voice quavered with an odd mixture of terror and belligerence. "Sorry we didn't invite you or nothing, but you don't gotta make such a big production of it."

"That's not why I'm here," Angel said simply. He glanced at the walls, covered with posters showcasing different cuts of meat, a pinup calendar of female demons, from a supplier to the butcher shop, and the state of California's required employment and OSHA regulation materials. A couple of file cabinets stood against one wall, and there was an old wooden teacher's desk with a computer on it, screen saver showing winged toasters flying around outer space.

"Why, then?"

"Fred."

"Who's that?" another one asked. This one's coloration reminded Angel of the aurora borealis—shimmering, constantly shifting patterns of light and dark working their way across his flesh at all times. The effect was disconcerting, and the demon played it up by wearing only an open vest and a pair of khaki shorts. "Fred Flintstone? Fred Astaire?"

"Burkle."

The demons all found their feet, but they looked at the vampire with blank expressions. "Don't know who you mean, Angel."

"She's a friend of mine," Angel said. "Part of my team, and under my protection. Someone grabbed her tonight, outside Caritas. I want to know who and I want to know now."

"We've been here all night, man," one of them protested. The demon's lips didn't move when he talked, because the words issued from a secondary mouth, inside the gaping maw of his external one. "We don't know what you're talking about."

"You're also tapped in," Angel countered. "There's not much that happens out on the streets that you guys don't know about." Which was why he had interrupted this little gathering—these five represented something like a hundred demons of various families, and their frequent gatherings were something resembling a United Nations of Southern California demon groups. They worked to keep the peace and facilitate communication—a necessary effort, given the difficulties of survival in a world dominated by a different, and often hostile, species. Sometimes when Angel thought about them he likened them to the infamous "Five Families" that controlled New York's criminal underground for so long, but while there were similarities, there were also crucial differences. Some of the demons lived outside the laws of city, state, and nation, but others were every bit as obedient and law-abiding as most humans were. "Now, tell me what you know, and do it fast," he continued, an edge of menace in his tone. "I wouldn't want to have to hurt anybody."

"Okay," the short, pink one acknowledged. "We might have heard something about a little trouble at Caritas tonight. Something about a fire and a drive-by. We're still tryin' to get the lowdown—it wasn't none of us, or ours, I can tell you that. You know we don't like to stir up trouble, man. It's hard enough out there without that."

"It's going to get a lot harder if I don't get Fred back, unhurt and in a hurry," Angel warned. "If anything happens to her, I'm on the warpath. So do whatever you can to get her back to me. Tonight."

"We'll put out the word, Angel. We find anything out, we'll take care of it, don't worry."

"I'll be worried until I know she's okay," Angel replied sharply. "You should be too." He turned and headed back out into the alley from which he'd come.

Behind him, he heard one of the demons grumble, "Who's gonna pay for that door?"

Wesley and Gunn had agreed to track down human informants, to see if what had happened to Fred had to do with crime on that level instead of on the demonic one. It seemed unlikely, but Angel was determined to shake down the demon world. And until they had some kind of information—even though the best guess was that demons, not humans, had kidnapped Fred—they could afford to leave nothing to chance. Wesley was the acknowledged leader of Angel Investigations, but he knew that in a situation like this, once Angel had made his mind up, there was no changing it. So he let Angel go off by himself while he and Gunn approached things their own way.

Which led to them finding themselves in a rough neighborhood of downtown Los Angeles. This time of night it was mostly quiet, but music and the muffled chatter of TV sets could still be heard from some windows, and every few minutes a car or truck rushed up the street. The sidewalks seemed deserted, though, which Wesley pointed out. "I don't see him," he said. In the stillness of night, he kept his voice low, and his British accent softened it even more. "Are you sure this is the right place?"

"This is the place," Gunn confirmed, sounding very sure of himself. "He's here. Just can't see him yet."

"He's human, though, right?" Wesley asked, afraid he'd misunderstood. "Not an invisible demon or spirit or anything?"

"He's human. He's just good at not being seen unless he wants to be."

"And you're sure that he'll know something about Fred's disappearance?"

Gunn glanced at Wesley, tossing him a quick smile. "You know what they say. Nothing's sure in this world except death, taxes, and Angel broodin' over some woman or other. But if there's anything to know, he'll know."

"Yes, well, in the present case there's plenty to brood about. Fred is fragile, still. The thought of her being terrorized like this is just . . ." He searched for a word. "Appalling. It's beyond the pale."

"Got that right, English."

Poor Fred, Wesley thought. *She's already been through so much. It's just not fair for her to be victimized in this way.* The young woman had barely survived her experience in Pylea—and being sucked, unprepared, through a dimensional portal into an alien land would, in itself, be enough to drive most humans stark raving mad. Winifred Burkle, physics student and library employee, would have had no way to know there was such a dimension as Pylea, or, beyond the purely theoretical, that there were other dimensions at all, much less strange beings that lived in them, enslaving humans and referring to them as cattle. It was no wonder that her behavior now was a bit off the beam, as it were.

And still, he thought, *she's already become such an important presence in our day-to-day life. Her natural good humor, grace, and charm have always shown through. And when she smiles, it's like a beacon on a dark night. She really is quite lovely, in fact.*

Wesley looked at Gunn, whose gaze was carefully combing the block looking for Strayhairn, the informant he was convinced should be here, and Wesley wondered if the other man had noticed that about Fred yet. Her beauty had not been so apparent at first, when she'd acted almost more like a wild animal than a person, and fear had etched her face. But as she had become more comfortable around them and smiled more frequently, Wesley had come to realize that she was indeed an extraordinary beauty.

"There," Gunn said sharply. He pointed toward a dark doorway at the end of the block. Wesley couldn't see anything at first, but when he stared into the shadows he noticed a faint gleam—a silvery zipper pull reflecting light from the neon beer sign in the window of a tavern across the street. "Come on," Gunn added. He started toward the doorway, and Wesley followed half a pace behind.

Strayhairn, if indeed that's who it was, waited in the doorway as they approached. Finally Wesley could make out some more detail. He was a little taller than Gunn, with skin a couple of shades darker and close-cropped hair that hugged his scalp and a mustache that drooped past the corners of his mouth. He wore a zipped-up jacket and track pants, and his sneakers must have cost three hundred dollars, Wesley speculated. They looked as high-tech as a space shuttle. He leaned in the doorway, as casually as if he'd been expecting them all evening.

"Gunn," he drawled. His easy smile showed a gold tooth in front. "'Sup?"

"Yo, dog," Gunn replied, putting on friendly airs. "Been lookin' for you."

"Been right here."

"All night?" Gunn asked. "Must get kinda lonely."

"Not all night, but for a while. My homies know where to find me, they got something to talk about."

"What are they talking about tonight?" Wesley asked anxiously.

Strayhairn turned his head slowly to look at Wesley, as if noticing his presence for the first time.

All of his movements were so languid, it almost looked to Wesley as if the man were under water. "Who's this?" Strayhairn asked.

"This is Wesley," Gunn said. "He's with me."

Strayhairn offered a fist, which Wesley, after a moment's hesitation, bumped with his own. "Any friend, yo," Strayhairn said.

"Likewise, I'm sure. But if we could get down to business . . ."

Strayhairn chuckled. "Oh, this about business?"

Gunn pulled a few bills from a pocket and laid them across Strayhairn's suddenly open palm. "Okay, it's business," Gunn said. "You know what we're after, right?"

"I might have an idea," Strayhairn said. "A brother—I don't know if you know him, Sam Rini?"

Gunn shook his head, and Strayhairn continued. "Anyway, Sam told me he heard rumors about some girl being snatched. She one of yours?"

"She is," Wesley confirmed. "What else do you know about it?"

"Rini's a good guy, smart as the dickens. I told him to find out more, let me know what he turns up. That kind of thing is always good business, you know what I mean? It's the information age."

Gunn turned to Wesley. "Strayhairn's kind of a broker," he explained. "He keeps his ear to the street, and he usually knows who to sell what he learns to."

"Sounds like a very, umm . . . honorable profession."

"I ain't driving a Jag and drinking Cristal every night, but I do okay," Strayhairn told them, a measure of pride creeping into his voice. He looked past them instead of at them, always keeping an eye on the street, Wesley noticed.

"So you don't know who took the young lady, or where she's being kept?" he asked. *There has to be more. Getting only a tiny piece of information is almost worse than none at all.*

"Told you what I know. So far, there's just some .rumors. Nobody knows anything for sure. At least, not that anyone's talking about."

"Which tells you something in itself," Gunn added. "Most times, something like this happened, everybody'd be talkin' about it."

Strayhairn nodded, his whole body seeming involved, bobbing up and down. "And since they ain't, what's that tell you?"

"That it's none of the usual suspects," Gunn said. "Not gang-related, not organized crime. Either some solo act, or something else entirely."

"By which you mean . . . ," Wesley prodded, not wanting to lose sight of their goal.

"How much does he know?" Strayhairn asked Gunn, inclining his head toward Wesley.

"More than just about anybody," Gunn answered quickly.

"Demons?" Wesley speculated.

Strayhairn nodded again. "People don't like to talk about 'em. So if nobody's talking about something everybody should be talking about, that's where I'd look."

"Which is what we thought from the beginning," Wesley said with a sigh.

"That's right," Gunn agreed. "But Angel wanted to cover that angle himself."

"You'll let us know if you hear any more?" Wesley inquired.

"Check in, time to time," Strayhairn offered. "I get more, I'll share. Long as you do too."

Gunn laughed softly. "I always take care of you, dog."

Strayhairn pocketed the bills Gunn had given him. "Always have so far, anyway. You keep it up, hear?"

"No worries," Gunn said. "Come on, Wes. We can't spend all night here. We got a girl to find."

CHAPTER FOUR

Nemchuks paired for life, Lorne knew, so when he sat down at the table with Mif'tal and his mate, he knew that this couple would beat the odds on California marriages. Once a male was mated with a female, their circulatory systems became linked together, and if they separated for any length of time, both of their bodies would go haywire. Death usually followed in three or four weeks, unless the couple was reunited in time.

Once he had been at the table for a few minutes, though, he thought that perhaps these were ancient enemies rather than committed lovers. At least, that was the impression he got from talking to them.

"It was a Camaro," Mif'tal announced. "I know my seventies cars, and that was a classic Camaro."

"You only *think* you know everything, Mif'tal!" The female's name was Urf'dil, and as was normally the case with Nemchuks, she was about six inches taller and a hundred pounds heavier than her male. "It was a Firebird—seventy-seven, in fact."

"You know, folks, the exact make of the car probably isn't the biggest issue we have to contend with tonight," Lorne suggested. They'd already been on the car for a couple of minutes—it was the first thing Mif'tal had started in on when Lorne had asked what they'd seen outside.

"Firebird?" Mif'tal mocked, ignoring Lorne completely. "Did you *see* any fire on it? Or a bird?"

"It's been painted—and badly, I might add. But that doesn't change the fact that it was a Firebird."

"Camaro."

Urf'dil crossed her massive arms over her chest and blew out a puff of air. "Lorne, tell him to behave himself. He's just so argumentative lately. He still thinks we used to drive a Nash Rambler, and I have to tell him we never did. I think he confuses it with our old Plymouth Valiant."

This was something Lorne really didn't want to get into the middle of. All he wanted to do was find Fred, not play Dr. Drew to a couple of combative kooks. *And how could someone confuse a Rambler with a Valiant?* But somewhere beneath their bluster was the chance that one, or both, of them had seen something useful. He needed to pry it from them if he could.

"Look, Mif'tal," he said, leaning toward the male and speaking in a conspiratorial stage whisper. "You're probably right about the Camaro, but it doesn't really matter in the long run. Why not just say it was a Firebird, for her sake? What's the harm?"

The Nemchuk gnashed its many teeth at him and lowered the bony ridge over its eyes. "Because," Mif'tal said slowly, as if addressing a not particularly bright child, "it wasn't a Firebird!"

Lorne buried his head in his hands, elbows resting on the glass tabletop. "Can we agree that it was a car?" he asked plaintively. "Four wheels, some doors, maybe some windows?"

"Of course it was a car," Urf'dil said. "I really don't see why you're making such a big deal about this."

Why me? Lorne wondered. *Why does it have to be me all the time?*

He believed they really wanted to help. At least, they'd claimed that they did, and he had no reason to doubt. Nemchuks were clannish demons, keeping to themselves and as far from human society as they could manage. Most, in fact, lived in remote rural areas—northern Scotland had a big community, as did central Mexico and the Russian Steppe. But some had settled in cities, including a small group that had somehow found its way to Los Angeles and decided to stay. They moved about in the dark, wearing clothing that shielded them from any human eyes to which they might accidentally be exposed. But Mif'tal said they had heard that Angel was a great hero to a lot of demons—he'd heard about the Scourge, and how Angel and a half-Brachen named Doyle had saved a lot of Lister demons. Urf-dil had interrupted to insist that they had, in fact, been Lubber demons, but Lorne had been able to set the record straight on that score. Angel, he said, was not particularly popular among the Lubbers, while Listers practically worshiped him. So they truly did desire to help, it seemed.

Lorne just wasn't sure how much more of their brand of help he could stand.

These two had sung for him already, but the most he had learned was that they would remain together—driving each other crazy—until Urf-dil's death many years hence.

"Okay," Lorne said, taking a deep breath and calling on any reserves of patience he might once have had. "We'll accept that it was some kind of car. And did either of you love-muffins happen to see who or what was in the car?"

"Sure," Mif'tal said. "I had a good view. Five demons, with semiautomatic weapons."

"Five?" Urf-dil countered. "Are you nuts? There were only four of them, and those guns were full auto."

Mif'tal shook his head so fast, Lorne was afraid it might fly off. "No. I'm telling you, I counted five. And any fool could tell by the sound they were semi."

"Let's back up a minute," Lorne interjected, trying desperately to bring some kind of sanity back to the conversation. "Are we sure it was demons in the car, and not humans?"

"I know humans when I see them," Mif'tal insisted. Lorne had to figure that was true. For all their fearsome appearance, Nemchuks were largely harmless to humans. His characterization earlier of the demon as a big pussycat wasn't that far off the mark, except that cats could turn on their humans in a heartbeat. Nemchuks had no particular love for humans, but they bore the species no ill will. Their lack of affection for humans stemmed more from their fear that humans would attack them, driving them to extinction as they had so many other races in the years since they had taken dominance over the earth. "These were not human."

Urf-dil raised her clawed hands into the air and waved them about. "Hallelujah," she declared. "He's right about one thing. They were definitely not human."

"Could you tell what they were, then?" Lorne asked, thrilled that at least there had been one area of agreement. "I'm guessing by not human you don't mean something like dogs or llamas, but more something of the demonic persuasion."

"Too dark," Mif'tal said flatly. "But I can tell you one thing: Urf'dil has never known squat about guns."

"I was blinded by the headlights," Urf-dil said, more or less simultaneously. "But I know what automatic weapons sound like."

"You know, if you guys don't want to help . . ." Lorne began. *Much more of this bickering,* he thought, *and I'll be the one reaching for an automatic weapon.*

"No, we do," Urf-dil said, suddenly sincere. She touched Lorne's hand with her claw. "Angel's never done anything bad to us. We have no hard feelings toward him. I'm really sorry that his friend is missing. Honestly, Lorne, if there's anything we can do, if we saw anything that might help him, just let us know."

"What she said," Mif'tal added. "We do genuinely want to help Angel out if we can."

"Then can we declare a cease-fire for long enough to get through this?" Lorne pleaded. "I don't have all night. Well, I do—I'm the original night owl, you know? But we don't know if Fred does, and she's what's important here."

"I'm sorry," Urf'dil said. She looked at her mate with what Lorne assumed were the Nemchuk version of soulful eyes. *Or, heaven forbid, bedroom eyes,* he thought, immediately wishing for a brain shower to wash *that* mental image away.

"Is there anything else you can think of that might be helpful?" Lorne pleaded with her. "Anything out of the ordinary that you noticed?"

"The whole thing was a bit out of the ordinary," Urf'dil pointed out. "But I do remember one thing: I thought I smelled cinnamon."

"How could you smell that?" Mif'tal demanded. "There was a burning building across the street, guns were being fired—how could you possibly smell cinnamon over the smoke and soot and gunpowder?"

"I don't know, honey," she said, almost sweetly. "I just have a very strong sense that I did. Like a sense memory, almost—if I put myself back there, mentally, I get a strong whiff of it."

Lorne took a physical whiff of the air, just in case she was picking it up from someplace more local. *No cinnamon,* he thought. *Maybe a couple of demons in here who haven't been bathing as regularly as they should. And demon b.o.—that's the worst.*

"Didn't you think you smelled vanilla on the night of our pairing ritual?" Mif'tal asked her. There was a mocking edge to his voice.

"Now that you mention it, yes," Urf'dil replied. The edge there, Lorne guessed, was suspicion. "And I also remember that my sister was wearing vanilla at our ceremony. I always meant to ask you about that."

Mif'tal laughed, a truly unpleasant sight that involved his several rows of teeth clacking together, strings of spittle joining them when they pulled apart again. "If you think I'd have anything to do with that ogre of a sister you have, you're even crazier than I thought!"

"Now, Mif'tal," Lorne said, putting his hands out to pacify both of them. "Remember our purpose here. Let's not get nasty."

"You want to talk about nasty, take a look at that sister sometime. She could get a job sitting outside a doctor's office, making people sick."

Urf'dil turned in her chair so that she was facing away from the table, and her mate. "Lorne, I will do whatever I can to help Angel and Fred, but I won't sit here and have my family insulted by that . . . that ridiculous male."

"He's sorry," Lorne said, hoping it was true. "He's really, really sorry." He turned to Mif'tal, a plaintive expression on his face. "Aren't you?"

"You can tell her that I'll apologize right after she does."

"For what?" Lorne asked. *Didn't I not want to get in the middle of this?* he thought. *Now look at me—if this isn't the middle, I don't know what is.*

"Ask her."

"What does he want you to apologize for?"

She didn't even look at Lorne. "I'm sure I don't know. Why don't you ask him?"

I have new respect for marriage counselors, Lorne thought. *Also hostage negotiators and anybody with the patience not to go berserk when surrounded by lunatics.* "Okay, we'll do it the hard way," he said. "Mif'tal, is there anything else you might have seen, or heard, or smelled, that could in any way be significant?"

Mif'tal *hmmmed* for a long time. Finally, Urf'dil interrupted. "He doesn't want to hear you clearing your throat. Tell him about the Polgara."

"I wasn't clearing—Lorne, tell her I wasn't clearing my throat. I was thinking. And then ask her what Polgara she's talking about."

"He wasn't—oh, you heard him," Lorne snapped. "What Polgara?"

"When I remembered the cinnamon, it drew me back there, in my mind's eye. And I thought I remembered seeing a Polgara demon standing right around Fred just before she disappeared. It seems like I even remember seeing it reach for her. But that's when the shooting started and we all ducked."

"There was no Polgara," Mif'tal declared. "You weren't even looking at Fred when the shooting started—you already said you were looking at the car, miscounting demons, and misidentifying weapons."

"I got a glimpse of the car," she argued. "But then I turned—maybe it was as I was ducking—and noticed Fred. I'm sure it was a Polgara."

"Maybe your sister was the sane one, after all," Mif'tal said. By now he and Urf'dil were both turned completely away from the table, facing in opposite directions.

Maybe life-bonding isn't all it's cracked up to be by the family values types, Lorne thought as he rose from his chair. "Thanks, you guys," he said. "If you think of anything else, I'll be around. Anything related to this, I mean. And that you both agree on."

"You're welcome, Lorne," Urf'dil said, sounding a bit miffed at Lorne's parting entreaties.

"I hope they find her," Mif'tal added.

A Polgara? There hadn't been a Polgara in the club all night, Lorne knew. He'd have noticed if there had been. Which didn't necessarily mean there hadn't been one lurking outside.

But if Fred had been taken by a Polgara, she'd be a meal by now.

And that was too horrible to even think about.

CHAPTER FIVE

The first thing she noticed was the headache, throbbing, as if every drop of blood that passed through the veins in her head carried a small explosive charge with it. For a while, the headache was her entire world. She couldn't remember pain like that ever in her life; she couldn't remember a life before the pain. She could only pray there would be a life after.

A bit later it occurred to her to open her eyes. She started to do so, but the motion sent a lance of fire through her temples, so she stopped with the eyelid a quarter open, admitting a little bit of light but nothing else. *Still is better,* she decided. *No movement at all. Movement is really, really bad.*

But thinking, she realized, *thinking doesn't hurt so much.*

She could think without moving. When that

enlightenment hit her, though, the first thing she thought was the obvious: *Where am I?*

She decided to go for the eye thing again. She would have gritted her teeth, but that would have required yet more movement. *Just the one eye,* she thought, *that'll do for now. I have another as backup if I need it.*

And so, doing her absolute best to ignore the screaming pain caused by the barest fluttering of her eyelid, Fred opened her left eye.

And saw floor.

A nice hardwood, she thought. *Could use some work. But it's not made of rock, so that's a good thing.* There were deep scratches in it, dust worked into the scratches. The finish was dull, without that gleam that lives inside good hardwoods but that needs tender ministration to bring out, polishing and rubbing and love. The pool of blood that would have been there if one of Angel's edged weapons really had been buried in her skull wasn't there, so most likely that wasn't the source of her pain.

She could see maybe six square inches of the floor. Probably a little less.

But you're a physicist, she thought. *If you can only see six square inches of the floor—thirty-nine square centimeters—there has to be a reason, and that reason will be grounded in your understanding of the physical world.*

And you're thinking—I'm *thinking of myself in the second person, which is odd. But at least I've fixed that part.*

A little success felt good, even though it was admittedly a very tiny triumph. So she turned to the next issue at hand, which was why she could only see a tiny patch of floor with her single open eye. She considered this from a variety of angles. Maybe she'd suffered partial blindness. This theory, she realized, could also explain the headache. *The* blinding *headache,* she thought, a flash of inspiration that almost made her smile until the slight upturn of her lips caused the pain to come roaring back like a hungry lion released from its cage.

But then another possibility occurred to Fred. Perhaps it wasn't blindness at all. And there didn't seem to be anything obstructing her view that she could make out from here. So maybe it was a matter of positioning.

When it finally came to her, she wanted to smack herself. Except not.

I can only see a small area of floor, she thought, *because I'm facedown on that selfsame floor.*

This theory had the taste of truth to it. Of course, as with any theory, it was only a hypothesis until it was tested and proven. Testing it, though, would mean more motion, hence more pain. *And I'm not sure I can really take more pain without screaming,* she thought, *and if I screamed, that would really really hurt and then I'd just have to hope I could scream my head off, because I definitely wouldn't want it anywhere near me.*

While she considered this predicament, she fell asleep again.

She was remembering a day, a long, long time ago. She had just been a little girl, nine, she thought. Maybe she had recently turned ten, or was about to. Somewhere in that zone, though, she knew. She had been outside under a bright, hot Texas sun. The sky was a gigantic, inverted bowl of pure blue, cloudless, the color of jeans worn to the point of perfect softness, of the awning at Fields' Drugs, where they had the old-fashioned soda fountain and made the world's best milk shakes, of the sea off South Padre Island, where her parents sometimes took her on vacation. The horizon was perfectly flat; the only thing that stuck up above the horizon line in any direction was the house her grandparents lived in. She knew that beyond the house there was a barn and a silo and a corral, but from this angle they were hidden, invisible. She also knew that beyond the miles and miles of fields there were roads, and towns, and even big cities, pulsing with life. There were oceans out there, and other continents, other countries, other people. And still farther, even beyond those things but no more invisible, from here, there were other stars and those stars had planets, and because, as it had been explained to her, there were billions upon billions of stars, that meant there were billions upon billions upon billions of planets, and somewhere in all those planets there might well be one with life on it, and if there was then there would likely be a little girl like her, looking out and thinking about other little girls, far, far away.

She gazed up into that blue, blue sky, trying to pierce the veil of color, to see through the blue. *There's nothing blocking my way,* she thought, *nothing like the farmhouse between me and the planets, just sky, and sky's transparent, isn't it?* She stared into the sky and started to turn in slow, lazy circles, hands out for balance. As she turned she felt her summer dress lift, like a ballerina's, with each circuit she made, and as she turned faster it lifted faster and it made her laugh. So she kept turning, staring straight up over her head and spinning, arms flashing at her sides, eyes trying to tear away all the space above her, until finally she became so dizzy that she fell down and struck the back of her head on a jagged bit of stone sticking up through the rich Texas earth. It hurt, and she thought maybe she was bleeding, but she couldn't check it because the world was spinning in an irregular pattern, practically looping around on itself and doing its best to throw her off, and until the world slowed down she had to hang on with both hands.

By the time she made it back to her grandparents' farmhouse, her scalp was matted with her own blood and her summer dress was ripped in several places and she'd even been a little bit sick, out in the fields. But her head would heal and her dress could be mended and her hair would wash, and she had made a very important discovery about herself and her world.

"When I grow up," she had announced that night at dinner, "I want to be a scientist. I want to be the kind of scientist who can figure out stuff, like stuff about the world. Why does it turn so fast and why can't you see through the blue part and how are we down here connected to people we don't even know exist on other worlds?"

She didn't know it at the time, but she had just discovered physics. The study of the world, why it is the way it is, what holds it together.

And it all started, she remembered, when she hit her head on a rock.

Fred knew there was a reason she was remembering that day, and after thinking about it for a while decided that it must be because of the pain in her head. She realized that she'd been asleep, and dreaming of that time, but here she was awake again and that pain was still there. Maybe a fraction of a fraction of a percent better than it had been, but still bad enough. She considered for a moment, and decided that she'd better risk opening her eye again. Maybe the hardwood floor had been the dream part. Maybe when she opened her eye now she'd be on South Padre Island, with an ice-cream cone in her hand and the headache would be an ice-cream headache and her dad would rub the back of her head and it would all be better.

There was probably not much chance of that, she decided. But it was worth a shot. There might be a floor there, or there might be something else. Maybe she was on the back of a giant moth, flying through a cityscape of graceful minarets. Maybe she was on the moon. *Just not Pylea. Or the kitchen of a fast-food restaurant.* She opened her eye, just the tiniest bit.

Hardwood floor.

What the heck, Fred thought. *Might as well go all the way. In for a penny, in for a pound, that's what momma used to say, and although I was never quite sure what she meant by it in the literal sense, the gist of it was clear enough.* Mentally bracing herself, she opened both eyes, wide.

Now she could see more of the floor, but still not a very large swath of it. The other eye was also relatively close to the floor, which only made sense because, as she had already determined, she was more or less face-planted on it. For the first time, she wondered about the positioning of the rest of her body. Though it was hard to tell through the headache, the rest of her seemed to be in quite a bit of pain as well.

She tried to isolate individual body parts, to figure out what condition they were in, but it was too hard, and her focus kept skipping around like a flat stone thrown sideways at still water. She would try to picture her left knee, but then the image of a carousel would pop into her head, its animal seats snarling and dripping saliva from hungry, chomping mouths. She felt as twisted-up as a pretzel, and it confused her nerve impulses. There was only one way to solve this, she decided. She had to actually move herself into some position from which she could see herself and her surroundings.

And as she had that thought, a chill ran through her, because she realized it meant she was coming to her senses, and that meant that she had been, at least for some period of time, out of her senses. It also meant that she understood now that, wherever she was, it wasn't a place she had taken herself. Something had been done to her, by somebody, and apparently her own personal comfort was just about the last thing that somebody had in mind. She remembered, suddenly, where it must have happened—outside Caritas, where they were watching the fire across the street, and then a car rushed toward the crowd, and then . . . and then, she didn't know what. Someone must have knocked her out then.

Was that person, or persons, still here with her? Watching her, maybe? That idea was terrifying, almost paralyzing. But she couldn't allow it to paralyze her, she knew. Her breaths became short and shallow, barely bringing in enough oxygen to keep her awake, and her heart started to pound rapidly in her throat. She was already physically in bad shape, practically frozen, anyway, by the stiffness of muscles that had been pushed into unfamiliar position and left there for she didn't know how long. She couldn't afford to let blind panic make her situation worse. She had to think this through, quickly and decisively, and do whatever needed to be done to get herself out of this. Getting control of her breathing, she took in deep lungfuls of air, trying to calm herself. Gradually, her heartbeat slowed.

Angel will help me, she found herself thinking. *All I have to do is wait, and Angel will rescue me. That's what he does.*

Which she knew to be true. But there was always the possibility that he wouldn't, this time. That he couldn't. *What if something has already happened to him? What if he was taken out first, before they even came for me? What if I've been portaled to some strange new dimension he can't even find?*

No—what she had to do was assume that she was on her own. If Angel did come—*and he will if he can, I believe that*—then he would save her. But even if he didn't, she couldn't just lie here on her face on the wooden floor and wait for more bad things to happen. She had to brainstorm a way out of this, and she had to start now.

She started by listening—really listening—for a moment. Her own breathing sounded loud, but when she held her breath she couldn't hear any other sounds that seemed to be coming from inside this room. No other breathing, no rustle of fabric, tapping of fingertips . . . nothing to indicate that there was anyone in the room with her. The only sounds, she realized, were faint, occasional bursts of a frantic buzzing noise, the source of which she couldn't locate. Resuming her own breathing, taking in the stale air, she knew the time had come to make the scariest move of all. She had to sit up.

Her muscles screamed with agony as she called on them to do their thing—pain shot up from her arms and legs, from her ribs, from her neck, almost driving her back to her awkward but now-familiar facedown pose. She bit down on her lower lip and worked through the pain, ignoring it as best she could. She was able to bend her knees, to bring her legs up under her, noticing as she did that her shoes were missing. Then she flattened her palms, pressing them against the cool wood floor, and pushing off.

Her right hand felt odd. Heavy. She looked at it.

A metal bracelet encircled her thin wrist. A chain extended from the bracelet to a similar one, looped around an old-fashioned radiator attached to the wall. She was handcuffed.

I really am a prisoner, she thought. *I really am trapped here.*

The radiator pipe came out of the wall about eight inches from the floor and ran straight up, joining the tubes that provided heat at the top. It gave her about eighteen inches of play, all vertical. Still, the cuff would slide up the radiator pipe far enough to enable her to sit up, so she did, in spite of the screaming pain. She let out a whimper, but that and the rattle of the metal bracelet on the pipe, and the slight rasp of her clothes rubbing together, were the only sounds she made.

She couldn't see whoever had put her here. But there was a door, across the room, and there was no telling who, or what, was on the other side of that door.

I have to get out of here. I have to get myself free.

When Fred had managed to get herself into a sitting position, back up against the wall next to the radiator, she took stock of her surroundings. The room she was in looked like an old apartment, or maybe an office. Old because of the crusty, peeling paint that had once been white, dotted with mold in spots, the apparent age of the radiator, all coiled metal, and the glowing lamps set into sconces on two of the walls. She guessed the building was from the nineteen thirties or forties, though architecture wasn't really one of her specialties and she knew she could be off by a couple of decades in either direction. There was a bit of a mildew smell to the room—*mildew and dust,* she decided. At the other side of the radiator, where she couldn't reach it from here, a dark, dust-caked window looked blankly out at nothing she could see.

At least everything looks and smells like Earth, Fred thought with a degree of satisfaction. *If there's a silver lining to this cumulonimbus, that's it.*

Halfway between her and the door was a dinette table with metal legs, and a flat top that she guessed was probably linoleum. Two chairs were tucked up underneath the table. The legs of the chairs were partially rusted where they met what looked like green Naugahyde seats. Against the far wall was an old, overstuffed chair with a brown fabric covering that was wearing through in spots. The seat of that chair looked uneven, and she suspected springs would poke at anyone who sat in it. The last piece of furniture in the room was the one nearest to her, tucked into the corner where the wall she sat against came together with the side wall. It was just a small piece, like an end table or nightstand, with a single hinged door enclosing a shallow space where there must have been a shelf. Other than that, it was open and its surface was empty.

Then there was the door.

All the way across the room, centered in the far wall. It was natural wood, which had maybe been stained once, but probably never painted. The wood was rubbed smooth around the knob, and splintering a bit around the lock and the hinges. But, from here, at least, it looked solid. Artificial light leaked in from underneath, where there was a quarter-inch gap, but Fred couldn't see anything through the gap, couldn't tell if there was another room, or a hallway, or what, beyond the door.

But it was clearly the only way in or out of the room, unless the window conveniently opened onto the ground floor, or a fire escape, or unless the walls were really secret hatchways that led into tunnels habituated by mole men. She *had* to get to the door, even though it might as well have been a continent away.

Quiet, she realized, was counterproductive. If there was actually someone on the other side of the door, then they meant her harm, anyway, and it wouldn't hurt to alert them to the fact that she was awake—and seriously ticked off. If she was completely alone, then a little noise wouldn't be a problem. But she wasn't going to get out of these handcuffs without making a racket, and obviously, the cuffs had to go. Anyway, she couldn't hear the slightest sound from the outside world in here—wherever she was, it was well insulated—so chances were that no one could hear her unless they were actively listening for her.

Most of the pain she'd felt had changed—she had a pins-and-needles sensation in her arms and legs as her circulation returned to something approaching normal, but the headache and muscle aches had dropped to a dull, steady throbbing. She knew she risked bringing it all back, but like the noise, that was just something she would have to live with. Readying herself for lances of agony, she drew her right arm back all the way against the wall, letting the cuff chain go slack, and then threw her fist out as fast and as hard as the could.

The manacle bit into her flesh, tearing the skin. The chain clattered, and the manacle wrapped around the radiator pipe clanged against the metal. But it didn't give.

It's got to, she thought. *This building is so old, the radiator can't be stronger than I am.*

She tried it again, and a third time, each time wincing at the sensation of the metal ripping her arm. After two more lunges, she gave up. The radiator was holding, but her arm wasn't. Blood ran down into her hand now, and dripped onto the hardwood floor. She elevated her hand as much as she could, trying to slow the bleeding, but it just ran the other way, down her arm to her elbow. She was still wearing the silk blouse and flower print skirt she'd worn for Lorne's party, and she was reaching down to tear a strip from the skirt with which to bandage her arm when she had another idea.

My wrists are skinny little things, she thought. *Like a stork's legs, or those needles you find in the carpeting months after Christmas. And the blood will make them slick. Just maybe . . .*

She brought her thumb and little finger together in the center of her palm, trying to make her hand as small as possible. The cuff fit fairly loosely about her wrist, so she thought she should be able to slip it off. But try as she might, even with the blood to lubricate it, she couldn't work the narrow circle over the base of her hand. It widened just enough that the manacle wouldn't let go. When she realized that she was just cutting herself worse, digging the steel bracelet into herself, she gave up on that attempt.

Fred had survived for five years in a place where humans were considered cattle and were often fitted with collars that would cause their heads to explode if they displeased their masters. *Earth can be a scary, dangerous place, but if I could make it in Pylea, I should be able to take care of myself here. All I need to do is not give up.*

The racket of the cuff slamming against the

radiator hadn't brought anybody charging in, which at least was one good thing. It meant she had more time to try a different approach—though she was running out of ideas. She took a closer look at where the radiator pipe came out of the wall, but that didn't seem at all encouraging—the pipe was solid, and she couldn't even seem to budge it. Short of sawing off her own hand on the metal bracelet, she wasn't sure what to try next.

Feeling panic well up in her again, she let her gaze dart about the room. The door, the table and chairs, the little end table, the impossibly distant overstuffed chair, the hardwood floor. *Not much to look at,* she thought, *although it's not like I came here for the scenery, anyway, right?* But then she stopped, swallowed, tried to calm herself again, and took a long look at the end table, nightstand, whatever it was. She wondered if she could reach it. Not with her left hand; it was too far away for that. But maybe with her feet.

She slid the cuff all the way down the radiator pipe to its lowest point and once again flattened herself against the floor. With her free hand and her feet, she scooted herself toward the end table, forcing herself to the limit of where the handcuff on her right wrist would allow her to reach. She felt about with her foot, but found only empty air. *No,* she thought. *It* can't *be out of reach. It just can't!*

Raising her head just enough to allow her to

locate it again, she realized that her foot had just barely missed one of the table's legs. She lowered her head, extended her foot as far as she could, arching it, stretching toes out, and swept the air again. Then her foot touched wood and she stopped.

The table was in the corner, and as far as she could tell from here, it was right up against the wall. Her fear was that it wasn't but that the pressure from her foot would push it back until she had shoved it out of her own reach. But she couldn't manage to hook her toe around the leg, so she had to risk it, anyway.

Pressing her toe against it, she pushed with what little force she could muster. The table rocked a little. Finding it with her toe again, she pushed once more. This time, the table clunked against the wall, rocking for a moment longer. She pushed again.

Finally, on the fifth push, the table hit the wall and rocked back toward her, and she was able to kick out again, catching one of the legs as it swayed. The whole thing tipped forward and crashed to the floor.

Well, if that noise doesn't bring people running, then I guess I really am alone here. I wonder, if I do manage to get out, if I'll even be able to figure out where I am.

Bringing down the table was the most positive thing she'd done since she'd found herself here, though, and it filled her with new hope. She hooked a leg around it and slid it up to where she could reach it with her left hand. Then she sat up again and flipped the table over so she could get at the door.

And now she saw the source of the occasional buzzing sounds she'd been hearing—a fly, trapped in a web that a spider had spun in the corner of the two walls. The fly didn't seem to be hopelessly entangled yet, and could jiggle the web by trying to fly out of it, but couldn't seem to make the break. The spider itself, no bigger than the fly, waited on the far side of the web, apparently confident that the fly could do nothing more than wear itself out trying to escape.

"I know just how you feel," Fred lamented. At this moment, all her sympathy was with the fly.

Fred turned her attention back to the table. There was nothing at all on the shelf behind the door, just a little storage space where someone might keep tissues or a book or a couple of magazines, maybe. But she hadn't counted on there being anything inside. She wanted the door.

Or more precisely, one of the small hinges.

Hinges, Fred thought, *have pins. Small hinges have small pins.*

Working the table to where she could use both hands, she waggled and jerked the door around, trying to loosen the two hinges. That wasn't notably successful, though, so she tried to pry the pin out of the top hinge with her fingernail. She almost had it, she believed, when her nail bent backward in the middle. It felt like a hot nail being driven down into her thumb. Biting back the pain, she tried a different fingernail. Still no go.

I need a tool. Pliers, a screwdriver, something.

Obviously, none of those things were close at hand.

But there was something, she realized. Hoisting the table up onto her lap, she went to work on it with the handcuff bracelet, trying to wedge the metal band against the top of the pin and force it out that way.

The pain was incredible. With each movement the bracelet was jammed against the part of her wrist she'd already mangled. Blood started to flow again, splashing her silk blouse and once-beautiful skirt with every jolt of the cuff. But the pin was moving—she thought a couple more millimeters of it were showing above the hinge than before. She slammed it a couple more times with the cuff, and it moved again.

Finally enough of the pin stuck out that she was able to grab it with her fingers and work it free. She held it in her hand—a narrow metal pin, not much bigger around than a toothpick—and tossed the rest of the cabinet to the side.

Now, Fred thought, *all I have to do is teach myself*

how to pick a lock. She giggled at the idea—it seemed so impossible, and yet, considering everything she had already tried and failed at, it was her absolute best hope.

She was still marveling at it when she heard footsteps on the other side of the door, and saw the knob start to turn.

CHAPTER SIX

After working for a while, Cordelia had taken a few moments to change out of her party dress into a pair of old sweatpants and a soft cotton V-neck shirt that she kept at the Hyperion, mostly for workout sessions or combat practice in the basement room Angel had converted into a gym. She hadn't wanted to spare the time, because she knew that every minute counted in trying to get Fred back, but she believed she'd be more productive if she was a bit more comfortable. Her strappy heels had been terrific shoes, but they too had been discarded and she sat at the computer barefoot.

Usually the problem she faced being research girl was that, since very few people knew about the demons, vampires, and other assorted nasties with whom they shared the planet, there was precious little info to be found about any given creepy-crawlie. And much of what could be turned up was wrong—a mixture of legends and lies, with the occasional nugget of reality thrown in almost by accident. *Which is,* she thought, *pretty much the whole problem with the Internet, at least the way I hear it. More info available more easily than at any other time in history, and most of it's wrong.*

This time, though, the problem was entirely the opposite. She had so little to start with that she had found herself deluged with data, virtually submerged under an ocean of info. Basically, her starting point had been demons who had some association with fire. *Well,* she learned, *that's kind of like trying to figure out which birds have something to do with the air.* There were demons who shied away from fire—although of course they came up in the search too, specifically because they did—but there were lots and lots of demons who had close kinship with fire. It was practically, she discovered, a hallmark of the demonic, or subterrestrial, world. Even demons who lived thoroughly modern lifestyles, with electricity and modern appliances, tended to prefer fire for heat and cooking. Something about it just suited their nature. *Like that whole ducks and water thing. Or attractive people and great wealth . . . although, since wealth is no longer mine or even on the horizon, it'd probably be best not to go there.*

She turned back to the mass of data before her. Trying to find what kind of demons might start a fire was akin to the cliché about the needle and the haystack. Her database returned more demonic types than she had known existed. What she needed was a way to narrow the field, to weed out the ones who couldn't be involved. Demons who only lived in Eastern Europe, for instance, could pretty much be written off. But there weren't enough easy calls like that one to make much difference in her masses of information.

If only Fred were here with one of her handy-dandy math formulas, she thought. *She could juggle some numbers in the air and make two-thirds of these things go away.*

Of course, if Fred were here, then we wouldn't be searching for Fred and I'd probably still be at Caritas, looking fabulous. Or else at home sleeping, which also has its advantages.

Sometimes Cordelia found herself envying Angel, Wesley, and Gunn—although Wes not so much, she knew, because often he was sucked into the research-boy role, going through his old dusty books to find this spell or that antidote or a picture of some particularly heinous breed of night thing. But the guys got to have the comparatively simple job of going out and knocking heads around until they got the answers they wanted. *Not particularly sociable, but sometimes the frustration of trying to do everything by computer makes a person want to knock some heads, and there aren't any around to knock.*

"If you had a head," she said to the computer, "you'd be in some serious trouble right about now. Of course, I guess one could say you're all head, or all brain, at least, so watch out."

And talking to inanimate objects, she thought, catching herself. *There's a sure sign of mental stability.*

She considered taking a break, trying to go away from the screen and coming back to it a little later with a fresh eye. *It works for jigsaw puzzles,* she thought. But jigsaw puzzles tended not to have deadlines, especially deadlines that involved actual dead-ness. And that's what they were facing, she feared, if they couldn't locate Fred. So she gave up on that idea, took a couple of deep breaths, screwed her eyes shut, and then opened them again. *There you go. Fresh eyes.*

I wonder if the others are making any headway, Angel thought as he steered his GTX through L.A.'s dark streets. He pulled a cell phone from his pocket and pushed the button that would scroll through his saved phone numbers. *Cordelia first, then Wesley and Gunn, and Lorne last.* Too much time had elapsed since he'd talked to them all— time that couldn't be spared, if Fred was to be saved.

But all he got from the phone was a weak *beep* and a LOW BATTERY display. He tried the glove compartment, looking for the car cable, but couldn't find it. He switched off the useless thing and shoved it back into his pocket. *Pay phone, then.* He started to watch the sides of the road for one.

He'd been shaking a lot of trees tonight, hoping some rotten fruit would fall out. He needed something to go on—anything would be more than he had so far, which was effectively nothing. Fred had been there, then she'd been gone. A complex combination of diversions, which had obviously taken considerable planning and split-second timing. Schemes like that didn't happen in a vacuum. Somebody knew something. *It's just that L.A.'s such a big place, with so many people—and nonpeople. Finding the right ones with no clues to go on is a huge job.*

The sidewalks were empty, and only the occasional car shared the streets with his. Block after block rolled by, and no pay phone came into sight. The neighborhood he was cruising was a mixed one, mostly retail and commercial on the ground floors, residential upstairs. *Everyone who frequents the area either uses a phone in a place of business, or in their apartment,* he guessed. For a brief moment he wondered if the proliferation of cell phones meant that there were fewer pay phones around, but then figured that the number of truly inane pay phone commercials on TV, whenever he made time to watch, suggested otherwise.

The glow of a twenty-four-hour convenience store on a parallel block caught his eye, though. *Those places usually have phones,* he thought, performing a sharp right turn from the left lane. His tires squealed, but there was no one else on the street at the moment, so no danger to other drivers or pedestrians. He gunned the powerful engine, swallowing the block in seconds, and turned into the convenience store's parking lot. A clerk inside sat behind his sales counter, seemingly engrossed in a tabloid, and didn't even glance his way. But there was a pay phone underneath the store's overhang. Angel climbed out of the convertible without opening the door and went to the phone. He stuck his hand in his pants pocket, looking for change.

And he came up empty. He checked his coat, also fruitlessly. He returned to the car, looked around the dash, the instrument panel, tugged open the ashtray he never used. Zip.

He went into the store. As he crossed the threshold, an electronic chime rang. The clerk didn't put down the tabloid. Angel saw that the cover story was about a baby born with two heads, one of which was that of a fish. It looked like a salmon, but he wasn't entirely sure about that from this distance.

"Can I get change for the phone?" Angel asked with forced casualness.

"I can't open the drawer unless you buy something."

Angel snatched a pack of gum off the candy rack. "Okay, pack of gum," he snapped.

The clerk slowly put down the paper, folding it carefully, as if it were something precious. *Probably hasn't paid for it*, Angel suspected, *and wants to be able to sell it as new*.

"Sixty cents," the clerk said. He was a young guy, under twenty, Angel guessed, with bad skin and greasy hair. He rang in the sale and the cash drawer *chinged* open.

Angel handed him a five. "Couple dollars in quarters," he said. "As long as your drawer's open."

The kid laboriously counted out Angel's change, and then eight quarters and two singles, and handed it all to Angel. "Phone outside's busted," he said. "So don't try using that one. It'll just eat your money."

"You couldn't have told me that before?" Angel asked, on the verge of losing his patience.

"You'd still need change if you went to a different phone," the kid said. Which was true. "And I still couldn't give it to you without ringing up a sale. Besides"—he opened his lips and showed Angel an enormous wad of green gum between his teeth—"everybody needs gum."

"It's kind of an emergency," Angel said. "Is there a store phone I could use?"

"Employees only," the kid said. "Sorry." He didn't sound sorry. He sounded amused. There were brief moments, on extremely rare occasions, when Angel wished he were still evil. This was becoming one of those moments. "You don't want me to lose my job, do you?"

Angel almost told the kid that he'd rather see him lose his head, but he managed to restrain himself. He also realized that even if he succeeded in gaining the use of the store's phone for his calls, the kid would surely listen in, and he didn't want that, either. He just turned away and went back out the door. As he left, he could hear the kid settling back into his chair, and the rustling as he unfolded the tabloid again.

Pocket jingling with change, Angel climbed back into his car.

"No human could have taken her right out from under us," Wesley insisted. "Therefore, by talking only to human sources, we're wasting precious time."

Gunn shook his head. The argument had been dragging on for a while now. "You're most likely right that she wasn't snatched by humans," he admitted. "But that don't mean that humans don't keep track of what goes on in the demon world. Look at us—we're both human, right?"

"Well, yes."

"And we know from demons, don't we?"

"I think it's safe to say that we're somewhat rare cases, Gunn."

"Yeah," Gunn acknowledged. "Rare, but not unique. My old crew keeps pretty close tabs on vamps, right? I didn't train 'em all—lots of us just found one another, because we had that thing in common. But we already knew about the vamps, for one reason or another." He stopped for a moment, listening. They were walking along a quiet, dark street in a neighborhood where most people who went out at night didn't have human kindness on their minds. But Gunn knew it was those streets, most often, where information changed hands. The mean streets were the first Internet, where word of any lawless activity passed from mouth to ear faster than the electrical impulses raced down wires and onto computer screens.

I wonder if we should look up the guys, he thought. *See if they've heard anything.* The idea had crossed his mind several times, and he'd dismissed it each time. Since he had chosen to go to Pylea with Angel, Wesley, and Lorne, he hadn't exactly been Mr. Popularity with the crew of vampire hunters he'd once led. *Maybe as a very last resort,* he decided. *Maybe.*

"I've learned a lot more about what's out there, hangin' with y'all," he continued. "But there's nothing to say that other people with different experiences from mine don't know about other types of demons or whatever."

"People have always known," Wesley agreed softly. "Those ancient books I have—they were obviously written by people, for the most part. Fairy stories, legends, tales of monsters and supermen and gremlins—they show up in every human culture, every race, in every country on Earth. They try—*we* try—to claim that we don't believe, that we really do consider it just a lot of fanciful nonsense. But we do believe. In the darkest hours of the night, if you ask any one of us, I think you'll get the honest answer. There's more to the world than we acknowledge in the daylight, and the things that move through the night scare us."

"That's what I'm sayin'," Gunn shot back. "People know, and the kind of people we're lookin' for tonight, ones who stay out when they shouldn't, they're the ones who might have some clue, right?"

"Not necessarily," Wesley replied. He didn't sound at all convinced. "Someone—a demonic someone, I'm positive—targeted Fred. That means they targeted Angel, because certainly they knew that to touch Fred would bring down Angel's wrath. No demon would take such a step lightly, and they'd be very sure that their venture, whatever its goal, wasn't compromised by interference from humans. They'd take pains to make sure they weren't observed. I mean, look at how they got in and out with Fred so easily. They must be teleporters, matter shifters, dimension hoppers, or something along those lines. Couldn't they guarantee that some vampire hunter didn't spot them taking her into a hiding place?"

This is so frustrating, Gunn thought. *Wesley's right, and I'm right too. But we can't both be right, and we can't take the chance that either one of us is wrong.* "What it comes down to is, we have to do whatever we can do," he offered.

"That sounds right," Wesley agreed.

"Because it's Fred."

Wesley almost smiled, Gunn thought. But then, it was dark out, so he couldn't be positive. "Because it's Fred," the ex-Watcher agreed.

They had covered three more blocks, walking together in silent agreement and purpose, when they spotted him. He waited in the shadows, far outside the glow of any streetlamp, no doubt for a hapless victim to come along. But Gunn was used to looking at shadows, and he saw the form, a black shape in the blackness of night. He nudged Wesley. "Up ahead, on the right."

Wes peered into the darkness for a moment. "I see him," he said. "Human? Perhaps a mugger?"

"Can't tell yet. Let's get a little closer, see if he tries to take us."

"He won't," Wesley speculated. "Two against one? The way he's hiding in the shadows, he doesn't appear to be particularly courageous. I imagine he'll let us pass and wait for someone a bit less threatening."

"Then we'll have to force his hand," Gunn said with a grin. The prospect wasn't at all unpleasant. At least it was action—doing nothing was what really killed him.

The figure kept its position in the shadows, apparently secure in its belief that it couldn't be seen, as they approached it. It was pressed up against the wall of a building on their right. When they were dead even with it and it still hadn't shown itself, Gunn and Wes both decided as one that it was time to act. They had fought together often enough that they didn't even need to strategize— they simply turned and charged to the right, slamming the figure up against the wall.

In response, the person—a male, they could see now—responded by vamping out and slamming them with powerful arms, knocking them both back across the sidewalk.

Gunn picked himself up and gave a low chuckle. "Dog," he said, a friendly tone in his voice. "I didn't know you was a vamp. Wouldn't ever have tried a move like that on y'all if I did."

Wesley sounded shocked. "Gunn, have you lost your mind?" he whispered.

"Look, man, he ain't lookin' to eat us, because if he wanted to, he would've already. But maybe he can help us out with our little problem. What do you think?" he said, addressing the vampire who held his position by the wall. "Can you answer a couple questions?"

Wesley was already advancing on the vamp with a stake clenched in his fist, though. Even in the dim light Gunn could see Wesley's knuckles, white because of the tension with which he gripped the wood. "I don't see any particular advantage to politeness," he said angrily. "You *will* answer our questions, vampire, or you will be dust."

"Chill, Wes," Gunn pleaded. "There ain't no call for this."

"There's every call," Wesley countered. "Time is of the essence. What will it be, bloodsucker?"

Gunn was now close enough to the vamp to make out his expression, which had shifted from one of rage to something that looked, beneath the ridged forehead, beady eyes, and fanged mouth, like concern. His gaze ticked from Wesley to Gunn and back again, as if he were watching a tennis match.

Maybe the good cop/bad cop routine will work on him, Gunn thought. It wasn't what he'd had in mind, at the beginning. And the brutality of Wesley's immediate response had surprised him—*sure, the guy's a vamp, and we dust vamps. But not until after we get the information out of them.*

The ex-Watcher, he figured, was just so stressed about Fred that it was making him act in ways he ordinarily wouldn't. But that was okay—Gunn could be the good cop for a change, play against type, as long as the routine ended with a vamp getting dusted. *We gotta keep this one intact for a minute, though, vamp or no, just because I don't want us to lose Fred.*

Because I don't want to lose Fred.

He decided to play his role to the hilt, though. "Ease off, Wes," he said. "I think this vamp'll cooperate when he sees we're not out to hurt him."

The vampire didn't look especially comforted, and Wesley continued to advance cautiously, stake held out before him.

"You—your name is Wesley?" the vampire asked.

"That's right," Gunn answered quickly, picking up on the real source of the vamp's concern. "That's Wesley Wyndam-Pryce. I'm called Gunn. Heard of us?"

The vamp nodded—*a little fearfully,* Gunn observed, with a degree of satisfaction. "Yeah, that's what I figured," he continued. "We work with a guy named Angel. You know who that is, right?"

The vampire nodded again. *He's definitely realizing this has all the makings of a bad night,* Gunn thought.

"So you know Wes there won't mind dustin' you if you give him half a reason, right? I mean, that's kinda what we're all about. But, your lucky night, you might've caught a break. Because tonight we're really looking more for talk than action, if you catch my drift."

The vampire nodded one more time. His gaze darted right and left, as if looking for an escape route, but Gunn and Wes had him boxed in. "Wh-what do you wanna talk about?" he asked in a quavering voice. Gunn speculated that he was relatively new at the whole vamp thing—most vampires who had been around a while knew never to show fear, even if they felt it. And most vamps didn't seem to feel it, as if all the human victims they took gave them the confidence to believe that they could always win, even up against humans, like Gunn and Wes, who'd been down this road dozens of times.

"If you know who Angel is, then maybe you've heard about something that happened tonight to one of his people."

"I don't know what you mean, man," the vampire said. "I don't really pay attention to talk, you know?"

"So there is talk?" Wesley demanded.

"Hey, there's always talk," the vamp said dismissively. "Most times it don't mean anything."

"But maybe this time it does," Gunn pointed out. He moved a step closer and put a hand out toward Wesley, trying to look as if he was reaching to stop him, but really closing the web around the vamp, making sure there was no place for him to run. "Don't stake him yet, man, let him talk."

"He's got nothing for us," Wesley said with a snarl. He pushed past Gunn's hand, pressing the stake right up against the vampire's chest. Gunn wasn't certain that Wes was playing a part—he looked like he really wanted to dust this one. "Let's just finish him and move on."

"No, I might've heard something," the vampire said, the words rushing out in a torrent. "I mean, I *did* hear something! I don't know if it'll help, but I'll tell you."

"Talk fast," Gunn warned.

The vamp looked uneasily at the stake jabbing into his chest. "Like I said, it's just loose talk, you know. I don't know how true any of it is."

"We don't need your editorializing," Wesley said, his voice icy. "Just give us the facts."

"Okay, okay." The vampire's head was nodding like a bobblehead doll on a dashboard. "What I hear is, there's some kind of plot against Angel. I don't know any more than that, just that something's going on, some kind of action being taken. Lot of folks in this town got no use for a vampire with a soul, you know what I'm saying? Me, I got no opinion, one way or the other, about that. But some people I guess finally got fed up enough to make their move."

"Who are these 'people'?" Wesley asked, pushing the stake's point harder into the vamp's chest. "We need names, where we can find them."

"I don't know any of that," the vamp said, desperate now. "I'd tell you if I could—you know that, right? I just know what I hear, you know, from a guy who knows a guy who knows a guy."

"So in other words, you're useless to us," Wesley said.

"Yeah . . . I guess," the vamp agreed, somewhat hesitantly.

"All right, then." Wesley drew back and then drove the stake forward with all his strength. The move took Gunn by surprise—by the time he realized what Wes was doing, the vamp was nothing but a cloud of black dust scattering in the evening's breeze.

When the vampire was gone, Wesley turned to Gunn, glaring at him as if expecting him to maintain his good-cop role.

"You heard him," Wesley insisted. He sounded as if he would brook no argument. "He had nothing for us."

Gunn shrugged. "If he knew a guy who knew a guy, we might've been able to backtrack."

"We don't have time to follow the vampire rumor mill," Wesley said. His voice was still so cold that it scared Gunn a little. "Fred's out there, in trouble, and she needs us. We're wasting our time with these insignificant sources. We need to find someone who matters."

Gunn couldn't argue with that theory. He wasn't

exactly sure how they'd go about it, because "someone who matters" could be just about anyone, depending on the situation. And since they were no closer to knowing who had it in for Angel, they were still looking at a big blank wall.

But he knew one thing for sure: *I never want to get on the wrong side of this guy.*

CHAPTER SEVEN

"The thing is, I'm pretty sure Angel killed my brother."

Virg was a Kailiff demon, as muscular as a pro weight lifter, and with four rows of pointed spikes erupting from the battleship gray skin of his head—two rows extending back from his forehead, on either side, and two following the line of his jaw—he looked, to Lorne, like an extremely menacing sort of individual.

Which, Lorne knew, *is actually a very accurate description of him.* Kailiffs tended to be enforcers, leg breakers, hired muscle. From the stories he'd heard, they were very selective about who they hired themselves to, most commonly working for Kedigris demons. But as dangerous as Virg might be outside, Caritas was sanctuary, and Lorne knew the demon wouldn't hurt anyone in here.

Even so, he almost hesitated to ask the next

question, but he figured there was no graceful way out of it. He steepled his long, elegant fingers and went for it. "What makes you think that?"

The big demon shifted in his chair and downed a swallow of ale before answering. "Griff was trying to collect on a debt. Guy named Doyle made some bad choices—horses, college ball, I'm not too sure of the details. But it put him in the position where he owed money to the wrong people, and all Griff wanted to do was give him the chance to make it right."

"Sounds like a reasonable fellow, that Griff," Lorne suggested. He'd heard of Doyle, of course. The half Irishman, half demon had been Angel's first ally in Los Angeles, and had been the one who'd gotten visions from the Powers That Be until he'd sacrificed himself and passed the power on to Cordelia. "Salt of the earth, right? Trying to help a guy out that way, I mean."

Virg blinked a couple of times, and Lorne believed, unlikely as it might seem, that the demon was trying hard not to weep. The Kailiff had reluctantly sung the first few bars of "Baby Got Back" for him, which Lorne had listened to with equal reluctance, and he had a glimpse of a future in which Virg went down hard, but not without taking many of his opponents out first. Once again, there was no connection to Fred's disappearance that he could see, and once again he wished he had more precise control of his own powers.

"Griff was the best," Virg said sorrowfully. "He was a couple years older than me. Used to give me rides on his shoulders, until his spikes got too sharp and he worried he'd hurt me. Our dad wasn't always around, you know, and Griff looked out for me." He fingered one of his own spikes, near his chin. "Folks think just cause we're tough looking, we weren't little kids once, we don't got families."

Lorne had to fight the impulse to pat the demon's hand, or maybe give him a soothing hug. Sanctuary or not, he didn't want a friendly gesture to be misinterpreted by such a dangerous fellow. He settled for trying to sound as sympathetic as possible. "I can tell you miss him."

"Every day," Virg said, swallowing hard. "Anyway, he was trying to collect this dough that Doyle owed. Doyle was dodging him, and I guess Angel was helping him do it. Griff might've been, you know, pushed to the point where he needed to make an example out of Doyle, and he said Angel talked him into backing off, letting the welcher pay."

"By 'example,' I'm guessing you don't mean letting him off the hook with an abject apology," Lorne said. A Sqirtol demon was onstage, caterwauling to a ZZ Top number, and Lorne found himself almost shouting to be heard over the din. The Sqirtol's path was destined to be a violent one, but not in any way that intersected with Fred, as far as Lorne could see.

"More like being threaded onto a hook and hung over the street for everyone to see," Virg clarified. From the tone of his voice, Lorne got the idea that the Kailiff didn't find it an unpleasant image. "But even after Angel promised him that Doyle would pay up, he still didn't. Griff got tired of waiting—there was pressure on him, you know, from his . . . ahh . . . employer. So he tracked old Doyle down to this chick's haunted apartment, Angel's other friend, what's her name, Cordelia. That was the last I heard of him alive. His body turned up a couple of weeks later, in the sewers. Just dumped like one of those pet alligators you hear about."

"I understand that's an urban legend," Lorne pointed out anxiously. "The alligators, I mean. Like the dog from Tijuana, or waking up in a bathtub full of ice, and . . . I guess I shouldn't go there, should I?"

Virg ignored him. *Probably for the best,* Lorne thought.

"Doyle couldn't have taken Griff," Virg went on. He seemed to have forgotten his drink, maybe even where he was. His gaze was distant, as if he were back with his brother's body. "And that chick couldn't have. But Griff's neck had been snapped, like it was a twig." He touched his own neck, which looked to Lorne more like the trunk of an oak tree than a twig. "Had to be Angel."

Lorne felt compelled to offer some defense for his friend, even if it wouldn't mean much to the Kailiff. "I've known Angel for a long time," he said. "He's really, when you get down to it, a pretty peaceful sort. I mean, he fights when he has to, but who doesn't? I like to think I'm a lover, not a fighter, but there's been a time or two when I've had to throw down, right? Isn't that what they call it?"

"You going somewhere with this?" Virg inquired.

"I'm just saying, if Angel really did kill Griff, maybe he had a good reason. Maybe Griff wouldn't lay off, maybe he even decided he'd include Angel, or Cordelia, as part of the example. Angel wouldn't just kill him for the fun of it. I don't think I've ever seen Angel do anything just for the fun of it, for that matter."

"Griff was doing a job," Virg countered. "Angel didn't like that, he should have stayed out of the way."

"Except he's got a real problem with friends of his getting killed," Lorne shot back. He was getting angry now. This Kailiff demon's attitude toward killing associates of Angel's was cavalier, to say the least. And as a known Angel associate, the Host found that he couldn't help taking exception to it. "I'm truly sorry for your loss, bro," he said, dialing back to the sympathy part. "But is all this by way of saying that you won't help me find Fred because you're still holding a grudge against Angel?"

The Kailiff studied him for a moment, his brown

eyes seeming to search for something in Lorne's face. He couldn't tell if Virg found what he was looking for or not, but the demon eventually turned away and stared into his half-finished mug of ale. "Not necessarily," he said finally. "I got a problem with Angel. I got no problem with you, and I don't even know this Fred chick, so I got no problem with her."

"You couldn't have a problem with her," Lorne said effusively. "She's just about the sweetest person to ever set foot on Earth. Or, for that matter, any other dimension she may have visited once upon a time."

Virg lifted his mug and drained it. "Then I'll do what I can."

"Excellent," Lorne said, flashing his pearly whites at the big guy. The Sqirtol had finished his song and was starting in on Hootie and the Blowfish, obviously intending to do as much damage there as he'd done to the trio from Texas. "What did you see that might help?"

"The demons in the car that shot at everybody," Virg began. "They were Roshons."

Which matches what the Skander told me, Lorne realized. "Are you sure?"

I'm positive," Virg announced with a sneer. "I'd know those creeps anywhere."

"Am I correct," Lorne asked, trying to phrase it as diplomatically as he could, "in believing that there's some bad blood between the Kailiffs and the Roshons?"

The Kailiff thumped his empty mug down on the table, hard. "I hate 'em. We all hate 'em, I guess. They're the enemy."

Lorne attempted a smile, but had a feeling it wasn't coming across quite right. "You make it sound like there's a war on."

"Might as well be," Virg said, without a trace of regret. "You know my kind—we're better at muscle work than brain work. We leave the hard thinking up to the Kedigris. They tell us what to do, we do it, everybody's happy. Except whoever we did it to, they're usually not happy, even if they're still alive."

Charming, Lorne thought. *Now he's confessing hired murders to me.* He kept his mouth shut and let the Kailiff continue.

"The Kedigris, you know, I don't always like them that much, either, but they pay on time and they don't tend to bother us much, so that's okay. They have their own ideas about things, how things should be run. Somehow, the Roshons, they seem to object to these Kedigris ideas a lot. You follow me?"

"I think so," Lorne said. "But to tell you the truth, I'm not really sure. You are being a bit . . . evasive, maybe?"

Virg leaned across the table toward him. It may have been just to be heard over the Sqirtol's wailing, of course, but to Lorne it felt just a wee bit intimidating as well. "Anything I say in here is just between you and me, right?"

"Yes, of course," the Host assured his guest. He wasn't entirely sure he wanted to hear whatever Virg had to say, with that kind of a preamble, but if it might help Fred, he'd take a chance. "Think of it as saloon keeper–client privilege."

"Good." Virg sat back in his seat, apparently satisfied. "The Kedigris kind of control what you might call organized crime, in the demon world. We don't think of it as crime, of course—it's just business. But I mean, if you were on the outside looking in, and you didn't know any better . . ."

"Of course." *I was right*, Lorne thought. *I really didn't want to go here.*

"Anyway, you know," Virg went on, "the human world has their businesses and their businessmen, and our world has ours. Somebody like old Doyle wants to play the horses, play the point spread on a U.C.L.A. game, he's got to have someone he can work with. Maybe someone needs a little something to get going in the morning, or to take the edge off at night. Maybe somebody needs a date, or a weapon. There's always going to be an organization that provides these services, right?"

Onstage, the Sqirtol had finished his Hootie massacre, and was bowing to the halfhearted applause of the captive audience. Lorne didn't want to walk away from Virg now that he'd started in a direction that might eventually prove to be helpful, but he still had a duty to his club, as well, and he knew it was important that everybody stay entertained since they were going to be here a while. "Listen, Virg, you'll have to excuse me, all right? Just for a second. Half a second. I just need to go do the hosting gig, and then I'm all yours. Undivided attention, okay?"

Virg waved him off. "Sure, go. What do I care? It's not like I'm going anywhere soon."

"The time's flying by," Lorne tried to assure him as he stood. "You'll see." He wove his way between the tables and took the stage, clapping as he did. The Sqirtol was already on his way to his own seat.

"Thank you so much, Slorvis," Lorne said into the microphone, beaming his smile toward the audience. "Brings a tear to the eye. In the good way. And just to clear up a common misconception, a Sqirtol is not a type of Pokemon." He waited for the audience's laughter to die, and then looked blankly about the room. "Okay, next up we have . . . who's next?"

A female Shrenli stood up at her table, where she'd been sitting alone all night. Lorne had seen her in the club earlier, but didn't think he'd ever met her before. "I'll go," she said quietly. Lorne had the impression that she had to force herself to the stage, like it wasn't something she was comfortable with. *If I looked like something that mutated out of the lobster tank at Trader Vic's, I'd be shy too,* he thought. He clapped for her, hoping to encourage her, and got the audience applauding for her too. When she reached the stage he took one of her pincers and helped her up. "What's your name, beautiful?" he asked her.

"Vizzsclorf," she replied, parting her beaklike mouth in what Lorne hoped was a smile.

"Ladies and gentlemen," Lorne announced into the mike, "I'm proud to present, gracing our stage for the first time, Vissclorf! And what song would you like to share with us tonight, darling?"

"I was thinking of 'R-E-S-P-E-C-T,'" she told him.

"She's taking on the queen of soul!" Lorne shouted. "Let's give her a great big honking Caritas hand! Give it up for Vissclorf!"

He got out of her way then, and by the time he got back to the Kailiff's table, her song had begun. She was actually pretty good, he was surprised to hear. Her voice was untrained but strong, and she put a lot of passion into the song. "She's not bad," Lorne said.

Virg shrugged. "Guess so," he said.

"I'm sorry, big guy—you were in the middle of a story and I interrupted you, just like someone in a Miss Manners rant. Something about providing necessary services."

Virg seemed to have no problem picking up where he'd left off. "Yeah, and the Kedigris, they're good at it. They're fair, you know? They take a reasonable profit on any transaction they do, and they're willing to show they mean business when they need to—that's where we come in, making sure people know they're serious folks. But they don't go out of their way to hurt anyone. If it comes down to keeping a customer happy so he'll still be a customer tomorrow, they're willing to be flexible, right? Where some types—your Roshons, for instance, they'd just as soon take the customer's head off and pull their insides out through their neck."

"I'm not eating right now, but I'd like to again before I die," Lorne interrupted. He understood that Virg was using the word *people* in its most general sense, but still . . . "So that kind of visualization I can do without, thanks."

"I'm just making a point," Virg said.

"Consider it made."

"Okay, sorry. I didn't realize you were a sensitive type."

"Very sensitive," Lorne assured him. "As sensitive as you can imagine. Maybe more so. I'm so sensitive, Oprah Winfrey took lessons from me."

"Can I keep going?" Virg asked.

"Please." He really hoped Virg would keep going, but without quite so much incidental detail, and with more getting to the point.

"So you have the idea about what the Roshons are like," he continued. "And some people are customers of one group at one time, and another group the next. Maybe there's someone who likes to make a bet with the Roshons but comes to the Kedigris for certain other amusements. If the Roshons get carried away and peel all the skin off his body, then we're going to have a problem with that."

"So if I'm getting this straight," Lorne attempted, "your employers and the Roshons have business methods that occasionally find themselves in conflict."

"You could say it that way," Virg agreed. "I wouldn't, but you could."

"I think I just did," Lorne pointed out. "The only part I'm still not clear on is why you're telling me. It's, like, you tell me that the shooters were Roshons, and then you tell me that I shouldn't take your word for it because you don't like the Roshons and you'd probably tell me that, anyway, just to get them in trouble."

"I got no problem getting them in trouble," Virg said. "But this time it's because they deserve it. I spend enough time keeping an eye on Roshons, I'd recognize them even in a car at night, with guns blasting. And that's who was in the car. I guarantee it."

"Okay, then," Lorne said, glad the point had been reached at last. "That's good to know. Do you know where we might find them?"

Virg gave him a look that clearly implied he

thought Lorne was hopelessly stupid. "They're Roshons," he said, as if that explained it all. "If I knew where to find them, they'd be dead already."

"Of course." *I should have known,* Lorne thought. *Foolish of me.*

And one more little piece of information, but like the rest, all it points to is a dead end.

CHAPTER EIGHT

As the doorknob turned, Fred glanced at the wreckage she'd made of the place—the little cabinet knocked over; door taken partway off; blood on the wooden floor, spattered over her clothes and coating her arm. *No way to hide any of it,* she thought, shoving the cabinet away from her. *Like whoever is coming in won't know I did it.*

The door pushed inward. *What kind of demon is it going to be?* she found herself wondering. *Something with long claws, dozens of eyes, and a thousand teeth? A creature with its face in its belly and its stomach on top of its neck? A hungry demon with a taste for human flesh and a weakness for petite physicists?* The beings she'd had to contend with in Pylea had been bad enough, but since coming back to Earth and working with Angel a little, she had learned that she'd had only the barest beginnings of an understanding of just how awful some demons could be. And some humans, for that matter, like those lawyers at Wolfram and Hart.

Notwithstanding those lawyers, her heart leaped when she saw that the person coming through the door was in fact a person, one hundred percent human-looking, and not some kind of hellbeast. The thought that flashed through her mind in that first instant—*he's come to save me*—vanished just as quickly when she remembered that humans could be just as inhumane as the ugliest demon, while some demons, like Lorne, were just as nice as could be. And some hummingbirds weighed less than a dime.

The man was about five nine, 170 pounds, with a broad chest and arms that strained the sleeves of his T-shirt. His hair was dark brown and windblown, his face—handsome, in its own rugged way—clean-shaven. He might have been in his late twenties or his early forties—his face was youthful, with few lines except for some creases around the eyes, so it was hard to tell. The first thing he did after he'd closed the door behind himself, before he even looked her way, was to sniff the air.

So maybe not so human after all? Fred wondered.

"Blood," he said, his voice calm and even. Fred

would have thought it was a pleasant voice, under other circumstances. "Cut yourself." It wasn't a question.

Now he looked at Fred. She'd tucked the hinge pin into the waistband of her skirt, but the rest of her mess was in plain sight. She held up the bloody arm. "A little, yes," she said. "I don't suppose you have a bandage on you? Or maybe an emergency room doctor?"

"You won't need one," the man said. He came farther into the room, stopping when he was close enough to see the broken cabinet. "You're a sloppy one, aren't you? Destructive. But then, that's what your kind are like, isn't it?"

"Look," Fred implored, her Texas twang making itself evident as it tended to when she was under stress. "I don't know who you are or why I'm chained up here, but I think there's been some kind of mistake. Whoever you think I am, I'm not. My name is Fred Burkle, in case you didn't know. I'm just a scientist, and I'm kind of new in town, in a way, and I don't have anything you might want. I don't have any family that can pay a ransom, if that's what you're looking for. So if you'll just unlock me, I'll be on my way out of here and we'll pretend all this never happened, all right?"

The man turned away from her, ignoring her as easily as if he'd been stone deaf. He crossed back to the other side of the room, and for a moment she thought he was going to go back out the door. She wasn't sure how she felt about that—on the one hand, she'd be able to get back to work with her hinge pin, except that she still didn't know anything about picking locks beyond her suspicion that it was harder than it looked in the movies. Most things were, like skydiving. That looked so free and easy on the big screen, but she had a hunch that in real life, it'd be just about as scary as anything.

But on the other hand, if he stayed maybe she'd be able to persuade him to free her.

He stayed. Instead of going through the door, he went to the big brown chair and sat down with a heavy sigh.

"You don't want to have to sit here all night watching over me, do you? I mean, a guy like you, you have better things to do. You could go to a ball game, or the library, or—no, maybe not the library, you probably wouldn't like that, sometimes I say the stupidest things. And as for a ball game, I guess if it's night, that wouldn't work either. Is it night? I'm not really sure how long I was, you know, unconscious."

He continued to ignore her. It seemed to be what he was best at.

"I'm sorry about the little nightstand or whatever," she said. "I guess I accidentally knocked it down. And I didn't mean to get blood on your floor, but I'll clean it up if you let me go."

Fred could see him, sitting in the chair, staring off into space as if he were all alone here. She had taken him for human, but could a human being really ignore someone else so completely, especially if that someone else was obviously injured and scared? What kind of man could he be?

She remembered that she had been talking to a human man in Caritas earlier. It had surprised her to see him there, since usually she and her friends were the only humans around on the few occasions that she'd been to Lorne's club. But she was coming back from the women's room—*well, females' room, anyway,* she corrected—and he had been standing in the hallway, by the pay phone, with a colorful drink in his hand. Even in the dark hall she had noticed his brilliant green eyes, which caught some wayward light in such a way, they almost seemed to glow from within. He'd been handsome, too, she remembered, in a kind of Angel-y way, with spiky dark hair and shoulders one could hang a swing from, and he'd grinned at her like she was the first human female he'd seen in ages. *Which, if he hangs out here,* she remembered thinking, *maybe I am.*

"Hi," he had said. "I'm Jack. You come here often?"

Which was maybe not as original as it might have been, but considering the type of club Caritas was and the clientele it drew, was not as mundane as it would have been in just about any other setting on the planet.

Suddenly shy, she had looked toward Jack's feet— *nice shoes,* she thought—and let her hair swing down in front of her face, in case she was blushing or making a funny expression or had a little bit of spinach between her teeth, except that she hadn't actually eaten spinach today, or even this month, that she could remember. She hadn't really spoken to anyone since returning from Pylea, except the gang at Angel's, and wasn't sure she could remember how to do it. "Oh, I don't really go anyplace often," she said. "From my room down to the lobby, I guess, and then back up to my room, but that's about it."

"Lobby? You're staying in a hotel? Just visiting?"

"No, I live here," she explained. "I mean, not here in Caritas, but in Los Angeles. In a hotel. I live in the hotel. It's—a friend's place. His hotel."

"A male friend," Jack said. He sounded a little disappointed. "I see."

She saw too. "Oh, no, it's not like that." *Not that I wouldn't like it to be,* she thought. *But there's no indication that it's going that way.* "It's just— you know, he has this hotel, and there are plenty of rooms there, so he lets me stay there. And we work together, sometimes."

"What do you do?" Jack asked. He closed the gap between them, moving forward to stand maybe a little closer than Fred found comfortable. But the hallway was fairly narrow and her back was already against a wall, so she stayed where she was.

"I'm a physicist," she said. "I guess I don't do much actual physics these days, though. But I help out with his work."

Jack laughed. Fred liked the way it sounded. "A woman of mystery, eh?" he said. "I can appreciate that."

She felt shy again, and resumed checking out his shoes through a curtain of hair. "I don't think I'm very mysterious," she said softly. "I think I'm kind of an open book."

"There are a lot of books," Jack replied. His voice sounded surprisingly intimate, and he looked at her—no, *into* her—with strikingly green eyes, like chips of emerald. "Some of them you can't read until you know the right language."

Fred hadn't had a lot of boyfriends in her life, she knew. *And why did I just think about that now?* she wondered. *He hasn't done anything except be polite to me. He's probably trying to figure out when I'm going to get out of his way and let him get to the telephone or the men's room.* But at the same time, she could tell he wasn't trying to go anywhere. It was almost as if he'd seen her go into the hall and had followed her, waiting until she'd come back through so he could talk to her. And he was certainly going beyond just politeness.

"I'm not written in code," she said. "Just English." *With a little Pylean thrown in, maybe. And some higher mathematics.*

"Well, I can read English," he replied, showing a friendly smile. Those remarkable eyes seemed to snare the hallway's dim light and cast it back toward her. "Maybe—"

He didn't get a chance to finish his sentence because a loud noise suddenly sounded from outside, cutting him off. Within seconds the club's occupants were on their feet and headed for the door, Fred and Jack carried along in the wake. She lost sight of him, then. Outside, she had been standing toward the back, behind the bulk of the spectators watching flames engulf the building across the street. She could make out, at the front of the pack, Angel, Cordelia, Wesley, and Gunn, and she was about to try to slip through the crowd toward them when the car approached, opening fire.

That was the last thing she could remember, until she'd awakened here on the floor with a headache like someone had used her skull as a target in a professional rock-throwing contest. Of which, unlikely as it seemed here on Earth, she'd witnessed several during her time in Pylea. Organized sports there had been very different from their earthly counterparts—the closest she'd seen here to Pylean athletic activities were the World's Strongest Man competitions on TV, where events seemed to include versions of Carry a Big Rock and Throw a Log, both of which were real crowd-pleasers in the Host's home dimension.

She wondered for a moment why the young man sitting in the chair, steadfastly ignoring her as he stared out at the ceiling and walls, had reminded her of the one she'd spoken to at Caritas. But now that she wondered about it, she could see right away. Although the two men looked nothing alike, this one also had luminous green eyes that looked like they could light up a dark room.

"I really don't mind sleeping on the floor, so don't let that worry you," she said to him, suspecting he'd pretend not to hear her, anyway. "I'm kind of used to it. Used to a dirt floor, anyway—wood is a different thing, harder to mash around into the right shape, but it's better than stone floors, and I've done that, too. I could use a pillow, though, if you have any around."

The man didn't answer. It was almost as if he'd left his body there and had gone somewhere else. But as she watched, she could see his chest rise and fall as he breathed. Every now and then he twitched, or brought his hand up to scratch behind his ear. He moved his head from time to time, changing his angle of view but never looking directly at Fred. The fly, whose buzzing had become less frequent and insistent, made more noise than he did.

"I could use a rest room, too. Do you think you could unlock me long enough for that?"

No answer.

"There were ten naked women here looking for you a few minutes ago. I think they were cheerleaders for the Rams."

Still no response from the man in the chair.

"You know, I've seen some pretty silly things— things you probably couldn't even imagine. I've seen a bird with four wings steal meat from a butcher's cart. I've seen people who didn't know how to sing celebrate a holiday by batting one another with long purple squashes, like giant eggplants, until there was only one standing. But you sitting there, acting like you can't even hear me talking to you when I know you can, that's got to be right up there with the most idiotic things I've ever encountered. Don't you feel stupid knowing that I know that you know that I'm talking?"

Now he finally shifted in the chair, putting his elbows on his knees and bending forward. But he wasn't looking at her, Fred realized. And then she saw what he was tracking, moving just his eyes but not his head. While she'd been talking, the fly had broken free of the spider's web. She saw the spider crawling rapidly toward where the fly had been, as if not believing it had slipped her trap. And she saw the fly, making excited, erratic patterns across the room. The man rose from his chair and walked toward the center of the room. Waited there, still, barely breathing. Then he reached out with one arm, a move so fast, Fred could scarcely follow, and snagged the fly, mid-flight. He held it up and examined it for a brief moment, then popped it into his mouth and swallowed. Finally, he looked at Fred. "I hear what you're saying," he said, his voice cold. "I am just not interested in talking to you, okay?"

"Well, sure, that's fine," Fred said, heartened that there had at least been some take in the give-and-take, but equally dismayed by the guy's dietary tic. She thought not mentioning the fly would probably be a good idea. "But what about my requests? That bathroom thing is getting toward urgent, you know?"

"Not interested in talking," he said again, "and definitely not interested in listening. Especially that. You have nothing to say that could possibly be of interest to me. So you might as well just be quiet. You're not going anywhere for a while, so get used to it."

At least that's something, Fred thought. *Not very helpful, but now I know that he's not necessarily planning to kill me, and expects that at some point I'll be moved away from this spot. Sooner would be better than later, but I'll take what I can get.*

Looking on the bright side had often proven to be difficult for Fred, but she considered it an important goal in life, and tried to focus on it whenever she could.

Now seemed like a particularly good time to practice it.

I'm not dead, she thought. *I'm not dead. And as long as I'm not dead, there's hope.*

CHAPTER NINE

"How are you doing, Cordy?" Angel asked. He'd finally found a pay phone that worked, outside a closed gas station on Figueroa. He was painfully aware of the precious minutes he'd lost looking for one. "Got anything yet?"

"A crick in my neck from sitting here staring at this computer screen," Cordelia's voice came back. "After we find Fred, I think we should schedule an ergonomics seminar. You know, getting kicked around by demons and stuff is bad, but who knows what kind of repetitive motion disorders we're risking without even knowing about it?"

"Talk to Wes about the seminar," Angel said wearily. "I was thinking more about Fred-related information."

"Well, Lorne called. He didn't have much, though—he said that one of the demons smelled cinnamon, which could mean a Kedigris demon or it could mean someone can't afford a decent perfume. And another thought he saw Roshons driving the car, but that one was a Kailiff, a natural enemy of Roshons."

"So really, nothing useful."

"That's what he thought, but he wanted us to make that judgment," Cordelia explained.

"What about your own progress?" Angel asked, hoping for a more substantial answer from her.

"I've been narrowing the field," Cordelia replied. "I've got it down to about forty-seven different types of demons who have used fire as a diversionary tactic. Oh, and humans. Apparently we do it all the time."

"What about a combination of fire and portals?" Angel asked. "Since they probably took Fred out through one."

"That takes it down to eleven," Cordelia reported. "But one of those can be discounted because they're extinct, and one because they can only open a portal *inside* the flames. I think we'd have noticed if someone had carried Fred across the street into the burning building."

"Seems likely," Angel agreed, impressed at Cordelia's efficiency. "So what does that leave?"

"Klakivan, Sholirt—"

"Sholirts don't live in Southern California," Angel interrupted. "Too cold here."

"Okay, strike them. Mumford, Divik, Bovissle, Zhoon, Skander, Korvitak, and McDonald."

"There's a kind of demon called McDonald?" Angel asked, surprised.

"Apparently they've blended almost completely with the human community," Cordelia informed him. "But I know a certain fast-food chain I'm keeping away from for a while."

"Okay, good work, Cordelia," Angel said. "Of those, the only one I saw at Caritas tonight was a Skander, I think. Did you notice any of the others?"

Cordelia hesitated for a moment. "There might have been a Klakivan," she said. "But it could have just been a badly dressed Davric. I get those mixed up sometimes."

"Who doesn't? Keep at it, Cord. You're making progress."

"I'm on the case, ex-boss," she replied. He could hear the smile in her voice, and as he hung up the phone he pictured it in his mind's eye. Cordelia's ready smile could keep him going through the long night. *Although a pint of blood wouldn't hurt.*

He tried to think of which of those demonic types might hold a grudge against him. There was a danger, he knew, in assuming that it was all about him, but it was less likely by far that Fred had managed to make such powerful enemies. The reasonable conclusion was still that she had been grabbed to get at him, somehow.

Trouble is, I've managed to tick off just about every kind of demon in town, at one time or another. That doesn't really narrow the field. But he was, he realized, not far from a Korvitak lair he'd had reason to visit, a couple of years before. One of Doyle's visions had sent him to a cocktail waitress, who had managed to become entangled with a Korvitak clan. The clan leader had visited the bar where she worked, shape-shifted into human form, and the two had seemed to hit it off. He had maintained the illusion whenever he saw her, for a couple of weeks. But she'd sensed that he was hiding something, assumed it was a wife and maybe a family, and followed him home one night. Peeking through the windows, she'd seen him drop the human guise and assume his real form. When he wouldn't answer his calls and stopped going to work, the Korvitak realized she had discovered his secret, and had gone looking for her, to silence her before she could reveal him.

She had no intention of revealing anything—she was utterly terrified of what she'd seen, and in Doyle's vision she'd been hiding out under a freeway overpass, afraid to go home, afraid to return to the bar, even afraid to draw money out of her bank account. Angel had found her, listened to her story, then had gone to the Korvitak and persuaded him to leave her alone. The persuasion had involved a few broken bones, but an agreement had been reached.

So that Korvitak might still hold a grudge, Angel reasoned. *Maybe it's time to pay him another visit.* He got back into the car, still jingling because he hadn't yet called Wesley and Gunn, or Lorne, and still had a pocket full of change. He'd have to call them soon, but first he wanted to check out the Korvitak lair since he was so close.

As he covered the blocks to the demon lair, he thought about how terrified Fred must be. She had managed to get through five years in Pylea, but not without serious damage to her mental and emotional stability. Obviously, he hadn't known her before Pylea, but anyone who spent most of her time back here in her room, writing on the walls, had to have some issues. She was a sweet young lady with a good heart and a brilliant mind—maybe the smartest person Angel had ever known, in a very long lifetime. But she had been left damaged by the experience, *frail,* he thought. Being kidnapped by demons wouldn't help her at all, and might even set back her progress. She had been starting to get better, willing to go out more, hoping to be a full-fledged member of the team. He wondered what state she'd be in when he found her this time.

Because I will find her, he vowed. *Before the sun rises, I'll have her back.*

There had been seven Korvitaks living in the bungalow when Angel had last dropped by. He couldn't remember the name of the one who had frightened the waitress, and had never known the names of the others. But he thought he'd recognize them again when he saw them, assuming, of course, that they were wearing their natural forms and hadn't shape-shifted into something else.

It was a smallish house, screened from the road by a hedge of oleander, with a narrow, rutted dirt driveway leading to it. The neighborhood was all residential, single-family detached homes, most with garages and long drives. Angel parked on the street and hiked up the driveway, listening. Just the usual night noises: crickets; somewhere a TV set on; cars passing on nearby streets. The windows of the bungalow were all dark.

Angel tried to reason the best way to go into the house. If Fred was imprisoned somewhere inside and he just charged in, her captors might panic and hurt her. On the other hand, if they were using Fred to draw him in, they might be waiting for him and he could be walking into a trap. What he should have done, he knew, was call the rest of the team together and gone into every entrance simultaneously, increasing the chances of finding her in a hurry and reducing the risk.

But he hadn't done that, and he was here now.

He went to the front door and rang the bell.

And he waited. He rang it again.

This time, he heard shuffling sounds inside. Someone approaching the door, feet thumping down the hall, claws clicking on the floor, tail dragging behind. A light over his head went on, and the peephole set into the door went dark. Then the door opened.

The Korvitak stared at him, an expression of sleepy annoyance on its long, hangdog face. Its yellow eyes, heavy-lidded with sleep, were the size of golf balls, its snout horselike, with drooping jowls that bracketed a disturbingly human-looking mouth. Its skin was a bright orange, like California poppies. An enormous robe, of something that looked like silk, covered its body. Angel was pretty sure this was the one he had fought before.

He was also pretty sure he'd woken the demon up.

"What are you doing here?" the Korvitak demanded in a voice that Angel instantly remembered, high-pitched and whiny. One of its clawed hands scratched its enormous belly, beneath the robe. "Do you know what time it is? Do you know my wrist still hurts when it's going to rain? What is it, you want to punch me around some more? I haven't been near Stella since that night."

That's right, Angel thought. *Her name was Stella, and the Korvitak's was . . .* he groped for it *. . . Frank!*

The greeting didn't seem like the kind of welcome he'd get if Fred had indeed been kidnapped by this clan, though.

"Hi, Frank," he said, trying to sound casual, like he'd just dropped by for a friendly chat. "What's new?"

Frank just stared at him.

Angel shook his head, shrugged, scratched the end of his nose. "I, uhh . . . just thought I'd drop by, you know. See how you're doing. All that old business with Stella, no hard feelings about that, right? Ancient history, water under the bridge."

Frank stared some more.

"Angel, you know we dream, right?"

"Sorry, what?" Angel asked, confused.

"Korvitaks dream. Some demons, they don't dream. They go to sleep and it's like they're dead, until they wake up. But Korvitaks dream, like people do, maybe even more intense. Stories, pictures, words, the whole bit. It's like watching a movie in your head, in Technicolor with Sensurround and Dolby. Do you know what I was doing when you rang the doorbell?"

"Dreaming?" Angel guessed.

"I was with the most beautiful Korvitak in all of creation. We were on a grassy hill, with the sun setting in front of us, the sky all indigo and rose and gold the way it gets sometimes, little puffs of cloud picking up pink highlights. A warm breeze wafting the scent of flowers. She was holding my hand and making certain suggestions that I won't go into. And then there was this horrible bonging noise, which I eventually realized was my doorbell, and I figured I had to come and answer it, even if it meant walking out of the dream, because at this time of night it just might be important."

"I, uhh . . . ," Angel stammered. "I'm sorry."

"Is it?"

"Is it what?"

Frank raised his hands, questioningly. "Is it important?"

"I thought so, for a minute," Angel said. "Have you seen Fred?"

"Who's Fred?"

"Part of my team. She was kidnapped, outside Caritas tonight. I thought maybe you—"

The Korvitak shook his head, which caused his jowls to sway like miniature sandbags on strings. "We've been home all night. We don't really get out much anymore, tell you the truth. Too much trouble out there in the world."

"I'm sorry to have disturbed you, Frank," Angel said sincerely. *This was a bad idea,* he decided. *But if I hadn't done it, I wouldn't have known that.* "I had to check," he said, by way of explanation. "I was in the neighborhood, you know."

"You checked. Satisfied?"

"I'm sorry," Angel repeated.

"Then you don't mind if I go back to bed."

"Sure." Angel started to turn away, then had another stray thought. "Oh, one more thing. Do you have a cell phone?"

"Now you want to use my cell?"

"No, I just need one of those car charger cords, you know, that stick into the lighter. If it's compatible with this." He fished his phone out of his coat pocket.

Frank glanced at it. "Hold on," he said. He vanished into the dark house and came back a minute later with a coiled cable. "Here, take it."

"I'll bring it back tomorrow," Angel promised.

"You know what?" Frank said. "Mail it. If I never see you again it'll be too soon." He turned, his heavy tail swishing behind him, and shut the door in Angel's face.

Well, at least that's one suspect eliminated, Angel thought. He hadn't smelled Fred's scent on Frank, and really didn't think the demon had been lying to him. If he'd taken Fred to get back at Angel, he didn't show it.

As he walked back to his car, twisting the cable in his hands, he wondered what it mattered if a given Korvitak wasn't the most beautiful one in all creation, since they could take virtually any form they wanted. But he guessed if one had to ask another to assume a certain appearance, it wouldn't be the same.

Back in the GTX, he plugged the cable into his phone and shoved the other end into the lighter socket. He started the car and pulled away from the curb, running through the other demon types Cordelia had mentioned in his head. Klakivan, Bovissle, Divik, Skander . . . and there had been a Skander at the club, he remembered. Maybe it wouldn't hurt to figure out where they hung out.

He had only gone a couple of blocks when his phone trilled at him. He snatched it up off the passenger seat. "Yeah?"

"Angel?" The voice was unfamiliar. Deep and masculine, a little gravelly. He couldn't tell if it was human.

"Yes, who is this?"

"We have a friend of yours. If you want to see her again, listen up."

CHAPTER TEN

"Who is this?" Angel demanded again. He jerked the wheel of his convertible, pulling it up to the curb at an awkward angle. A car speeding down the street behind him had to swerve out of the lane, and the driver leaned on his horn as he passed. Angel ignored the blare, focused on his cell phone.

"Don't ask questions, Angel," the voice warned him.

"If you've hurt Fred, the world isn't big enough for you to hide from me," Angel said darkly.

"She's fine. Now listen—"

"No, you listen," Angel interrupted, reflexively making a fist of his free hand. Fury threatened to engulf him, a volcano of anger inside him that, once it began to erupt, couldn't be halted. "You can still save your own life. Release her, and have her call me at this number as soon as she's free. Once I know she's okay, I'll stop looking for you. If that doesn't happen, you're dead."

"You're not really in a position to be dictating to anybody," the voice replied calmly. "We could snap her neck in a second. Maybe you'd find us, maybe not—it doesn't really matter to me. We're working for a cause bigger than my life, vampire."

Great, Angel thought with a frown. *Idealists.* He'd lived long enough to know that people with an emotional attachment to a specific idea or ideology could accomplish marvelous things—but they could also be extremely dangerous because they really did consider their lives secondary to their mission.

"What cause could Fred possibly have anything to do with?" he asked.

"She has nothing to do with it. She's just a tool, that's all. A way of getting your attention."

"Okay, you've got it," Angel admitted. "What do you want?"

"We'll happily let the girl go if you agree to our demands," the voice told him. "She means nothing to us."

Angel's mind churned with possibilities. *What could they be after? Money?* That didn't make sense—kidnappers looking for a big payoff could pick plenty of targets in Los Angeles with more to spend than Angel had. No, it had to be something more germane to Angel, to his ongoing struggle against the evil that targeted innocents. Maybe this was some new scheme of Wolfram and Hart, the law firm that he'd gone up against so many times in the past.

There's only one way to find out, he thought. *Listen, but agree to nothing.* "Okay, keep talking. What are your demands?"

"Do you know Pershing Square?"

Angel didn't even have to think about it. Everybody in L.A. knew Pershing Square. It was a downtown park between 5th and 6th Streets, and Olive and Hill. Once, it had been overgrown, drug-infested, and crime-filled, but the city had remade it, filling it with modern art sculptures. Now it was one of L.A.'s loveliest landmarks. "Of course," he said, trying to disguise the rage he felt.

"If you want the girl back safe, meet us there. The very center of the park."

Angel pictured the spot in his mind, wide open, very little to hide behind except some of the sculptures. "When?" he asked.

"Sunrise."

Angel choked back a laugh. "You do understand that I can't do that, right? Sunlight and I don't exactly get along."

"We understand that," the voice said, still composed. Angel hadn't detected any real emotion in it— the speaker's tone remained flat and expressionless no matter what he said. "That's kind of the point."

And, like the sun coming up over the horizon,

the real plan dawned on Angel. *They'll turn Fred loose,* he realized, *but only if I sacrifice myself for her. I stand in the park, with no cover, no escape, and let the sun come up. Once I burst into flames and burn to a crisp, then they have no reason to hold Fred anymore. Simple.*

And, in its own sick way, brilliant.

At the center of Pershing Square, Angel would be exposed. They'd be able to watch from any number of vantage points, on the ground or in buildings, to make sure he wasn't pulling any tricks. There'd be no way he could have a secret underground exit route ready, because it was a public park. Even if he'd known farther in advance where the meet was to be held, there wouldn't have been a chance to dig any escape route.

They held all the cards, in this case. *Well, almost all,* he corrected himself.

Dawn was still hours away. Which gave him time to keep looking for them, to locate them and free Fred himself before he had to face the sun. "What assurance do I have that you'd let Fred go free after I flame on?" he demanded. "How do I know you'll follow through?"

"I guess you just have to trust us."

Now Angel did laugh. "Because you've proven so trustworthy so far?"

"That's the deal, Angel. Take it or leave it. You for Fred."

"I need some time to think about it."

"There isn't any time," the voice countered, still calm. "What'll it be?"

"There's time," Angel said. "Dawn is still a ways off. Remember, the other option is I let you kill her and then I kill you. One at a time, slowly. I don't know how many of you there are, but I'll save you for last, because I'm developing a personal hatred for you."

"You won't let us kill her," the voice said. "That's not the way you work. You're not put together that way."

"You think you know me?" Angel said with a wry edge. "You don't. You don't have any idea of what I've done. I already have plenty of lives on my conscience, one more wouldn't really make a difference one way or another."

"Somehow I don't think I believe you."

"Believe whatever you want," Angel said. He had to keep the caller on the phone, try to get him to give some sort of clue to his identity or whereabouts. He had been listening for any background noises that might help, but the cell phone connection was not great, and the caller seemed to be in a very quiet place. "Maybe you want to take a look in my eyes and then tell me what you believe. Although I'll be tearing your throat out at the same time, so you might not like that part."

"Sadly for you, you won't get the chance," the voice said. "Unless you sacrifice Fred, of course. And I just can't see that happening."

"You keep saying that," Angel replied. *Have they been watching me? Studying me?* He tried to run through any demons he'd encountered recently, or anyone he'd seen who might have been following him, putting him under some kind of surveillance. None came to mind. Few of his enemies survived, and not many of those would intentionally tick him off again. *Except Wolfram and Hart,* he thought again. They would definitely bear looking into. "Do you know me?" he asked. "Have we met?"

"I'm surprised at you, Angel," the voice answered. "Haven't I already proven I'm too smart to answer such a stupid question?"

"You haven't proven you're anything except suicidal." He'd have Cordy hack into the cell phone company's computers, to see if she could locate the phone that was being used by the caller. He would turn over every rock in Los Angeles and see what scampered out. One way or another, he would find Fred, and those who had taken her.

"You going to answer, Angel? Or don't—it's all the same to me as long as you show up. We're wasting time here. Morning will be around sooner than you think. And if you're not dead at sunup, Fred will be."

Angel glanced at his watch. It was after one in the morning. Still plenty of time, but the caller was right: The hours would pass quickly.

He tried to remember what it was that professional hostage negotiators demanded. *Proof of life*, he thought. *That's it. If the hostage isn't really alive, then there's no point to any discussion at all.* And if these people—or whatever—expected Angel not to survive the morning, they might have already killed her.

"I need to know that she's still alive and unhurt," Angel insisted. "Without that, there's no deal."

"You'll just have to take my word for that," the caller said.

"No!" Angel shouted, the anger taking him again. "Not for that. I need to talk to her. I need to have her tell me she's okay. If she is, then we have a deal. If she's not, then you're walking dead."

The voice didn't respond right away. *Does that mean they've already done it?* he wondered, fear rising in him. He wasn't sure how he'd be able to face that.

"I'll have to call you back," the voice said finally. "I'll need a few minutes to set it up."

"Make it fast," Angel warned. "If I find you before you get it done, you'll be very sorry."

"You're just full of empty threats tonight, Angel. Let me just remind you that I'm not afraid to die. Stay close to the phone."

There was a click, and the connection was broken. Angel sat looking at his own cell phone—gratful that Frank had been able to give him a cord for it—as if it were some foreign item that he'd just found in his hand. Without the voice on the other end to focus his rage at, he felt a sudden hollowness. He knew that, for all his threats, he was right where he'd been the moment they'd realized Fred was missing. No clues, no ideas, no real way to track her down. He had made solving the impossible into his business, but this case was looking even more impossible than usual, and with the stakes so high, the pressure was almost paralyzing.

Except that he couldn't let it be. He had to stay active, stay mobile, keep checking any leads he could turn up. Only action would fix this. And only action would keep his mind off the choice that would have to be made as morning drew near. He checked the street behind him. It was empty, so he pulled out, put the car into drive, and headed down the road.

Headed for Wolfram & Hart.

As he drove he punched out the number of the Hyperion Hotel on the phone. After a moment, Cordy answered. He cut off her greeting with a gruff, "Cordelia, listen."

"What is it?" she asked, concern evident in her voice.

"Don't ask questions, I can't stay on the phone long. I need you to hack into the cell phone computer, find out what phone called mine just a few minutes ago. It's the only call I've had all night, and it was a long one. Find out where the phone is and don't call me back until you know, okay?"

"Got it," she said, now all efficiency.

He hung up. If the kidnapper called back with Fred on the line, he didn't want to miss the call. And he didn't want them to get a busy signal and think he was calling for help, or the police. Not that he'd do that. He knew the police would have no interest in helping him—or the ability to, for that matter.

Cordelia would be a little miffed at his brusqueness, but she'd understand and get over it, he knew. She understood that he counted on her, leaned on her probably more than anybody else. No one had worked with him as long, no one knew him better. Even a past love, like Buffy, didn't really know him anymore. She knew the Angel he had been back in Sunnydale, years before. *Years, and a lifetime.* He didn't think he had changed a lot in that time, but realized that he must have. He had come to Los Angeles without a real plan, just trying to get away from Sunnydale, away from a love that could never work. It wasn't until he had arrived in town and met Doyle that he'd learned what the new direction of his life would be. And ever since then, he knew, it had continued to change, to evolve. Cordy had been there almost since the beginning. Then he had taken on Wesley, and Gunn, and finally Lorne and Fred had joined their little family. Even though Wesley was nominally the leader of Angel Investigations now, Angel knew that he was still the guiding force, and the one ultimately responsible for them all.

And that included Fred. *I have to find her,* he thought.

IIis phone chirped again, and he answered it right away. "Yeah."

The voice was different this time, but similar in a way, with the same kind of timbre and a menacing quality Angel didn't like. "Someone wants to talk to you. Hold on."

There was the sound of another phone ringing, as if the first caller was conferencing in another phone, and then, a moment later, Angel heard Fred's voice. She sounded scared, but trying to hold herself together. "A-Angel?"

"Fred, it's me. Are you okay? Have they hurt you?"

"I'm fine," she said. "I hurt my arm a little, but I'm okay."

"Who has you? Where are you?"

"Angel, I—"

"That's enough," the voice said, cutting Fred off. "And Angel, I want you to understand how serious I am."

"I get that," Angel started to say. But a loud, shrill scream interrupted him. Fred's voice. "What did you do?" Angel demanded. "If you hurt her—"

"It's just a little cut," the voice replied calmly. "Tiny. But I'll keep doing it, cutting her, now and again, until morning. Just so you understand that you'd better be at that park or she'll hurt a lot and then she'll die. Got it? She's okay now, just cut a little. She can stay that way, or she can be very much not okay. Your call, vampire."

My responsibility, Angel thought again.

There was really no choice at all.

"I'll be there."

CHAPTER ELEVEN

"Yeah, kiddies, your help is greatly appreciated," Lorne said, shoving the chair he had just vacated back under the table after another useless interview. The pair of Snoalmish demons had seen nothing, heard nothing, smelled nothing, and reading them had been every bit as helpful. They weren't sure who Fred was, and only knew Angel because they'd been present once when he'd dusted four vampires on the street in front of the Boyle Heights apartment they rented. They had been impressed with his prowess, on that occasion, and claimed they'd help if they were able, they just didn't know anything.

Well, I can believe that, Lorne thought, frustrated. He wasn't entirely sure they even knew their own names.

I'm just not getting anywhere, he thought. *Maybe a Polgara is involved, but maybe not. Maybe there's a smell of cinnamon, but wait—that just could be from somebody's cappuccino. Maybe Roshon demons are responsible, but of course we hate Roshons and would blame them for global warming if we could get away with it.*

Lorne loved his customers, he loved music, and he appreciated that here on Earth, as opposed to Pylea, he could make a living by bringing the two together. *There's no better way to earn a buck,* he believed. But tonight, he thought he could throttle the whole lot of them. Sure, they were being kept against their will, but they didn't *have* to stay—if they really wanted to leave, there was no way he could stop them. They had stayed because he'd asked them to, and then they'd been argumentative, indecisive, uncertain, and uncommunicative.

There were still interviews to be conducted, but he no longer held out much hope that they'd be any more useful than the previous ones. He was trying to pick which table to approach next when Luis, his tuxedo shirt and bow tie–clad bartender, approached him. "Boss, you got a phone call," Luis said. He held out the cordless toward Lorne.

"Who is it?"

"I don't know, but she said it's important. Sounds kind of upset," Luis opined.

Worried about what that might mean, Lorne took the phone and went to a corner of the club where he could have a modicum of privacy. "This is Lorne," he said into it.

"Lorne, it's Cordelia." She sounded terrible, frantic.

"What's up, Princess? Take a deep breath before you answer. Maybe two of them."

She didn't listen to him. *Like anybody does,* he thought. "It's Angel. He just called me. Again. I mean, he called me before and now he called me back."

"Well, he is kinda sweet on you, you know," Lorne offered.

"He *talked* to them. The ones who have Fred."

Now Lorne understood the frantic part. "Tell me what he said, Sugar. Everything."

"He said . . . " Her breath caught. Lorne thought she sounded like she'd been crying, and maybe still was. "He said they offered him a deal. They'll let Fred go if he shows up in the middle of Pershing Square, at sunrise."

"Let me guess. There isn't a big umbrella or a gazebo or anything in the middle of Pershing Square."

"No such luck," she said. "Just open space. He'll be fried."

"But he told them to forget it, right?" Lorne asked. "I mean, he can't do that."

This time he distinctly heard a sob before she answered. "He told them okay. I mean, he still wants to track them down before morning. But he agreed to the deal."

"Well, sure," Lorne guessed. "To keep them off guard, right? But he doesn't really intend to go through with it."

"I asked him to tell me that," Cordelia said between sobs. "He . . . he wouldn't. Or couldn't. Oh, Lorne—"

"Calm down, cupcake," he said as soothingly as he could manage. "This is Angel we're talking about. There's not a rabbit he hasn't pulled out of his hat at one time or another. Maybe they were listening to him or something. I'm sure he's got a plan in mind. He's not the type to just hand over the world to the forces of darkness, even to save Fred."

"I'm not sure he sees it that way," Cordelia argued. "I think he just sees it as saving Fred. He'd sacrifice himself for her—for any of us, I think. But he might not think of it as sacrificing the rest of the world, too."

"Darlin', he's saved the world more times than I've made my bed. And I'm a pretty neat house-keeper, considering the hours I work. He's got to see the big picture."

"Only, Angel's not so much the big picture kind of guy, I think. He's more the 'oh no, Fred's in trouble, got to save her' kind of guy."

"We'll just have to make sure he understands," Lorne said. "I'll call him."

"He said not to," Cordy countered. She was sounding a little calmer, and had at least stopped openly weeping. "He wants to keep the line clear. He said unless we had real information for him, to not call."

"Then I guess we'd better find some, right? Have you got anything yet?"

"Not much," she admitted. "Not enough. And Wesley and Gunn are drawing blanks too. I was hoping you'd found out more since the last time I talked to you."

"I wish I could say I was doing any better, but I'd be a big fat liar if I did. There are still some folks I haven't questioned yet, though."

"Well, get busy," she urged him. "What are you doing talking to me?"

You called me, he thought. But he didn't say it, didn't want to set her off again. "I'm on my way," he said. "Stay in touch, and let me know if you hear from him again. As soon as I have anything promising I'll let you know."

"That's good. Thanks, Lorne. You're a good friend."

"You too, gorgeous," he told her. "Talk to you soon." He broke the connection and carried the phone back to Luis at the bar. "Keep this line open," he instructed. "No calls in or out unless they're for me."

"You got it, boss."

"And this free-drink thing has gone on long enough. Start watering a little."

Luis nodded, crisp efficiency in action. As Lorne turned away from him, he felt his knees wobble as a wave of anxiety washed over him. *Apparently, frantic is catching,* he thought.

"So you're a Brachen demon?" Lorne asked. Misty, the woman he sat across from, looked purely human—*and quite an attractive human, at that,* he'd decided. She had apparently dressed to make a statement. Her minidress was fire engine red silk that clung in places where Lorne couldn't blame it for clinging, and gapped in others, where the physics of curvature and suspension demanded. Her dark hair was pulled up in back and held into place with two wooden rods that looked like chopsticks. Her eyes were wide and dark and regarded him with what seemed like frank curiosity and maybe some amusement. She was not shy and she was not timid, he gathered.

"Half," she said. "And half human. On my mom's side. See?" She let her demonic self come to the fore, soft blue spikes emerging from her skin until she looked like something a giant might use to brush the dog. After he nodded, she retracted them. "But I can pass," Misty said. "And I usually do. I have a regular job, working with humans, in a bank. I've dated humans, although not exclusively. I live in a condo complex in Santa Monica. Nobody knows."

"A lot of mixed-blood Brachens blend in, right?" he asked. He knew the answer, but wanted to keep her talking.

"Sure, I think most of us do, to some extent. Maybe not to the degree that I do, but for sure, lots of us. I don't know about everyone, but for me, sometimes I start to feel like I'm losing touch with that part of myself. I mean, it's easier to get along in life if people think I'm like them. But I don't ever want to lose who I really am, what my heritage is, you know? So sometimes I come here, or some other function where I know there'll be plenty of other demons." She glanced down at herself, as if she'd forgotten how she dressed. "And, you know," she added, "maybe I hook up with somebody, now and again. Nothing wrong with that, right?"

"It makes the world go 'round, honey," Lorne said appreciatively. He remembered the other Brachen in the club tonight. "You saw Stark sing earlier, right? The golden throat."

She nodded. "I know him, a little," she said. "He's nice, but a little dull."

"Believe me, I know the type," Lorne said. "But you have an advantage too. You're one of the demon breeds that can mate with humans—makes the chances of getting a date that much better," Lorne continued. "Did you know a half Brachen named Francis Doyle?"

She smiled, a languid, leisurely smile that took its time spreading across her face but finally landed in her eyes with a mischievous gleam. "Not in the hooking up sense, but I had seen him around, I guess. I knew who he was, even before . . . well, you know."

"Before he died?"

"Before he sacrificed himself. I mean, that was just about the bravest thing I've ever heard of. He's a hero to me, he really is. I think to all of us. You know, if he hadn't done what he did, anything with human blood within the range of the Beacon would have been killed. Humans, and even demons with as little as an eighth or less of human blood in them. But Doyle stopped it. I can tell you one thing, if I ever had the chance to meet him, you know, in that way . . . I'd have jumped at it."

"From everything I've heard about him, I'm sure he'd have appreciated the opportunity," Lorne told her.

Misty smiled her slow grin again. *When she does that, it makes her look like someone with a secret,* Lorne thought. *A good, juicy one, which is always the best kind. I think I like this woman.* "I like to think I'd have made it worth his while," she said.

Lorne shook his head slightly, not wanting to get distracted from his mission by thoughts of how she could do that. "You know what I'm asking people about tonight, right?"

"About Angel's little friend, and what happened to her outside."

"That's right. Did you see anything?"

Her smile vanished, and she was all business now. "I sure did. I saw her get shoved into a dimensional portal."

"You did?" Lorne couldn't contain his surprise. "Are you kidding me?"

"Of course not. She was standing right there, not ten feet from me. We were outside, watching that fire across the street. Then someone said something about a car coming, and somebody said there were guns, and then the noise and the bullets and everything. I was so scared, I don't mind telling you. It's like, I know trouble kind of follows Angel around, and whenever I see him at someplace like Caritas, I worry a little. But not inside Caritas, because, you know, nothing's ever going to happen in there."

"Not if I have anything to say about it," Lorne said with a degree of pride.

"Well, you've done a great job with the place. I mean, I have always felt so safe in here."

"That's the idea," he said. "But you were saying what you saw outside."

"Right, I'm sorry." Misty swept at a lock of hair that had come loose and tickled her cheek. "So when the guns started going off, I hit the deck, you know? Because that's what everybody else was doing, pretty much, and it seemed like the best plan at the time. But as I was down there on the sidewalk, I looked up to see if it was safe yet, and I just saw the edge of the portal, kind of shimmering, right? And I saw Fred disappearing into the portal, and an arm around her, an arm with a red robe on it, it looked like. But I can't be sure about that. It seems like there was red, anyway. But then the portal just kind of blinked away, like a TV set's picture used to when you turned the power off and it faded down to that little dot and then the dot blinked out."

"So you didn't see anyone left on this side who had maybe pushed her in? Just the arm on the other side that was keeping her from getting away."

"That's right."

He could barely believe what he was hearing. "And why didn't you say anything about this before?"

"Well, I came back in when you said to. And then you and Angel were still outside, and then you came back in and said you would be talking to everyone, and not to plan on leaving until you did. So I thought I should just wait my turn. I mean, probably lots of folks saw more than I did."

"You'd be astonished," Lorne said dryly.

"I mean," she continued, "I hardly saw anything, did I? But the portal was right there, and everybody was outside by then. It seems like someone must have grabbed her and shoved her in. Or grabbed her and jumped in with her."

"That's what it seems like," he agreed. "But so far, you're the first one I've talked to who even saw a portal. Or even so much as a port. Or an al."

She laughed and shook her head. That wayward lock bounced off her exceptionally lovely cheekbone again. "I guess everyone was a little too concerned about their own necks," she said. "I mean, I was too. But Doyle trusted Angel, right? So if there was ever anything I could do to help Angel, I would."

Lorne thought maybe he could follow that logic if he didn't think about it too hard. "Was there anything else you saw? Maybe inside the club, beforehand? Anybody hanging around Fred that you saw? Or after, anybody acting strangely? Anything suspicious?"

"Let me think about it a minute," she replied. She took the end of the stray lock of hair into her mouth and sucked on it as she considered. "No, I guess I didn't see anything else," she said finally. "I might have smelled something."

Might have, Lorne thought with disappointment. *Again with the maybes and the possibles. I need some certainties, and I need 'em fast.* "What do you think you smelled?" he inquired.

"Cinnamon," Misty answered, tugging the hair from her mouth and tucking it up behind her ear.

"It was the strangest thing. All those demons around, each with their own individual scent, and the fire burning across the way, and then suddenly I thought I caught a strong whiff of cinnamon. It was very noticeable until the smell of the gunsmoke or whatever drifted over us, and that covered it up. What do you think that means, anything?"

Lorne couldn't stifle a deep sigh. "Well, it could be a sign of a Kedigris demon. But then it could also be a sign that someone had stopped at a bakery, or that Luis had made himself a double capp, so by itself it's not all that definitive." Although he knew it wasn't necessarily unsupported—Urf'dil had thought she'd smelled it too. So that was looking more and more promising, with only the minor exception that he hadn't seen any Kedigris, and since they were shape-shifters he might well be surrounded by them without even knowing about it.

"Sorry I don't have any more information for you. The portal, the arm in a red sleeve or red robe, the cinnamon smell that went away. That's pretty much everything I know." The expression on her pretty face was sincere and a little sad. Lorne believed her—if she could help, she would. *Or she's a heck of an actress*, he thought.

"Listen, I appreciate as much as you have done. I'll get these interviews wrapped up and cut everybody loose as soon as I can," Lorne promised her.

"But it's going to take a bit more time. So if you haven't, umm . . . hooked up yet, you still have a chance."

"You know, after everything that's happened tonight, I think I just want some time alone," Misty said. She reached across the table and put a hand over the back of Lorne's. "But maybe another time I'll come back. Do *you* ever get a night off?"

If Lorne could have blushed, he would have, but fortunately his flush didn't really show on his green skin. "Honey, I own the joint. If I need to take a night off, I just ask myself for permission. And I happen to be very permissive."

She squeezed his hand once and crinkled her nose in a happy grin. "That's what I wanted to hear," she said. "Until next time."

"I'll be counting the hours," Lorne said. He gave her hand a gentle squeeze in return and left her table. That interview hadn't shed much more light, but so far it topped the night in fringe benefits. He wondered if the next one would be half as entertaining.

CHAPTER TWELVE

The building that housed the offices of Wolfram & Hart was dark at this hour, with just scattered lights showing through the windows. After driving past it, Angel parked a couple of blocks over and went down into the sewers, from which he had a well-established path into the building's interior. He emerged in an abandoned hallway, near the elevator. The building's security system would, he knew, recognize that there was a vampire on the premises, and armed guards would be dispatched. He'd dodged them—or fought them off—before, and he was sure he could do it again.

The elevator came quickly, since no one else was using it this late at night. A few moments later he was standing in front of Lilah Morgan's office. Light spilled out beneath her door, and he could hear hushed voices inside. Angel smiled. *She's here, and she's got a man in there with her,* he thought. *Undoubtedly the one who called me.* He tried her office door and found that it was unlocked, so he walked in.

"Who—oh, it's you," Lilah said, startled. She regained her composure quickly, though, and gave him an exasperated stare and added a layer of ice to her voice. "I'm a little busy right now, Angel. Is there something you need? Other than a stake in the heart?"

Behind Lilah, a big window on the dark night sky reflected the office, except for Angel, who of course had no reflection. Lilah sat behind her desk, which had a mound of paperwork on it. She inclined her head toward the man sitting across from her in one of the visitor's chairs. He was a round little man, with a big belly and a round, bald head, and a small white mustache under his big round nose. He looked at Angel with a mixture of curiosity and concern, his mouth falling open a little. The hairs on his mustache quivered.

"I'm Angel," Angel said to him. "Who are you?"

"I'm . . . I'm Stanley," he said. As soon as he spoke, Angel knew it wasn't the voice on the phone. This guy's voice was high-pitched, almost squeaky. There was no way he could have pulled off the deep, gravelly voice that Angel had heard before.

"Stanley is a client," Lilah explained. "And I'm on his clock right now. And his business, oddly enough, doesn't involve you."

When Lilah wanted something from him—*even when she just wants to dust me,* Angel realized— she would put on flirtatious airs. Now, though, that tone was completely missing. He couldn't tell if it was because she truly was busy, and distracted, or if she was hiding it because of Stanley's presence. Either way, he had the distinct sensation that she was telling the truth—she wasn't involved in the kidnapping of Fred or the plot against his life. *Which doesn't mean that the entire firm is equally innocent,* he knew. "Let me just ask you a quick question, Lilah, and then I'll get out of your hair."

"It had better be quick," she said. Her firm jaw was set, her mouth a grim line. "Because the guards are certainly on their way up."

"Is anyone at Wolfram and Hart trying to kill me? I mean, currently. Or is there any ongoing plot involving the capture of one of my team?"

Lilah drummed on her desk with her fingertips as she considered the questions. "Not that I know of, and not that I know of. How's that?"

"If there was such a plot, would you know about it?"

Waiting for her answer, Angel glanced at Stanley. The little round man had reddened noticeably, and he seemed to be pressing himself into the chair as if he wished he could hide beneath it. Lilah saw where his gaze was, and she tapped her index finger against her forehead.

"He's not right," she explained to Stanley. "Up here. Paranoid delusions. Every law firm has a few of 'em running around." She looked back at Angel. "I would, and I don't. Now if you'll say good night, Angel, Stanley and I can get back to preparing his incorporation papers."

"Yeah, sorry for the intrusion," he said. Before he left he bowed close to Stanley. "Read the fine print *really* carefully," he warned. Then he backed out of the office and closed the door behind him. He ran down the hall, back to the elevators, and punched the button. He could hear cables and pneumatics working in the shaft. Both elevators reached his floor at the same time, but in one he spotted a brown shoe and a length of leg, wearing gray pants with a gold stripe down the middle. Angel slipped into the other elevator and punched the button for the ground floor, then the DOOR CLOSE button.

The doors slid shut just as the guards emerged from the other elevator and started up the hall. Angel flattened himself against the control panel. The back of the elevator was mirrored, and in the glass Angel could see one of the guards toss an inquisitive glance inside, as if wondering why an empty elevator would be closing just now. But since he cast no reflection, and the guard didn't actually come into the elevator, Angel remained unseen.

• • •

"Did you know that Wolfram and Hart takes on regular people as clients?" Angel asked after describing the scene in Lilah's office to Wesley and Gunn. They'd met at a street corner, and Wesley sat beside him in the car now, with Gunn lounging in the backseat.

"Stanley? Regular?" Gunn laughed. "Old Stanley is the consigliere for one of L.A.'s most prominent mobs. They keep him around because he has a good head for numbers and that innocent look that makes people believe he couldn't possibly be up to anything crooked. Bankers and judges love Stanley, until they hear how many murders he's been associated with."

Angel swiveled in his seat. "Are you kidding? Do you think I should go back there? Maybe he *is* the one I talked to."

"Angel, please watch the road or let someone else drive," Wesley said quietly. Angel turned back to the front and swerved around a city bus that was pulling away from the curb with a huff of its air brakes and a growl from its engine. *Wesley has a point*, Angel thought. *If I need to look at Gunn, that's what the mirror's for.*

"I never heard about Stanley being involved with anything supernatural," Gunn said. "And I never heard about him changing his voice. Every Stanley story talks about that little mouse squeak he's got. It just don't fit that he'd be mixed up with demons."

"He's mixed up with Wolfram and Hart," Angel insisted.

"Which only goes to prove," Wesley added, "that they represent criminals of the human persuasion as well as of the monstrous. Nothing more."

"I guess," Angel said.

"Besides, you ain't done anything to make the mob angry, have you? Why would they care about you?"

"I guess you're right," Angel said again. He felt disappointment that his hunch hadn't paid off, combined with a gripping fear because he still had no clue as to where Fred was, and the hour was growing later and later. "I was just so sure that Wolfram and Hart must be involved."

"They still might be," Wesley suggested.

"No, I think if they were, Lilah would know about it."

"But she wouldn't necessarily tell you, would she?"

"Usually, she would," Angel said. "One way or another. She's good at keeping secrets from her coworkers, I think, but when it comes to me, she seems to get some sort of satisfaction from taunting me. I think it makes her feel like she has power over me."

"And that's what she's all about," Gunn said.

"Power is that chick's middle name. Why she fits in so well at the firm."

"That, and a complete lack of conscience," Wesley suggested. "They must comb the law schools for signs of sociopathology before they recruit." The ex-Watcher shook his head in disgust.

"Nice to know they got standards, though," Gunn said.

Angel made a couple of right turns and headed for a market that a demonic informant had mentioned to Wesley and Gunn. He drove in silence for a few blocks, but then Wes broke the quiet. "Angel, we have to talk about it," he said solemnly.

Angel decided to play dumb. "About what?"

But Wesley wouldn't buy it. He almost never did. "Cordelia told us about the offer, the deal. You for Fred. You know you can't do it."

"Nothing to it," Angel insisted. "I go to the park. They free Fred."

"You really want to tell us that Fred is more important than you are?" Gunn asked. "Because that's bogus, you know what I'm sayin'? I mean, I love Fred, she's great. Kinda brings a breath of fresh air to the team and all. But long run? She'll never be the demon killer you are."

Angel negotiated a left turn, then a right, before he answered with a question of his own. "What makes you think that's the only consideration?"

"What other consideration might there be?" Wesley wanted to know.

"My word," Angel said simply. When no one spoke, he elaborated. "I promised Fred that she'd be safe with me. When we wanted to bring her back to Earth from Pylea, I told her she'd be protected. I offered her the sanctuary of our team, of the hotel, of my abilities. And I did that even though I knew—I know—that anyone who is near me is in danger, all the time. You guys all know that. So does Cordelia. You accept it, anyway, and that's your decision, but you knew the ground rules when you decided to play the game. Not Fred. She didn't have that luxury. She was just brought in, and I told her she'd be okay, and now she's not. She's already been hurt."

"Hey, English," Gunn called from the backseat. "Check and make sure that's really Angel."

"What do you mean?" Wesley asked, confused.

"I never heard him say so many words at once," Gunn clarified. "I think maybe he's been switched for an exact duplicate, except one with a bigger vocabulary."

Angel ignored the gag. Part of him was glad that Gunn could still crack wise, despite the circumstances, but another part thought it was inappropriate. Until Fred was safe, he didn't want to see smiles and hear laughter.

Fred had offered Angel sanctuary in her cave, on Pylea, even when he had turned into a full-fledged demon, an Angelbeast. She had not thought twice, had not turned him away no matter how gruesome he'd become. She had never once seemed to worry that he might be a danger to her, always trusted that his human side—even when she couldn't see it— would overrule the bestial. When he had brought her back here, he had meant to offer her the same kind of unquestioning, unconditional acceptance and security. She had looked up to him—even, in a few of her less-guarded moments, made comments that made him think she had a pretty major crush on him. That made him responsible for her, no matter what. That meant he had to sacrifice himself, if necessary, to save her.

"Gunn's right," Wesley said, matching Angel's serious mood. "I love her, too, as we all do. But Fred can't do for humankind what you can. If it weren't for you, she'd still be in Pylea, living in a cave. You've done what you could for her, you returned her to her home dimension, you helped bring her out of her shell so she can function in the world. But you can't give your life for her, Angel. Just think rationally about it. Compare the contribution you can make to the world, versus hers."

"Fred's a physicist," Angel said, leaning into a turn. He was driving too fast now, tires screeching as he rounded the corners. He knew he should slow down, but couldn't seem to take his foot off the gas. "Probably a brilliant one, with life experience that no other scientist on Earth has ever had. Who's to say she won't make a contribution that way? She could be the next Einstein. Even better. She could open the way to the stars, she could bring about world peace. We just don't know. But she's young and smart and good, and I made a promise to her. I've lived plenty long enough and done so much damage, I can never hope to make it all right."

No one had an argument for that.

On the next straight section of road, Angel gunned the engine and roared toward a market on a corner, three blocks up. As the car hurtled over the cross streets, he glanced at Wesley, who braced himself with a stiff arm against the dashboard, and realized that his driving was causing his friends to worry, for no reason. He lifted his foot off the gas and applied the brake, slowing to a smooth stop just down the block from the market. "Look," he said as he turned off the ignition. "My plan is still to find Fred before morning. I want to avoid either of us dying, okay?"

"Good to hear, dog," Gunn said, climbing out of his seat. "We're behind you on that idea."

"Absolutely," Wesley confirmed.

Angel stood on the sidewalk and looked at the little corner market, its windows almost totally obscured by hand-lettered signs advertising bargains on cigarettes, beer, steaks, soft drinks, and other staples of life. Neon signs indicated that the store was open, and the soft glow of fluorescent lighting spilled out into the street through double glass doors. "Tell me again what you heard about this place," Angel said quietly.

"Front's a regular little food store," Gunn explained. "In back, though, there's a hidden second shop. Sells food items, if you wanna call it that, and other goods that a demon might need. Things your average human would flip out about if he ever saw 'em for sale in a store. Demon we talked to says he was in there shopping a few nights back, and heard the counter demon talking to another employee about some bad stuff comin' your way."

"So we thought that perhaps the demons working in this store were part of the plot against you," Wesley picked up. "Or aware of it, at any rate. At the very least, the timing is curious, wouldn't you say?"

"That may not be the word I'd use," Angel said. "But okay. Let's pay them a visit."

He went first, through the double doors and into the store. A bell tied to one of the door handles jingled to announce their entrance. To the left was a counter with racks of cigarettes above it and a cash register almost hidden behind counter displays of lottery tickets, magazines and tabloids, and a jar of rubber squeeze balls designed to look like eyeballs. Sitting on a stool behind the counter was a man who looked human, a grizzled, unshaven guy with a Yankees cap over long, straight hair, and a haunted look in his eyes. Angel had heard that look referred to as a "thousand-yard stare," and it seemed to fit in this case. The guy looked at them, or through them, with no change in his flat expression.

"Don't get up," Angel said. "We're just going in back."

The guy didn't even acknowledge them, but he kept his seat. Angel led the way through the store, between aisles of shelving overflowing with products, and through another door into a back storage room. It was dark back here, but the dark didn't slow Angel down. He was a creature of the dark; after all these centuries of vampirism he could see as well, or better, in the dark than in bright sunlight. Another door led out of the back room. The casual observer would think it opened onto a loading dock, but since it was the only door back here, Angel thought otherwise.

He was right. He passed through that door and came into a second store at least as big as the first, if not a little larger. The shelves here were crowded, too, but with a different assortment of goods. One shelf, for instance, contained nothing but jars of eyeballs, real ones, this time, floating in liquid—the same type of jar, Angel noticed, as the one that held the rubber balls in the front store. The eyeballs were all different types and sizes:

goat, rabbit, tiny pigeon eyes, great big camel ones. He didn't look carefully, but he was pretty sure one of the jars contained human eyes.

There were displays of weapons and armor, various foodstuffs—including, Angel noted with interest, different types of blood—magickal implements and accessories, and human-styled clothing in an astonishing variety of sizes and cuts. Angel crossed to the refrigerated section, where there were two shelves of blood, found a jar labeled PIG, and unscrewed the lid, sniffing it. *Smells right,* he thought. He carried it to the counter. A scrawny, bored-looking demon with aqua skin and four ear flaps, each pierced and dotted with a different type of stud or ring, watched them with curious eyes.

"That do it for you tonight?" the demon asked. Then he lowered his voice. "We don't usually like their kind to come back here," he said, nodding his head toward Wesley and Gunn.

"That'll do it," Angel said. He lowered his own voice and leaned in close to the demon. "They're friends of mine. They go where I go."

The demon rang up the sale and shook his head slowly from side to side. "Hey, whatever, man. I think it's a little sick, but whatever floats your boat, you know?"

"We'll leave my personal life out of it," Angel said, extending a twenty-dollar bill. "But as long as we're talking, let me ask you something. Have you ever heard of me? Name's Angel. Vampire with a soul. Apparently I have a bit of a reputation."

The skinny demon pressed a button on the front of the register, and the drawer popped open. "I . . . uhh . . . I don't think so." He took the twenty from Angel's hand and fumbled, trying to make change.

Angel heard the chuff of a door opening somewhere behind him, but didn't take his eyes off the demon at the register.

"Angel." Gunn's voice was odd, but not panicked. "Somethin' here you might want to see."

"I'd like my change first, please," Angel said to the cashier, ignoring Gunn.

"Sure, uhh, just a minute," the demon said.

"Angel," Wesley put in, "Gunn's right. You really should take a look."

Angel sighed and turned slowly, backing a step away from the counter so the demon cashier couldn't make a move for him while he wasn't looking. From a door at the back of the store, four demons like the cashier had emerged. But these were not scrawny ones. They were thickly muscled, and in their hands they carried metal or wooden clubs.

"Angel, those are Tik'lets," Wesley said carefully. "I didn't recognize the first one, because they're usually built like this lot here."

"Are Tik'lets bad?" Gunn asked.

"They're often merchants, as we see here,"

Wesley replied. "But they're also quite bloodthirsty when riled up."

"You guys riled?" Gunn inquired.

The Tik'lets didn't answer, at least not verbally. But they charged down the main aisle of the store, two abreast, clubs raised. Angel took another step forward. He didn't want to crowd Wes and Gunn, but he didn't want the cashier to get any clever ideas, either.

Gunn dropped into a defensive stance, hands raised in front of his face, legs coiled and ready to spring. Wesley snatched a square metal container off a shelf and raised it over his head. The label said BATWINGS, and Angel had no reason to doubt that it was true. The aisle wasn't narrow enough to allow Angel past them—he'd just have to wait for a chance to get into the action.

When the first rank of demons came too close for Wesley's comfort, he hurled the tin at them. The targeted Tik'let simply swung his metal club, swatting the wings container away, and came on.

Gunn landed the first blow. He stepped into the Tik'let's advance, dodged a downswung club, and brought the side of his hand in a short, sharp arc up and into the Tik'let's exposed ribs. The creature huffed and slipped against the shelving unit. Boxes and cans tumbled to the floor. Gunn pressed his attack, feinting with a left jab and then raising his right leg, releasing a snap kick that caught his opponent just above the knee. Even from where he was, Angel could hear bones snap. The Tik'let screamed and started to buckle. Gunn grabbed the club and yanked it from the demon's hand, then swung it around and into the demon's face. Bright blue blood jetted from its nose and mouth, splashing Gunn and the merchandise littering the floor.

Wesley, meanwhile, had engaged his own opponent. The Tik'let attacked again and again with its own club, and Wes dodged and wove like a practiced boxer. At the same time, he jabbed out with his fists, reaching the Tik'let only occasionally. Then the club caught him behind the ear, on a backswing, and Wesley's legs went out from under him. Angel was about to leap to his friend's defense when Wesley swung his own legs, catching the Tik'let in a scissors grip and knocking it down. The Tik'let flailed as he fell. Wesley scooped up a fallen can and brained the Tik'let with it, then clambered over the demon, getting a grip on its club hand.

Behind them, though, the other two Tik'lets were coming in, clubs brandished and ready to do some damage. Angel vaulted over the struggling pair on the floor. His feet slammed into the chest of the nearest demon, and the creature fell back, gasping for breath. The other one brought its club down in a savage arc. It struck Angel's temple, tearing the flesh there. The vampire saw bright flashes of light and felt a searing stab of pain. The Tik'let followed up with two jabs into Angel's midsection. As Angel doubled over, the demon he had knocked down caught him from behind, wrapping massive arms around Angel's own arms and chest. Angel struggled, but the Tik'let held him fast. The one still bearing a club moved in, jabbing a couple more times and then swinging the weapon up and across, smashing into Angel's lower jaw. Angel felt his teeth clash together, tasting blood.

When the demon raised his club for another blow, Angel tensed. Once the club was in motion, Angel lurched forward, bending at the waist. The demon who held him from behind shrieked as it realized it had just moved into the weapon's range, but the other Tik'let couldn't stop the blow in time. The club slammed down against its fellow's skull, and Angel felt the grasp on him loosen. He took another half-step forward and spun, hurling the injured demon at the club-wielder. They collapsed in a pile of aqua-colored limbs, and Angel lashed out with his booted foot, knocking them into unconsciousness.

He turned to see that Wesley and Gunn had subdued the demon Wesley had fought. Wes and Gunn both had clubs in their hands now, and the demon leaned against one of the shelf units, breathing hard, blue blood running in a steady trickle from between black lips. A cut over the demon's eye bled as well, and the eye was already swelling shut.

Angel stepped through the detritus on the shop's floor and stood before the Tik'let. "Where's Fred?" he demanded.

The Tik'let looked at him defiantly at first, but as it processed the question, its expression changed to one of confusion. "Fred?" it asked.

"My friend. The kidnapping, the deal, Pershing Square?"

The demon shook its head. "Man, I have no idea what you are talking about."

Angel pressed his thumb against the Tik'let's head wound. The demon grimaced in pain, and its knees wobbled. "You can hurt me all night if it makes you feel better," it said, "but I just don't know. Tell me who Fred is, maybe."

"Fred is part of my team," Angel explained. "You guys kidnapped her."

The demon tried a smile, but the effort seemed to hurt too much, and it stopped. "News flash," it said. "Wrong. We haven't kidnapped anybody."

Angel glanced at Gunn and Wesley. Gunn shrugged. "Just know what we heard."

"What'd you hear?" the Tik'let asked.

"We heard that a couple of demons working in here were talking about something bad headed Angel's way," Gunn said. "This, apparently, just days before our partner was snatched and Angel's life put in jeopardy."

Now the demon did laugh, a brief, throaty bark. "We're always talking about bad stuff for Angel," it said. It held Angel's gaze with its own eyes. "No offense, you know. But you never shop here. You're constantly takin' out some of our best customers. Do you know how hard it is to run a business in this town? I mean, it's not like we can advertise on TV or anything. And just when we get a big spender, you're liable to come along and dust him or send him to some other dimension. Man, you're the worst thing that's happened to the small business since the rise of the chain superstores. And I gotta tell you, we still don't get a lot of competition from them."

"Well, then, what about this?" Angel swept his hand around the room, indicating the carnage. "Why attack us when we came in?"

"Heh," the demon said, smiling again. This time it looked more than a little abashed. "Ka'reith over there gave the signal you were here," it said, pointing at the cashier. "We made a pact, long time ago, that if you ever came in here you'd be history."

"He was asking a lot of questions," Ka'reith said, as if that justified the attack.

"But I was a customer," Angel protested. "I bought something. In fact, I still don't have change for my twenty."

Give him his change," the injured Tik'let instructed Ka'reith. "Will you take it and go?"

"You're sure you haven't heard anything about Fred being kidnapped?" Angel asked, still hopeful.

"Not a thing. You talk about your private business in front of shopkeepers?"

"He may have a point there, Angel," Wesley said, finger-combing his hair back into place after the brawl.

Ka'reith counted Angel's change into his hand. Angel picked up the pint of pig's blood he'd purchased and unscrewed the top again. "I'll drink it here," he announced. "So I don't have to carry the jar around." He noticed that Gunn and Wesley both turned away, beginning to stroll, almost casually, toward the door that led back out toward the front store. Angel downed the pint quickly, felt the warmth and energy rush through his body, and put the empty down on the counter. "Nice place," he said as he followed Wesley and Gunn out. "You might want to try a little more positive word-of-mouth, though. Could bring you a better class of customer."

"Thanks," the Tik'let called after him. "Don't hurry back!"

When he caught up to them outside, Angel noticed that Gunn had bought an Energy Bar and a sports drink. "What's in that thing?" he asked, indicating the dark brown bar that Gunn was munching on.

Gunn swallowed. "I don't know. Oats, I guess. Cornmeal, dates, prunes, soy nuts, some crisped rice. Stuff like that." He took another bite.

Angel made a face. "At least I gave you a chance to turn your back before I ate."

"Well," Gunn said, his mouth full of Energy Bar, "I guess you're more polite than me."

For the first time in hours, Angel laughed.

CHAPTER THIRTEEN

It had been bad enough knowing that Fred was missing, and probably in grave danger. But now Cordy knew that the danger Fred was in was only part of the story, and the other part, the really really awful part, was that Angel was apparently willing to put his own life on the line to save Fred's.

Of course, she thought as she paced around the hotel's empty lobby, *everybody knows that the bad guys don't really mean to let the hostage go in the first place. That after they get the ransom, they kill the person they've kidnapped because she can identify them. Angel doesn't watch much TV, but surely he's seen that movie a hundred times. So by sacrificing himself, he has nothing to gain and everything to lose.*

But the only way she could see to prevent him from making that sacrifice was to locate Fred before the sun came up. The phone calls to Angel's cell had been made from two different public pay phones, and she had no way to determine who'd made them. And, in spite of her hours of staring at the computer screen and digesting so much data on demons that she felt capable of writing an encyclopedia, she still had not been able to narrow the field of suspects enough to help much. Even with all the experience she had, as part of Buffy's Scooby Gang back in Sunnydale, and here in L.A. working with Angel, she had never realized just how many different breeds of demon shared Earth with humanity. And that wasn't even including those who could drop in from other dimensions, like relatives who aren't really liked but who can't be turned away because they're family and might be bringing gifts.

Pylea had been a real education for her, in that respect. An entirely new dimension, a new world filled with its own various types of creatures, and it was all accessible to Earth through the use of a magick spell, or apparently, as in her case, and Fred's, entirely by accident. And who knew how many other worlds there were out there?

In that context, trying to figure out who had snatched Fred was much like trying to isolate what particular human being had touched a certain drop of water in the middle of the Pacific. Too many possibilities, too broad a field.

Anyway, Cordelia thought, *I've gotten good at*

this whole online research thing, but mostly by default since Angel and technology don't really mix, and Wes is always too busy with his books to bother joining the twentieth century, much less the twenty-first. But my real gift is the one Doyle passed to me: the visions. Why can't I just have a stinking, nausea-inducing, skull-splitting vision of where Fred is, and get it over with? Why won't the Powers That Be let me have some control over the power instead of just using it to torment me and occasionally ruin an otherwise entirely acceptable date?

Since returning from Pylea, where she'd had an opportunity to give up the visions and the accompanying physical and emotional distress but had chosen not to, the vision power had seemed to be evolving in some way. She wasn't quite sure where she was headed, but she could feel change in the air. The visions took more out of her than ever, wracking her body in ways she could not have imagined, and probably would not have accepted, in the early days. She had retained the power not only because it had become part of her, defining her own mission, but also because she knew it helped connect Angel with the Powers That Be, which seemed to be an essential part of whatever path he was on. She figured she owed Angel that much—or if *owed* wasn't the right word, it was, at least, a gift she wanted to give him.

But just now, it was incredibly frustrating knowing that the power lived within her but that she couldn't draw it out when it was most important. Cordelia wondered if the Powers That Be even realized they were on the verge of losing Angel, when he could be spared with the simplest little TV broadcast into her waiting brain. Once, there had been a way to contact the PTB, via the Oracles, but they'd been slain by a powerful demon called Vocah, and with them went the only way Angel and his team knew to get in direct contact with The Powers. *If only they had an e-mail address like everybody else,* Cordy thought, *or Instant Messaging. They're as bad as Wesley.*

She stopped her aimless pacing and stood in the center of the art deco lobby, blankly noticing a dust bunny up against the foot of one of the banquettes. For a brief moment she felt it was very important to get a broom and sweep the floor, but it didn't take long to identify that impulse as a way to avoid the genuinely pressing issue before her. *Finding Fred is all that's important,* she thought. The idea occurred to her, as it had once or twice before, that she should be able to force a vision to come if she tried hard enough. She had never made the attempt before, and didn't really know how she might go about it.

But hey, she thought, *the old cliché is that there's a first time for everything, right?*

Just in case it worked, Cordelia sat down on the padded banquette, ignoring the dust bunny. She put her hands on her thighs, clenching her fists so tightly that her nails dug into her palms, screwed her eyes shut, and summoned a mental image of Fred. Fred's pretty face, her long brown hair framing it in a cascade of loose curls, the smile that could dominate a room as easily as she could disappear from it by turning off the glow and retreating into herself. Goofy Fred, queen of the non sequitur, and brilliant Fred, who could apply her scientific mind to a problem and come up with a solution faster than most people could understand what the problem was. Shy Fred, torn between doting on Angel and hiding from him in her room. Winifred Burkle was a mass of contradictions—*but then, who isn't?*

She relaxed her fists, opened her eyes. She could bring up details about Fred, but she couldn't force a vision. Of course. Because the Powers That Be didn't operate in such a convenient way. They always had to be mysterious, aloof, with their own agenda that no mortal could know. . . .

"Big fat idiots!" Cordelia shouted toward the ceiling. "I just need a little vision here!"

And it hit her with the force of a tsunami, driving her off the banquette and to her knees on the cold, hard floor. A flood of images washed over her, threatening to carry her consciousness out to sea.

A woman retreating from an angry man who held a bottle in one hand and a knife in the other. A man surrounded by predators—vampires, maybe, or thugs, on a dark European street. An African man running from a raging mob. A young girl swimming desperately against a ferocious rip current, with a backdrop of paradise and palm trees in the distance. An ugly, purple-skinned demon advancing on unseen prey. Then the images started to rush at Cordelia so fast, she couldn't even make out situations, only momentary flashes of detail: a gun, flames, a jackknifing semi, more guns, fangs and claws, stones and steel and bombs and blood. A roar in her ears deafened Cordy, the images swirled behind her eyes, and the sheer volume of pain and fear and misery upon Earth rose within her, swelling until it had pushed all other awareness from her and she'd collapsed on the lobby floor.

When she blinked back to consciousness a little while later, it was gone. There was just a remnant inside her, a dull ache between her temples, a slight ringing in her ears. She hadn't seen Fred, or if she had, it had been only a momentary glimpse along with everything else. What she had seen, she believed, was a cutaway view of the world's pain: people in danger, in trouble, everywhere around the globe at that moment. It had been as if the Powers That Be were trying to demonstrate why asking for a vision was not the brightest thing to do—it was their job to prioritize these things, not hers.

So much for trying to force a vision, she thought. *Bad idea. Really incredibly bad idea.*

But she also realized that the experience drove home the continued necessity of having Angel around. The world could be a dark, scary, dangerous place. It needed a champion.

It needs Angel.

Cordelia pushed herself up off the floor, went to her desk, and grabbed her purse and a jacket. She couldn't do any more good sitting around here. She needed to get out, to find Angel and Wesley and Gunn, and to help them find Fred.

There's just no other way, she decided. *No other option that's acceptable. We have to find her.*

"I'm sorry," Fred said, sniffing back tears. She hated to cry, especially in front of strangers. She knew she shouldn't care what this guy thought of her; *after all,* she reasoned, *he's the bad guy.* And he'd cut her, whipped out a sharp-bladed knife and drawn it across her upper arm for no reason but to make her scream and shake Angel up. But she couldn't help the way she felt, and it was embarrassing to lose control of herself this way. She wiped at her eyes and nose with her free hand and glanced at the guy. He sat in his chair, barely seeming to notice that she was even alive.

"Look, I know you don't really care about me and are probably just going to kill me and everything, so you don't want to think of me as a person, but I am, you know?" she said. "So if you're going to be sitting in here with me you might as well help pass the time by talking to me, okay?"

"Nothing to say," the guy said.

"Well, that's kind of a contradiction, isn't it?" she asked. "You can only actually open your mouth to say that you have nothing to say? You're a funny man. Evil, I'm sure. But still funny, in the peculiar way. Maybe when Angel comes to save me, he won't kill you. Or maybe if he does it won't hurt very much."

Now the guy focused on her, a cloud of anger crossing his face. "Angel isn't going to kill anybody," he said curtly. "Angel is the one who's going to die. I promise you that."

"I talked to him on the phone," she said. The guy had handed her his cell phone as soon as it had rung, after he'd worked out the details in a brief call from a compatriot somewhere. "He'll just trace the call and find out where I am and he'll come get me. It's really not that complicated."

"Angel made a deal," the guy said, a sly smile spreading across his face. The smile didn't reach his eyes, which seemed cold to Fred. Vibrant green, but cold as glass, or emeralds frozen in ice cubes for safekeeping. "Him for you. Fast and easy."

She'd heard enough of the conversation to know that he was telling the truth, although if details of this deal had been worked out, it had been arranged with some confederate, not with this guy directly. But she couldn't bring herself to believe that Angel would go through with it. "That's what you'd like to think."

"It's what I know," the guy said. His smile grew now, as if he understood that each of his words stabbed her like daggers, and he was enjoying the torture. "Come sunup, I'm turning you loose, but only once Angel is bursting into flames, standing in the rays of the rising sun. He fries, you fly. It's a simple trade."

"But . . . but he's a hero," Fred protested. "He saves people, helps people. I don't . . . I'm just a scientist, a *nobody*. I've never saved the world, or even been to Greece. Not that going to Greece makes someone a hero, but you know, a lot of them came from there, in the old days. Angel helps more people in a week than I have in my whole life, probably."

"That doesn't always make him popular," the kidnapper pointed out. Fred noticed that he seemed engaged in the conversation now, leaning toward her, responding immediately when she spoke. "In fact, it's a good way to make enemies. Powerful enemies."

"Like you?" Fred asked, sensing that he wanted to talk about himself but that he wanted to be drawn out. It wasn't something she was good at—letting people stay in their shells was more her style. "Who are you, anyway?"

He looked away from her, toward the floor—but more, she thought, as if he were looking through the floor, at something she couldn't begin to see. "You couldn't pronounce my name if I bothered to tell you," he said. "If you must label me, call me John."

John, Jack, Fred thought. *If this is all some kind of plot with fake names and everything, they could at least put a little more imagination into it.*

But then again, it seems to be working, doesn't it?

"And you consider Angel an enemy?"

"Angel is most assuredly an enemy," John answered. "The worst enemy I know, because he is the most powerful. Fortunately, he'll soon be the most dead."

"The more evil enemies someone has, the better he is, I think," Fred pressed. "Even if you get mad at Angel because he goes after your friends, don't you recognize that he makes the world a better place to be? For everyone?"

"Let me explain something to you," the guy said. "I don't really care much about saving the world. I'm the one it needs saving from. I am interested in one thing: power. My associates and I have some, and we want more. A lot more. But there's something in the way of us getting it—of me, getting my just due—and that's Angel. I get rid of him, then I'm a hero, to my kind. And by capturing Angel's power, I am instantly the most powerful of all. Do you get that?"

"I get that you're an evil, nasty man with a killer inferiority complex that you're trying to hide by pretending it's a superiority complex," Fred replied. "And you're not someone that I think I would like, even if you weren't also a kidnapper and . . . well . . . a jerk."

John lurched out of the chair, rage flashing in his eyes, and she thought maybe she'd gone too far, because he looked like he had every intention of messing up the deal by killing her right now. He dug the knife from his pocket again and opened it, advancing on her. "I guess it's time to cut you again," he said. Fred tried to shrink back against the wall, but the handcuffs rattled against the radiator and there was no place she could go. She tried kicking at him, but he simply caught one of her legs in his strong hand. Fred writhed, trying to twist it from his grasp, but he was too powerful. With a thin smile, he drew the knife across her ankle and then released her, stepping back quickly out of her reach. A line of blood appeared where he had sliced her.

She started to cry again as he returned to his chair. But halfway across the room, a cell phone buried in one of his pockets rang, and he stopped, fishing it out and answering it. "What?" he growled.

He listened for a moment, said, "Okay," and clicked it off, returning it to his pocket. He looked at Fred for a long few seconds, green eyes still smoldering, and then turned and walked out of the room, locking the door loudly after he went through it.

Fred was alone again. *Which is just how I should be,* she thought. She realized that her big mistake had been returning from Pylea with Angel and friends. Back there, she had lived alone, been responsible for no one but herself, couldn't put anyone's life in danger. *Okay,* she thought, *I lived in a cave and slept on rocks and had to hide from the priests so they didn't explode my head. But at least there was no one whose life might depend on my ability to not get captured, except me. If I messed up, I might get killed, but no big loss since I wasn't really offering much to society in my cave, anyway.*

Here, though, she had become part of a team. And being part of a team meant that she was dependent on them and they on her. Which also meant that she could endanger others, and they, in turn, could endanger her.

But right this minute, she was not particularly concerned about the danger she was in. Even the cuts, while painful, were minor injuries. It would take a lot of those to put her life in danger. She was mainly worried about Angel.

John was gone, though, and that meant she could continue with the only thing she could think of to do, which was to try to pick the lock on the handcuffs holding her to the radiator. She worked the hinge pin out of her waistband and studied it. It was nothing more than a tiny rod of metal, and she didn't know if it would even work. From what little Fred understood about locks, there were some number of tumblers inside, the exact quantity depending upon the complexity of the lock. The tumblers had to be caused to line up, at which point the lock could be tripped. The ridges and slots in a key were configured in such a way as to push the tumblers into the correct alignment, but without a key, painstaking work would be needed to achieve the same result. And once the tumblers were lined up, tension was required—the turning of the key part. Even if she could manipulate the tumblers, she didn't know if she could hold the tumblers in line with the hinge pin and also use it to turn the lock.

As with any scientific experiment, there were multiple stages. One started with a hypothesis, and then proceeded to test that hypothesis, eventually arriving at a result. Her hypothesis was how she believed locks worked. The only way to test it was to get started with the hinge pin—*at hand,* she thought wryly. She raised the cuffed wrist to shoulder height so she could watch what she was doing, even though there wasn't enough light to see much inside the dark chasm of the lock, and she slipped in the hinge pin. The cuff's lock was probably a fairly simple one, so it wouldn't be too hard to figure out.

At least, that's what she hoped.

CHAPTER FOURTEEN

The stage was empty now, just recorded music filling the silence. Everyone was tired, Lorne included, and there were murmurs of resentment at being kept here so long. Lorne didn't care—nobody was leaving until everyone had been spoken to, and whatever clues this bunch might have about Fred's disappearance revealed. Subdued conversation took place at some tables, and at others silence reigned. In one corner, facedown on a blue table that glowed softly from within, a furry purple demon snored loudly. Sinatra played over the PA system, Lorne hoping the music would subtly remind the customers just who was Chairman of the Board tonight.

Lorne sat across from the pseudo-crustacean Shrenli who had come in alone and who sang soul and blues tunes like every phrase brought some fresh heartbreak. "You can really sing, Visssclorf," he said.

"Did you like it?" she asked. He thought she was smiling, but what with the beak and no teeth, it was hard to tell. Lorne knew that the beak was useful for ripping and tearing—Shrenli demons usually ate the young of other demon species, which made them less than popular to have around, even at Caritas. Lorne felt a little uneasy himself, sitting here with her—the other tables around her were pointedly vacant.

"Don't quit your day job," he admonished her. "But to someone who has to listen to people who not only can't carry a tune but wouldn't recognize one if it climbed up their leg and got friendly, it was . . . well, sometimes the old cliché is the best cliché: It was music to my ears. You sang those songs like you felt them, which is really what music is all about. If you don't have the passion, it's just talking loud with instrumental accompaniment." He took a sip from his mug—he'd moved on to coffee as the hour got later, just to help him stay alert.

"Did you . . . did you happen to read me?" Visssclorf asked. She sounded hesitant about the question, possibly afraid of the answer. "You know, my aura or whatever?"

Lorne set his mug down on the table. He knew

what it had taken for her to come out in public like this. She was safe enough inside Caritas, but Shrenlis were such an unpopular species that she must have worried about leaving, afraid that she might be attacked and killed on her way home. *And*, he realized, *I don't have a lot of sympathy for her. I mean, most of us can modify our diet if we have to. To her, of course, it's not cannibalism, because they're other species, but it's still far from socially acceptable behavior.* He reminded himself that she was a customer, one who had been particularly brave to come here, and that he might need information from her. "No, sweetheart," he lied. He had, but what he'd gotten had nothing to do with Fred, and since she hadn't asked him to, he didn't want her to think he was prying. "Did you want me to? I'm sorry, I just have other things on my mind tonight, and didn't even think to ask you."

"Well," she said, looking away from him and toward the floor, "kind of."

"Is there something in particular you're looking for?" he asked her, hoping she was maybe considering a dietary change. "Something troubling you?"

She nodded, still looking down. He guessed shyness was exhibited in similar fashion by many creatures. At this moment, she reminded him of Fred looking for an excuse to go to her room. "I have a . . . I guess, a major life change to consider."

"Getting a job?" he prodded. "Boyfriend, girl-friend, new house?"

Finally she looked directly at him. Her eyes were small, round beads of black, like drops of ink that had been spilled on her hard shell. "I don't know how much you know about Shrenlis, other than what everyone talks about, that we eat things we shouldn't. We don't seem to have much choice in that—we eat what sustains us, what gives us life, and whenever we've tried to change, it hasn't really worked out. Many of us have gotten sick, and died, from avoiding the food that we know works for us."

"You're right," Lorne admitted. "That's about all I know."

She took a sip of her beverage through a long straw. "Well, that's part of what we are, but not the whole thing," she told him. "That part makes us hated, and feared, and targeted. Your friend Angel, he's killed several of my clan, some of my sisters. I try not to hold that against him, because I know how the rest of the world sees us. But something else about us is that we reproduce asexually. We divide. My time has come, and I've been giving serious thought to dividing. But do I want to bring a new Shrenli, my own shell and blood, into a world where she'll be despised from the outset? Is that fair to her? That's the question I've been struggling with, and I was hoping maybe you could help me."

Lorne started to say something, and then held

back, which was unusual for him. He knew that he had a habit of speaking first and thinking later. He'd occasionally been accused of loving the sound of his own voice, and there was, perhaps, some factual basis for that accusation. He turned his mug around on the glass tabletop for a few seconds, listening to the dull ringing sound it made as it spun. His first thought was that she should not divide, not reproduce, and that if every Shrenli made the same decision and this generation of Shrenlis was the last, he would have no problem with that.

But should I say that? he wondered. *To her, eating the young of a Mofo, a Kailiff, or a Lister demon is no different from a human eating lamb or veal. Virtually every sentient species eats some form of meat, which means preying on some other creature's offspring. For that matter, there are demons who'd object to the presence of a Shrenli in their midst, but would think nothing of feasting on humans. What's repugnant to me is simply survival to her.*

"You said Angel has killed some of your sisters," Lorne said finally. "Does that mean you're not willing to help me find his friend Fred?"

"Not at all," Vsssclorf said quickly. "I want your help, and I'm happy to help you. Like I said, Angel is just doing what he thinks he needs to do. That's all we do too. So I'll help if I can."

"Fair enough," Lorne said. "You help me, I'll listen to you sing again and give you a reading. Maybe not right away, because I still have more folks to talk to, and the clock is ticking. But before you leave here tonight."

"I think it's more accurately this morning, at this point," she observed.

"Oh, a stickler for detail, eh? Did you see Fred tonight? Last night, I mean, now that it's tomorrow."

"I saw Angel and his friends all sitting at the table together, yes. I've been here a couple of times before, not very often, but I've noticed them here before too. I remember feeling worried because I knew what Angel had done to my sisters, but inside here he always leaves me alone."

"Those are the rules," Lorne pointed out.

"Right, I know. So when I saw them tonight, or last night, whatever, I noticed that there was someone new. I gather that was Fred, the young lady with all the brown hair."

"That's Fred. If she shaved her head I think she'd lose a quarter of her body weight."

"I saw her again, later on," Visssclorf continued. Her words were perfectly understandable, but her beak clacked a little when she spoke, which Lorne found distracting. The color of her skin reminded Lorne of seafood restaurants near the shore, painted bright red long ago and then sun-faded to a pale rose. "I had gone to the females' room, which is where I feel most comfortable, even though we have, you know, just the one gender. When I came out, Fred was standing in the hallway, kind of blocking it, talking with a young human male."

"Another one of Angel's people?" Lorne asked. He hadn't seen any other humans in the club all evening.

"No, someone else. Someone who hadn't been at Angel's table. Like I said, I recognized everyone sitting there except Fred, so this male was definitely not part of that group. This was just before the explosion that made everyone go outside. I didn't go out, but when everybody came back in, some were starting to talk about Fred having vanished. I looked around then for the human male, and couldn't find him. I didn't see him again all night."

Bingo! "Are you sure?" he pressed. "I didn't notice any other humans in the club at all, so this could be an important point."

"I'm positive," Vissclorf confirmed. "I had to stand there in the hall while they talked—flirted, I'd say. I was about to finally say something, when the explosion happened."

"What did he look like, this young man?"

Vissclorf considered the question for a moment before answering. "I can't say if he was handsome

191

or not," she said eventually. "Shrenli standards of beauty are very different, I'm sure, from human standards, or even yours. But Fred was looking at him as if she thought he was. He was a good deal taller than she was, I remember. Powerful looking. Wearing a blue shirt with dark pants. His hair kind of stuck up all over, like yours does, but darker."

Lorne unconsciously ran long green fingers through his own spiky blondish hair. She could have been describing Angel, except that his shirt tonight had been a deep maroon instead of blue. But that would make sense—Fred definitely had a crush on the hunky vamp, and if she had been as attracted to this guy as Vissclorf described, then it wouldn't be surprising if he bore a resemblance to Angel.

Then the question became, was it a coincidental resemblance? Or did whoever had plotted this specifically send in someone who looked like Fred's ideal man in order to catch her off guard?

There was a vague, indefinite goal that Lorne had had now and again during the years he'd been on Earth. In his pipe dream, instead of owning a downtown nightclub, he owned a resort in some balmy South Pacific paradise. The southern coast of Mexico, maybe, or some Polynesian island. Vampires like Angel could come and enjoy the nightlife, but for other demons there would also be daytime activities—snorkeling in impossibly clear blue waters; lounging at the beach; sailing, tennis, and golf—the whole tropical fun package, all rolled into one vast sanctuary.

That dream came back to him now because he thought if he had a place like that, he could welcome his guests at a private airstrip, all Ricardo Montalban in a lightweight silk summer suit, and then see them off again when they left. And that way, he'd never have to feel responsible for anything that might happen just outside the doors to his place, because he would have seen them safely come and go. Before they arrived and after they went, they were on their own.

The same applied at Caritas, of course, but there was always the freak event—like whatever had happened to Fred, where she had just stepped out of protected ground for a couple of minutes—that threw a monkey wrench into his whole theory. On his beachfront hideaway, there would be no stepping out—sanctuary would extend to the border of international waters, and anyone who went beyond that would know what they were opening themselves up to.

He shook his head to bring himself back to Caritas and the business at hand. "Let me just get this straight," he said. "You didn't see this guy in the club before you spotted him talking to Fred, and you couldn't find him after. He just showed up for those few minutes?"

"That's all I saw of him. I couldn't say he wasn't there before—I was kind of nervous, waiting my turn to sing."

"And then you finally did sing, and I wasn't paying close enough attention," Lorne said. "I'll make it up to you, Visssclorf honey. I promise. Did you see anything else that might help?"

"No," she said firmly. "Like I told you, I didn't even go outside when the explosion went off. I know I'm not well liked around here. I didn't want to leave the confines of the club when all those others were outside. I wanted to just sing my songs and then go, by myself, so I could get home before anybody spotted me. If anybody ever followed me home from here, or caught me outside, I'd be dead for sure."

Virtually every demon felt that way from time to time, existing in a world that had become so overwhelmingly dominated by humans. *But it's too bad,* Lorne thought, *that she has to feel that way because of something beyond her control.*

Absolutely disgusting and heinous, but nonetheless, not exactly her choice.

"Okay," he said. He wanted to pat her pinchers, to reassure her if he could. But who knew if that would even be taken the right way by such an alien breed? She might see it as an attack, or an insult. "Thanks, Visssclorf. I appreciate the assist, and I know Angel will too." He left her sitting there, sipping her drink through the long straw, and marveled at the courage it had taken her to come to this place knowing she was universally hated by the rest of the clientele.

Just goes to show you, he thought, *you can never tell what's in someone's heart by the way they look on the outside.*

CHAPTER FIFTEEN

Having left Gunn and Wesley on the trail of another informant's tip—*though informants,* Angel was beginning to think, *are not exactly proving their worth tonight*—the vampire was back behind the wheel of his GTX, heading for the Hyperion. He'd had another idea, but it would take some online research to pin down the guy he needed to talk to, and Cordy was already on her way out to join the guys, having had just about all the online time she could stand. Angel understood. *There are times when you just can't take the sitting and sifting data anymore, and you just have to find someone you can hit.*

The more the night dragged on, the more frustrated he grew, and the more hitting sounded like a good idea—especially after having heard Fred get cut. The fight at the demon market had been pointless, as it turned out, but at least it had dissipated some of his restless energy. Without that break, he might not have been able to look at the problem with a fresh enough eye to come up with this new approach.

It all started with the fire, he had realized. He wasn't sure if the explosion was what had started the fire, or if the fire had set off the explosion. But either way, the building across from Caritas had been burning, and that's what had drawn everyone out of the club and onto the sidewalk, where the drive-by car could shoot into their midst and distract them long enough to snatch Fred.

And yet, in trying to find a new way to come at the problem, he had completely ignored the fire. Lorne had speculated that it was arson, a fire set by the building's owner to claim insurance money since he couldn't afford to finish construction. It had sounded plausible to Angel—certainly it had happened just that way, many times—so he'd put it out of his mind. But after the market brawl, when he, Wes, and Gunn had been standing around outside shaking out sore knuckles and reliving the best parts, it had suddenly struck him as odd. Any other time, the explanation would have been fine. But tonight, the timing had been so precise that the fire must have been intentionally set to draw out the clientele of Caritas.

Which meant it was still arson—but maybe arson with two completely different purposes in mind.

He wouldn't know until he could find out who owned the building, and what his real financial situation was. And who his friends were—that would be key. If he had any dealing with Wolfram and Hart, for instance, or any known connections with any demonic groups, that would be a definite starting point.

Angel stomped on the accelerator and gunned the car through a yellow light, then down the street, barely slowing to turn into the hotel's driveway. He stopped in front of the doors, killed the engine, and jumped from the car. Inside, he found that Cordelia had left her computer powered up and online. *Good,* he thought. *Saves me at least three minutes.*

And this was one of those occasions, he knew, in which every minute might literally count.

"I'm tellin' you," Gunn said, for what seemed like the sixth or seventh time, "this is where we said we'd meet her."

"I just don't want to be standing on this corner waiting when Cordelia is, in fact, standing on some other corner waiting for us," Wesley said. He glanced up at the street signs again, as if they might have changed since the last ten times he'd looked at them. When they didn't seem to have, he looked back down at the sidewalk and crossed his arms impatiently. Gunn found himself almost wishing Cordy would be even later, just so he could see if Wes would actually explode.

But since Fred was still in danger, he figured that should be a pleasure saved for some other time.

"You could try her cell again," Gunn offered, with a wry grin. "But she'd just think you were worrying for nothin'. Or insane—there's always that."

Wesley was about to say something else—probably another variation on "I just want to be certain," Gunn suspected—when Cordy's Jeep rolled up to the corner and stopped. She lowered the passenger window. "You guys going to stand out there all night?" she asked cheerfully.

Gunn went to the front passenger door and climbed in. Wesley took the seat behind him. "You always pick up any men you see on street corners?" Gunn asked.

"Just the cute ones," Cordelia replied. "And believe me, most guys you see standing around on street corners look more like someone else's leftovers than cute ones."

"We're going to Fourth and Hartford," Wesley told her. Gunn thought there was still a trace of impatience in his voice, though really she'd only kept them waiting a couple of minutes longer than she had promised.

"Meter's running," she informed them. "Seriously, you guys, thanks for letting me come out with you."

"You're part of the team," Wesley replied stiffly.

"The part of the team who was going stir-crazy in that hotel," she announced. "I felt about as useless there as that bottle of Bain de Soleil we got Angel as a gag gift but that he refuses to just throw away."

"Not completely useless," Wes said, and this time Gunn caught an undercurrent of humor in his tone. "You did tell Angel that one of the demon species that might possibly be involved was a Zhoon."

Gunn picked up the narrative. "And I happened to know a Zhoon, from the old neighborhood. Used to freak some of my boys out, see me talk to this freaky-lookin' demon like it was just one of the locals. But that's what it was. Demon wasn't suckin' blood or anything like the vamps we took down. It used to collect bottles and cans in a shopping cart, for the money it could get down at the recycling place."

"Was it homeless?" Cordelia asked, sounding genuinely sympathetic. "That's so sad."

"No, it had a crib. It just liked a clean neighborhood, and it had a lot of time on its hands. Zhoons never need to sleep, and this one loved to talk. Thing would talk all night long and never get tired."

He had caught Wesley yawning. "A trait more of us could use, apparently," Wesley put in.

"No doubt," Cordelia said, squealing around a hard right. She drove the Jeep well, but faster than Gunn was quite comfortable with. Gunn thought she had probably been riding with Angel too much before she'd gotten her own L.A. wheels.

"So you found this sleepless streetcleaner . . . ," Cordelia prodded when Gunn failed to resume his story.

"It wasn't quite that simple," Wesley told her. "First we had to go to Gunn's old neighborhood, which, quite frankly, isn't on the Fodor's list of top Los Angeles tourist attractions—"

"Well, it ain't as cool as the La Brea tar pits or the Bradbury Building," Gunn interrupted. "But I think it beats Forest Lawn and that diner shaped like a hot dog."

"Hey, I love Tail O' the Pup!" Cordelia shouted. "I mean, the building. It's classic Southern California architecture. I don't actually eat the hot dogs." She paused, reconsidering. "Well, almost never."

"Yes," Wes humphed. "As I was saying, we had to tour the high points of Gunn's misspent youth—"

"I lived there two years ago," Gunn interjected.

"Quite. Before you moved to your current slice of heaven. And when we finally did find the Zhoon, he didn't so much want to talk to us as to use our headlights to see if the plastic bottles and jars he had gathered were number ones, twos, or fives."

ANGEL

"Recycling place only takes ones and twos," Gunn explained.

"Is going out with you two always so entertaining?" Cordy asked. "Because it just occurs to me that maybe there's some online research I could be doing."

"You did ask," Gunn said.

"Did I? I don't remember that."

"Actually, you didn't," Wesley corrected. "But we started to tell you, anyway."

"And once we start somethin', we don't stop," Gunn threatened. "So you might as well listen to the rest of the story."

"If it's short," Cordelia said. "We're almost there. And if I keep jabbering, maybe I'll get to miss the rest."

"Not that easy," Gunn said, playfully punching her shoulder. *Joking through hard times,* he thought. *I'm glad we can do that. Makes things easier.* Families had that kind of comfort level, he knew—he and his sister Alonna had had it once, before she had been turned into a vamp and he'd had to dust her. But if he started thinking about her, he'd think about Fred being in danger, and he'd ruin the mood that made coping with it possible. "Troublemaker."

"That's me," she agreed, rubbing her arm where he had hit her. "Trouble with a capital C, and that stands for Cordy. And hey, ow!"

"Okay, long story short—," Gunn began.

"Little late for that."

He ignored her. "We found the Zhoon who likes to talk. He'd been talking, to someone who talked to someone else, you know how it goes. And this someone mentioned an abandoned car that had turned up near the corner of Fourth and Hartford. Not just a car, but a Z-28, which is what the shooters drove. So we thought we'd check it, see what's up."

"Ahh," Cordelia replied. She scanned the street ahead, dark and silent. "So that's why we're in this neighborhood that seems to have gone to sleep hours ago."

"Well, most bad guys don't dump cars where there are a lot of people to see 'em," Gunn pointed out. "Except for the really stupid ones."

Cordelia turned onto Hartford and slowed the Jeep. At the curb, badly parked behind a rust-pocked pickup truck, a dark Z-28 sat. There was no light falling directly on it, so Gunn couldn't tell if it was black or dark blue, but it sure looked like the car he'd seen on the street outside Caritas. Cordy pulled in behind it, and in the wash of her headlights, he decided it was dark blue.

"That looks like it," he said.

"Or like a hundred thousand identical vehicles," Wesley observed. "I think we need to take a closer look before we decide for sure that's the one."

Gunn already had the Jeep's door open. "That's what we're here for," he said. He stepped to the sidewalk and approached the car, peering into the windows. It was definitely empty. And smelly. "Kinda stinks," he said.

Wesley and Cordelia joined him. She made a face. "Kinda," she said, breathing through her mouth. "In the sense that mustard is kinda yellow, or Prada is kinda better than Kmart."

Wesley bent close to the car and then turned away, wrinkling his nose. "I'm afraid we're going to have to get closer," he said. "Like, inside."

"What do you see?" Gunn asked.

"Take a look." Wesley pointed toward the car's ceiling, right around the dome light. Gunn hunched over and followed the line of his finger and saw what he was looking at. The ceiling was caked with something that looked like green cottage cheese. As he watched, a big droplet of it formed and fell between the front seats.

"That's nasty," Gunn said. "I mean, truly gross."

"The door's unlocked," Cordelia observed. "So if you guys want to really get into the spirit of this, feel free."

Wesley looked at Gunn. "We really need to," he said. "So far, we just have a car that smells bad. But there's no indication that it was the car that fired at us."

"Wasn't actually the car shot at us, but the

demons inside," Gunn countered. "And if we're gonna find out what demons they were, I guess we gotta go in." He put a hand on the door handle, lightly, as if expecting it to be white-hot, but then yanked on it and tugged open the front passenger door. The stench billowed out like heat from a blast furnace, catching him full on the face and making him gag. "Wow," he said when he could speak. "That is some rank demon-stink."

Cordelia turned away. "You're not joking."

Gunn looked back at Wesley, who was putting his head inside the car and taking a deep whiff. "Careful, man," he said. "That stuff might be toxic."

"No, I don't think so," Wesley replied. His voice sounded a bit strained. "It smells familiar, though. . . ."

I don't even want to think about how that could be true, Gunn thought. *Can't imagine I'll ever forget that stink, though.*

Wesley stepped away from the car and walked in a slow circle on the sidewalk. Gunn watched him, mouth-breathing and trying not to think about the fact that smells are caused by minute particles of the offending substance actually wafting into one's nasal passages. As Wesley paced through the arc of his circle, again and again, he held his face to the sky, almost like a man trying desperately to remember a name that eluded him.

"Sulfur and ammonia," he muttered. "But with a trace of onion—no, grilled onion. . . ."

Gunn risked another sniff. "Don't forget the sweat socks," he said, half-joking.

"That's it!" Wesley cried. "Thank you, Gunn. You've done it."

"What'd he do?" Cordelia said. "Besides making me not care if I ever eat again. You guys should partner up with Jenny Craig."

"This car has been occupied—and recently—by Roshon demons," Wesley announced. He went back to it and pointed excitedly. "Look, see the mucousy drippings?"

"Who could miss them?" Cordy asked.

"Well, Roshons breathe oxygen, as we do," Wesley said. "But they don't exhale carbon dioxide."

"And that goo came outta their noses?" Gunn inquired, not sure he wanted to know the answer.

"No, not directly," Wes replied. "It's a reaction of the bacteria in an enclosed space to the gaseous substance they exhale. It isn't something they excrete, it's just what happens when they breathe heavily in a tight space."

"Why wouldn't they just roll down the windows?" Gunn wanted to know. "Let some air in. Or out, whatever."

"It doesn't bother them in the least, according to what I've heard," Wesley pointed out. "It's repulsive to us, but just as normal to Roshons as our own bodily processes are to us."

"They sound like fun people to hang out with," Cordelia said. "But how is this helping us?"

"Well, it lets us know that Roshons have been driving this car."

"How long does it last?" Cordy asked.

"What do you mean?"

"The gunk. If it comes from their breath, does it stay there until someone cleans it off? Does it go away on its own after a while, what?"

"I'm not sure," Wesley said after a moment's consideration. "I think it lasts for a while, at any rate. So we probably can't determine exactly when the car was last driven, if that's what you're getting at."

Cordelia smiled like a student who had just scored a major point with the prof. But Gunn knew that understanding what they couldn't figure out was less important than figuring out what they could.

"Wes," Gunn said.

"Yes, Charles?"

"I'm amazed and disgusted that you know all this. But good job."

"Thank you," Wesley replied, still smiling.

Cordelia bent over and looked in the car again, still keeping her distance from it. "Okay, which one of you is going to look in the glove compartment and see if they left some identification behind, or maybe a map with a big 'X marks the Fred' drawn on it?"

Gunn realized that she was right. "Good point. All we know now is that Roshons dumped this ride here. We don't know for sure they were the shooters, even though we think they were. We don't know for certain if the drive-by is connected to the snatching of Fred, even though we think it is. And we don't know what any of that means in terms of who's got Fred, or where."

"Well, it means that Roshons are involved," Wesley said. "We at least have a direction to work in. That's progress from where we were five minutes ago."

"We know where these Roshons hang out?"

"Not precisely," Wesley answered. "We could find out, given time."

"Which is exactly what we don't have," Cordelia said archly, pacing the sidewalk.

"Yes, indeed."

"Think Angel would know?" Gunn inquired. It was frustrating to have what was almost definitely a clue but not know exactly what the clue pointed to. It was a step in the direction of saving Fred—*and Angel,* he reminded himself—but he didn't know how many steps would be needed, or how many changes in direction, before they reached the final goal.

"He might," Wesley said. "And he'd certainly agree that finding some Roshons and forcing them to tell us what they know is a reasonable approach."

"That sounds right," Cordelia said. "Except isn't he on his way to try the same trick on some presumably-human building owner?"

"Then we'll have to take it upon ourselves," Wesley said. "The Zhoon said the car was just dumped in the past couple of hours. Unless they were picked up immediately by some other vehicle, there may be traces around that will lead them to us. Perhaps they left traces on the sidewalk or the walls. We'll just have to see if we can find any."

"This night," Cordelia said, almost to herself, "just keeps getting funner and funner."

"Is that a real word?" Gunn asked her. "Funner?"

"It is now. You got a better one?"

He shook his head and started combing the sidewalk for drips of green mucus. "Nah," he said finally. "I think *funner* kind of sums it up."

CHAPTER SIXTEEN

"Lorne," Mif'tal said, "we're going to leave now." The Nemchuk's voice was soft and almost apologetic, but the club had gone completely silent when he and Urf'dil had started for the door, and Lorne knew that every eye in the place was upon them. He had turned off the recorded music a few minutes before, figuring that everyone, himself included, was too tired to care anymore.

"No, listen, Mif'tal, honey," Lorne stammered, palms out and pressing against the air as if he could shove them back toward their table from here. "Just wait a little bit longer. I have to talk to four more tables and then we're done, we're all done. I appreciate your patience so much, but—"

"Urf'dil is exhausted," Mif'tal told him, sounding sleepy himself. "She can barely keep her eyes open, and she gets cranky when she's tired, and—"

"I get cranky?" Urf'dil interrupted, in a tone that

was all about crankiness. "*I* get cranky? Listen to you, Mr. Cranky-Pants, trying to blame it all on me. The truth, Lorne, is that Mif'tal just gets put out if he doesn't get his eight hours right on schedule, you know? His whole routine goes screwy, he becomes irregular, and I have to listen to his complaints for a week while he gets back to normal."

"Just let 'em go!" someone shouted from the shadows.

Okay, Lorne thought, *time to put this down before it becomes all-out revolution.* He crossed to the stage and stood in front of the microphone. "Listen, I know what you all have been through tonight," he said. Enthusiasm was hard to drum up, even within himself, but it had to be done. "You've put up with a lot, what with the excitement outside and then me insisting that everybody stay put until I've talked to each of you individually. You've been magnificent, and I mean that. Why not give yourselves a hand?" He clapped his own hands together fiercely, but nobody joined in, and he tapered off. "It's been a long night," he said. "For you and me both."

"You're not kidding," the heckler shouted again. Lorne tried to see who it was, but with the spotlights aimed at him, everyone beyond the first few rows of tables was indistinct.

"If you don't have a suspect yet, Lorne," Mif'tal said from where he and Urf'dil stood, near the door, "you're probably not going to."

"I'm not looking for a suspect," the Host tried to correct. "I'm just looking for information, a witness, any little detail."

"Anybody remember anything? Anybody see the girl get snatched?" That, Lorne could tell, was Virg, the Kailiff. "Well?"

A chorus of negatives met his inquiry. *You're losing them,* Lorne thought. As an entertainer, he'd faced that situation before, and knew there was a point beyond which a lost audience couldn't be reclaimed, no matter what. He'd usually managed to catch his crowd before that point was reached, but this one had fallen so fast—seemingly with him one moment, against him the next—that he feared it might be too late. *I could try a few jokes, a crowd-pleaser like Lady Marmalade, but I don't think they're going to bite.*

Or, given the nature of this group, they just might.

He decided to go for the direct appeal instead of trying to jolly them anymore. "People, friends, give me twenty more minutes. That's all. Four more tables, five minutes each. Short and sweet, and then we're all out of here."

"Why not just talk to the last four tables after we're gone?" someone else asked. Lorne peered through the gloom and saw that it was Visssclorf, the Shrenli. He'd thought she would stay on his side longer than most because she wanted him to listen to her sing and give her a reading. Maybe she'd decided that could wait for another time. *Or she'd waited in here so long, she was past her dividing years.* "What difference does it make if we all stay or not?"

For a moment, Lorne, near exhaustion himself, couldn't even remember his own reason. "Because . . . because if someone at one of those tables tells me something that clicks with—or contradicts—something I heard earlier tonight, I have to be able to cross-reference. The last thing I need is to hear something that could be a clue except I can't make sure because the one of you who actually saw something critical has already gone home."

"That's not really our problem," Virg growled. "Getting out of here before daylight is our problem."

Murmurs of assent met this statement, much to Lorne's dismay. *When ordinarily peaceful demons are agreeing with a Shrenli and a Kailiff, that's really a bad sign. Maybe not quite* Apocalypse Now *bad, but* Apocalypse Soon. "I know most of you don't really know Fred, so you don't know how important this is to me," he said. "So let me tell you something about her."

There were groans, but no actual objects thrown at the stage—though, of course, because of the sanctuary spell covering Caritas, nothing could be thrown at the stage as a weapon. Mif'dal and Urf'dil had stopped by the door but still hadn't gone out. Lorne took this as a positive omen, and continued. "She hasn't been in town very long, and she doesn't really know anyone that well except for the gang at Angel's. Even they don't really know her, I guess, because she kind of keeps to herself. And I have to take some responsibility for that, since it was her five years in my home dimension that sent her over the deep edge, if you know what I mean. I didn't know her before that, but I have a hard time believing she went into Pylea the same way she came out.

"She kind of reminds me of a creature, a kind of field mouse called a shrackle, in my homeland. It lives in cultivated fields or woodland meadows, it comes out of hiding when no one's looking for it, it's apparently sweet tempered and friendly, but hardly anyone ever gets a good look at one because as soon as you focus on it, it dashes back under cover. Well, Fred is a shrackle. You couldn't hope to find a more pleasant young lady, or a smarter one, for that matter. And she'll come out and take part in a conversation, as long as it's not about her. But shine a spotlight on her and she's gone. Sometimes she brings the spotlight on herself, because of what she says or does—it's hard to ignore a girl who could take an old toaster and a couple of rubber bands and whip up a thermonuclear MacGyver bad-guy blaster, if that's what she needs. But she can do it. And then when everyone's looking at her like she's just pulled off a miracle, which she has, she blushes and hides because everyone's looking at her. How can you not love a kid like that?"

"Fine, we love her," Virg announced. "But the Nemchuks are right. We've been here too long and we're going. I am, anyway."

Lorne shook his head, feeling hopelessness well up within him.

"Sure, the Kailiff wants to go," another demon said. Lorne saw a Wifflin resting its four massive fists against its table as it sneered at Virg. The many folds of its cheeks flapped when it spoke, like chicken wattles in a high wind. "He probably did it."

Oh, no, Lorne thought. *This is just what I don't need.*

"What," Virg countered, sounding insulted. "Just because I'm a Kailiff, you think I'm guilty?"

"You Kailiffs are all thugs," the Wifflin said. "You didn't do this, you're guilty of something else. Or you just want to get out of here so you can join up with your gang and get back to terrorizing innocent demons."

"Hey," Lorne said. But demons were starting to take sides, chairs screeched as some leaped to their feet, a glass fell from a table and shattered against the floor. "Hey!" he called louder, trying to be heard over the noise. "Everybody just calm down!

We don't want this to turn ugly." *Of course, considering the nature of this crowd, "ugly" is pretty much a given, at least physically.* With few exceptions, demons didn't tend to be easy on the eyes. Maybe one reason that so few of them were in show business, despite having such a large population in the entertainment capital of the world. *A couple of pop singers,* Lorne thought, *one or two actors, a fair number of directors. And that one family singing group, but who doesn't know about them?*

"It's been ugly ever since that girl was taken," Urf'dil said. "That was ugly, wasn't it? If the Kailiff had something to do with it, he should say so."

"We could make him talk," the Wifflin suggested. "Kailiffs work for Kedigris demons, right? Someone said they smelled cinnamon, right? But there's no Kedigris demon in here, so it must have left with the human. This Kailiff is covering for his Kedigris masters, and we just need to persuade him to come clean."

"No!" Lorne boomed, right into the microphone. The single word echoed like a gunshot. "Caritas is a sanctuary," he continued, softer now that he had everyone's attention again. "I can't believe you're willing to forget that this is a place for music and joy and peace . . . to turn it into a place of violence and vengeance, just because you've been inconvenienced a little bit. You can't fight in here. No one is going to force Virg to say anything."

"Take him outside, then," someone else suggested. "And make him talk out there."

"That's the same thing," Lorne protested. "Do you still want to go outside, Virg? Because if you do, there's nothing I can do for you out there."

"What makes you think you can do anything for him, anyway?" an angry voice asked. The room no longer consisted of dozens of different demon types at their own tables, but had turned into a mob, milling about, anxious and scared and teetering on the edge of violence. "You going to stop all of us if we decide to do something?"

"You won't," Lorne argued, feeling desperation swirl about him like a whirlpool. "You can't. Sure, there's a spell on the club that prevents demon-on-demon violence. But it only extends as far as the door. The real reason Caritas functions as a sanctuary is not because I enforce it, not because I prevent you from hurting one another, but because *you* enforce it. All of you, by agreeing to it when you come here, and living up to it as long as you're inside. If you break that pact now, then Caritas is gone. Without sanctuary, we're never going to be able to have a place where you can all relax and sing and enjoy the music and drinks and atmosphere. We'll just have one more battleground, in a city that's already got plenty of those. What would be the point?"

"He broke the rules first, by using this place as a

trap for the human," the Wifflin pointed out. Others shouted their agreement.

"That doesn't matter," Lorne countered. "Even if you were right it wouldn't matter. If you're driving down the freeway and you're speeding and a cop stops you, do you think you can tell him it's okay because you saw someone else speeding first? What the Kailiff—what Virg may or may not have done is beside the point. You are—each of you—responsible for your own actions. If you choose to break the sanctuary of Caritas by committing violence outside, that's not Virg's doing, it's your own free choice. Don't look to blame it on anyone else."

The Wifflin and a few other demons had massed together, and now started to move toward Virg, shoving chairs and tables out of their way as they came. The clatter and screech of falling furniture was the only sound for a moment. Lorne knew that a flashpoint had been reached, that what happened in the next few seconds was going to decide if there would be a Caritas tomorrow night, or the next, or ever again. He felt himself sinking further into hopelessness. *Well*, he thought, *there's always the island resort. I do look great in white.*

Now Virg was on his feet, his gaze moving back and forth between the demons approaching him and Lorne, as if pleading for assistance that Lorne could no longer provide. "This isn't fair," he said.

"I'm tellin' you, I had nothing to do with it. Okay, I got a grudge against Angel, but not the girl. I didn't even know she was with him until tonight. How could I have planned something like this without knowing she existed?"

"Easy," one of the others replied. "You didn't plan it. The Kedigris did; all you had to do was follow orders. Everybody knows Kailiffs aren't smart enough to plan anything."

"Hey," Virg said. "We're plenty smart. But not— well, I just didn't do it, that's all. You can take me outside, you can work me over, whatever, but you're not going to get me to admit to something I didn't do." He looked at Lorne again. "Come on, Lorne, help me out here, you know I didn't . . ." He let the thought hang there, unfinished.

Lorne didn't know anything anymore. In ten minutes his entire world had been turned upside down. He could sing and he could make an audience laugh and he thought he could keep the peace, but now that was proving not to be true. And without the peace, he didn't have the rest of it. He sure wasn't going to get work in a human nightclub, not looking like he did. David Letterman might bring him on the show, but just as a curiosity, not to perform. *If there were still an Ed Sullivan, maybe I'd have a career,* he thought. *Right up there with the little mouse puppet and the talking hand wearing lipstick and the guys who spin plates on sticks.*

Lorne tried to understand why he felt so hopeless in the face of the disintegration of his nightclub, and then he realized what it must have been. He had Angel and the gang, of course, and they would always stick by him. But since he'd left Pylea and come to this dimension, alone, leaving behind everyone he'd grown up with, his mother and Numfar and the rest of the Deathwok Clan, Caritas had been his real home, its habitués his real family. Sure, it had been a sanctuary for all demons, but mostly it was that for him, a safe harbor, a place where he was always accepted, even loved, a place where everybody knew his name and where they always had to let him back in.

Without Caritas, what did he have here on Earth? Angel, the vampire detective who seemed likely to sacrifice himself for Fred? Cordy, Wes, Gunn? He loved them all, and knew they cared about him, but they had their own lives to live, their own problems and challenges. And since Fred had been taken from under Lorne's nose, they might not even be so happy to see him next time he came around. And Fred . . . Fred had accepted Lorne immediately and unthinkingly, but she was gone too.

And that brings us full circle, he thought despairingly. *If I let Caritas be destroyed in the name of getting Fred back, then I have no more*

Caritas. If I let Fred die, then I have no more Angel Investigations.

Virg had backed up against a wall, and could go no farther. Most of the demons were, Lorne was pleased to note, still keeping to themselves and not joining the small mob that had circled Virg. No one had touched him yet—the spell would cause an instant reaction if anyone tried. But it only prevented actual violence, not the threat of it. *Most of them want to maintain the sanctuary,* he thought, feeling a momentary glimmer of hope through the sadness that had gripped him.

"Listen," Virg pleaded. "I . . . I didn't—it's not me. It's that Skander, I bet. Where's that Skander?"

This brought a new outburst as some disagreed with Virg and others looked about, in vain, for the Skander that Lorne had talked to earlier. *What was his name?* he wondered. *That's right, we settled on Quort when his name turned out to be bigger than he was.* "Who, Quort?" he asked into the microphone. He realized he hadn't seen the demon for a while. "Quort, where are you?"

He didn't want to point the mob at another demon, but as long as he could keep them off their toes a little, he hoped, maybe he could prevent any violence from taking place.

"Yeah, it's gotta be the Skander," Virg went on. "They can manipulate dimensional gateways, right? How else could they have gotten the girl outta here, with all of us standing right there? Open up a gateway, shove her through."

"I might have seen a Skander grab her," a feminine voice said. It was Misty, Lorne realized, the half Brachen.

"You said you saw a Polgara take her through a portal," he reminded her.

"I know, but it was dark, and there was all that smoke. It could have been a Skander, I guess. Anyway, it could have cast a glamour."

"Did you even see a portal at all?" Lorne demanded angrily. "Or was it too dark for that, too?"

"I . . . I guess I'm not sure. You know, I wanted to help, and I thought I saw . . . something . . ."

"Well, I don't see a Skander," someone said. "I guess it *portaled* right out of here."

"There you go," Virg shouted, redeemed. "That proves it. He wouldn't have run if he wasn't guilty."

"You were trying to get out of here a few minutes ago," the Wifflin reminded Virg.

"We all were," Virg said. "I just spoke up for all of us."

"I still don't trust you, Kailiff. Your kind is always up to something."

"What about the Shrenli?" someone else asked. "That girl, Fred, she's young, right? Maybe the Shrenli ate her!"

"Folks, let's not get carried away," Lorne said

into the microphone. As long as he had the mike, at least he could still be heard over the general din. *For what little good that does,* he thought.

"Well, we should at least check her. Smell her breath or whatever."

"What we don't want is for everyone to start suspecting everyone," Lorne said. "We don't want chaos. I'll admit that if the Skander is gone, that looks bad, because he knew I wanted everyone to stay." He peered out beneath the spotlights, looking to see if the Nemchuks were still here, and finally spotted them. They had taken another table, this one close to the door, but they hadn't left. "And I'll tell Angel that, and he'll decide what action to take."

"Maybe the Kailiff and the Skander are working together," someone suggested.

"Like I'd have anything to do with one of those portal-hopping jamokes," Virg said with a sneer. "Gimme a break."

"Gladly," the Wifflin said. "Arm, leg, or neck?"

"Come on and try me, buddy," Virg replied. The two were barely separated by a few feet now, and well out of Lorne's reach. All he could work with was his voice.

"People, calm down," Lorne pleaded. "No violence. Look, we're already making progress. We need to find out what happened to the Skander, and we need to do it without hurting one another or breaking the rules of sanctuary."

He heard a reaction, but he couldn't make out the words coming from the crowd in the back of the room, or even tell if they were reacting to him or to something else. But as he tried to bore through the gloom, he saw the crowd part and a figure approach the stage. A strangely familiar figure. As it stepped up and into the lights, he couldn't believe he was seeing it.

Green skin, red horns and eyes, blond hair. A strikingly powerful jaw. All wrapped up in a terrific iridescent yellow suit.

"Very convincing," the figure said, extending a long-fingered hand toward him. "You almost had me convinced you were me. Only when you took my physical form you didn't bother to duplicate the personality. Now hand over my microphone and get off my stage."

CHAPTER SEVENTEEN

Allen Cavanaugh lived up in the Hollywood Hills, off Laurel Canyon, in a Spanish-style house set back from the road and shielded by enormous hedges. Angel parked on the street and approached on foot, watching the windows for signs of life before he went to the door. The house was one of those gone-to-seed places that would have commanded a medium-range price on the flats but up here would cost more than a million. From a second-floor balcony it looked as if Cavanaugh would have a terrific view of the lights of L.A. At ground level, all Angel could see was the house and fence, and the tops of some eucalyptus trees on the downslope property next door.

From what Angel had learned online, Cavanaugh was a couple of months behind on his mortgage payments, so he might be losing this place soon. Of course, any insurance settlement he collected because of the fire across the street from Caritas might help there. Cavanaugh had pumped a lot of money into buying the land and starting up the building, but then the economy had flattened, commercial real estate leasing slowed, buildings were standing empty all over town, and he hadn't been able to sign any long-term tenants to help cover the cost of finishing the building. He was on the hook for the whole cost of the job. And without long-term tenants, he ran a good chance of paying to finish the building and then finding himself with a mostly empty building that drew no income. He'd have the additional expenses of paying for utilities, maintenance, and taxes. All in all, he either needed an economic miracle or a fire.

He got fire.

I've got to look myself up online sometime, Angel had thought on his drive into the hills. *I hope my entire life isn't laid out for anyone to find, like this poor schmuck's is.* He figured the police would have no problem finding the same information on Allen Cavanaugh that he had, which meant there would be an investigation into the fire and Cavanaugh would still lose his Hollywood Hills home. *But he'll be trading it for an eight-by-eight cell.* If he was lucky, he'd go down for insurance fraud instead of arson—fraud would earn him federal time, and federal prison was Club Med compared with State.

Satisfied that he wasn't walking into a trap, Angel approached the house's big front door and rang the bell. Nine-inch iron bars caged off a little panel the occupant could open to look out through, which meant the door was from the days before home invaders wouldn't think twice about shoving a gun barrel in someone's face as soon as they opened the panel and demanding entrance. Angel pushed the doorbell button again, leaning on it, and after another minute or so he heard shuffling footsteps from the other side. Allen Cavanaugh—Angel had seen pictures, online—yanked open the little panel and scowled at him. "Haven't you guys wasted enough of my time?" he demanded. His eyes were puffy and ringed with dark flesh, probably from lack of sleep, and his short hair was matted on his left, sticking out at every angle on the right. He had a white sleeveless T-shirt on.

"I don't know what guys you mean," Angel said. He thought he'd go for sympathetic and polite, and then if that didn't work, turn to scary and hitting. *You catch more flies with honey than vinegar, Cordy always says. Of course, raw meat brings them out too. I still don't get why I'd want a bunch of flies, but I'm trying.*

"You. Cops, insurance, whatever. My lawyer left twenty minutes ago, and do you have any idea how much money a lawyer wants to come to your house in the middle of the freaking night? If I have to get him back there, I'll be better off just taking the loss of the building."

"I'm not with the police or an insurance company, Mr. Cavanaugh," Angel said. *Polite*, he reminded himself. *Honey*. "I just want to ask you some questions about the fire at your building."

"Press?" Cavanaugh asked. He said the word as if he'd just bitten into something rotten, causing Angel to believe that this option was even less popular than the others.

Angel handed him a business card through the bars. "Let's just say I'm a concerned citizen," he said.

Cavanaugh studied the card for a moment, blinking and holding it close to his eyes. "Private?" he asked.

"That's right, sir," Angel replied.

"That means I can tell you to take a hike. And then maybe I can finally get back to bed. So take a hike."

Screw honey, Angel thought. *Vinegar's better.* He willed the change to come over him, felt his fangs extend, his forehead ripple and bulge, his brow lower. As he went vamp Cavanaugh's sleepy eyes widened and he gripped the bars with one hand, knuckles white against the black iron. Angel closed a hand around Cavanaugh's.

"Let me in," he said, voice low and menacing.

"Or I'll pull you out through the bars. And you won't fit in one piece."

Cavanaugh trembled under Angel's hand. "I . . . I can't . . . ," he managed to squeak.

"Can't what?"

"Can't open . . . the door . . . with you holding me."

That made sense. Angel let him go, and Cavanaugh fiddled at the lock, then swung the door open. "Invite me in," Angel commanded.

"Come . . . in," Cavanaugh said hesitantly. He stepped out of the way, and Angel, now that he'd been invited in, crossed the threshold. When he was inside he closed the door behind him, shutting the little panel as well. Cavanaugh had crossed the tiled entryway and had pressed himself against the far wall as if trying to merge with the white stucco.

Once in, Angel lost the vamp face. It had done its job. Cavanaugh was plenty scared, but he might talk more easily to Angel the man than Angel the vampire.

"I just want to hear about the fire," Angel told him. "I already know about your financial troubles. But why tonight? Why at that precise moment? Who are you working with?"

Cavanaugh shook his head. With his T-shirt he wore red cotton pajama bottoms, and in his fear, arms wrapped around himself as if he were freezing, he looked very small and alone. "I . . .

don't know what you mean. I didn't have anything to do with the fire. I told the police that."

"I'm not the police and I'm not interested in prosecuting you," Angel said. "I just want Fred back."

"I don't know who that is," Cavanaugh insisted, shaking his head again. "I don't know anyone named Fred."

"Did you pay someone to start the fire?" Angel asked. "Maybe they picked the time?"

"No, honest, I . . . look, I wouldn't lie to you," Cavanaugh told him. "Whatever you are, you scared the stuffing out of me with that, that face thing you do. I'm not going to try to lie to you. I had nothing to do with the fire. Nothing."

"But it helps you out financially, doesn't it?"

"It helps a guy I owe money to," Cavanaugh said. "A lot of money. And he's a guy you don't want to owe anything to. I didn't tell the cops about this, but I'm sure he must have set the fire. He's the kind of guy who wouldn't think twice about doing something like that. Unless it was easier just to dunk somebody in cement and toss them into the Pacific."

Angel thought he understood, but wanted to make sure. "You're into a loan shark?"

"Whatever you think you know about me isn't all there is to know, not by a long shot," Cavanaugh said. He seemed to be in confessional mode now, so Angel just let him talk. "I've been living on credit and loans and the occasional basketball game that goes my way. But not enough games do, and when the building turned out to be yet one more disaster in a whole string of them, I was sunk. I've taken so many loans against the place, I'm like that guy in *The Producers*—if I had a hit I'd be in trouble because I'd owe two thousand percent of what I made. My theory is, the guy I owe the most to finally decided to make back what he can by torching the place, so I'll collect an insurance settlement that I can just sign straight over to him."

"Where can I find this guy?" Angel demanded. "What's his name?"

"His name's Johnny Sacco," Cavanaugh replied. "But you can't find him, at least not right away. He's in the Bahamas. You don't think he'd be stupid enough to pull something like this when he's in town, do you?"

"But he's got guys who do it for him," Angel pressed. *Guys, or demons.*

"Sure, he's got guys. I don't know who they are, though. I only deal with Johnny, and except for a couple of times he's sent goons around to rough me up, he's always the one who talks to me."

Angel crossed the entryway, and Cavanaugh tried to collapse in on himself, as if he could vanish altogether if he made himself small enough. Angel removed his business card from the man's grip. "Don't tell anyone I was here," he said.

"No . . . no problem," Cavanaugh answered, looking at Angel through slitted eyes. Angel thought he was surprised that Angel hadn't come over to beat him up. "I never saw you."

"That's the spirit," Angel said. "Stay out of trouble." He headed for the door, pocketing the business card as he went.

"A little late for that," Cavanaugh said. He sounded bitter. All of his problems had come home to roost, and they were all of his own doing. *That might be enough to make anyone a little bitter.* Angel went outside and closed the door, leaving Cavanaugh behind, alone with his own troubles and recriminations.

As he sat down in the car, Angel realized that this whole adventure had gotten him exactly nowhere. He had the name of the guy who'd most likely ordered the torching, but the guy was thousands of miles away. He probably relied on human thugs to do most of his dirty work, but sometimes humans subcontracted muscle work to demons. He didn't know if it had been humans or demons, or maybe both, who had put together the plot against Fred. But unless he could locate Sacco's gang, he was right back where he'd been, which was nowhere.

He glanced toward the east, and thought he

could sense the sky beginning to lighten. *Maybe it's an illusion,* he thought. *Can't be that late yet. Can it?*

Wesley had finished combing the car's glove compartment for nonexistent clues to the Roshon demons' whereabouts and was standing outside the vehicle wiping his palms against the stone surface of a nearby shop, trying to scrape off any remnants of Roshon goo.

The glovebox had been useless. Roshons liked candy, apparently, as there were wrappers from every imaginable sort of chocolate bar inside, some split open and licked clean. He had also found torn-out pages from tabloid newspapers with stories about incredible giant babies, extraterrestrials who lived among us and supported political candidates, and giant squids that sought victims by reaching thousand-yard tentacles up sewer pipes and snatching people through their own toilets. *Oh, and a half-empty package of tissues.* But nothing that identified the car's owners, no loose addresses or telephone numbers, no handy map with "X marks the Fred" scrawled on it.

Gunn had examined the boot but had already declared it a waste of time.

Cordelia, meanwhile, had been scouring the neighborhood. She came back around the corner to see Wesley desperately rubbing the wall. "Does it like that?" she asked him cheerfully. She pointed to her own back, between her shoulder blades. "Because if you're good at it, I have this knot here that I can't seem to loosen."

"It's just, I want to get this substance off my hands. Who knows what horrible thing it might do to me?"

"Oh, I'm sure it's nothing a little soap and water won't fix," she admonished him. "Stop being such an old lady. Here, let me see."

Wesley held his palms up to her. She looked at him—and then her face blanched. "Yaaah!" she shouted.

"What? Oh my God, what is it?" he asked, turning his hands around to inspect them.

"I think she means behind you, English." Gunn tapped him on the shoulder and gestured over his own. Wesley looked that way.

Five Roshon demons stood staring at them. They were all quite a bit taller than Wesley, with lean bodies that nonetheless appeared stringily muscular beneath their coats of dense blue fur. Their muzzles jutted forward, and a couple of them pulled back their lips, baring sharp fangs. Wesley was put in mind of hyenas or jackals, if hyenas or jackals were dark blue in color, walked upright, and wore baggy trousers and athletic shoes.

"What you doing with our car?" the one in front

asked. Wesley could make out the words, even though they came in a growl that wasn't really suited to human language.

"We . . . thought it was abandoned," Wesley said, trying to sound friendly. "We were simply trying to find out who owned it. What a relief to know it's yours."

As he spoke, one of the demons went to the car and stared in. When it looked up again, its canine face was twisted into what Wesley thought was an expression of despair. "The clippings!" it snarled. "Been at the clippings!"

Or perhaps anger, Wesley realized, *judging from its tone.*

"You look at our clippings?" the one in front wanted to know.

One of the others asked a question in a tongue Wesley couldn't understand, a mixture of growls, clicks, and yips. This one's muzzle was scarred in half a dozen places, and one of its ears had a chunk missing, in a shape that remarkably resembled a bite. A rapid-fire conversation followed, the result of which was immediately clear.

The demons sprang at them.

Thinking they were only examining an empty car, Wesley, Cordelia, and Gunn had brought no weapons out with them. They stood in a loose triangle, and braced instantly for battle when the Roshons charged. But the demons were bigger and stronger, and armed with claws and fangs. And there were more of them.

And that breath . . .

Wesley caught the first one that attacked him, grabbing its wrists as it swung its claws toward him. The demon leaned in toward him, snapping its vicious teeth at his throat, and on its exhale Wesley got a face full of the worst breath he'd ever encountered. The smell put him in mind of burning tires, with perhaps a light sewage glaze. He reeled, his eyes watering. *It's no wonder the inside of the car was so bad.*

The Roshon took advantage of his discomfiture to yank one of its paws free. As Wesley tried to recapture it, the demon jabbed forward with it, driving a fist into Wesley's solar plexus. The wind shoved out of him, Wesley doubled around the blow, and the demon tugged its other paw away. Both paws flailed at him then, one glancing off his cheek and the other slamming his shoulder. Wesley aimed a snap-kick at the creature's shin and connected solidly, causing it to whine in pain and step back. But it retreated for only a moment and then resumed its attack, claws out and tearing, cutting Wesley's shirt and skin. Wesley was driven backward until he felt the stone of a building, the one he'd used as a hand cleaner, most likely, against his back. The Roshon made a face that might have been a smile and pressed Wesley's shoulders against the wall. Wesley grabbed its arms, but couldn't break its grip. With its muzzle just inches from his throat, the demon paused.

"Shouldn't steal someone's car," he thought it said.

"Pardon me?" Wesley asked, not sure he'd understood. "Did you say 'steal'?"

The demon looked at him, eyes blinking in confusion. "'Course I say 'steal,'" it answered. "What you call it?"

Wesley's gaze darted around to see where his friends were. Gunn was on the ground, rolling around wrestling with one of the blue beasts while a second one pounded on his back. Cordelia stood her ground. One of the Roshons sat awkwardly on the sidewalk near her, rubbing its eyes, in obvious pain. The last demon orbited around her, looking for an approach but afraid of the weapon she bore. Noticing Wesley's curiosity, she held it up. A perfume bottle. "Never without it," she announced. "You guys really should carry purses."

"Yes, well," Wesley said, straining to hold the demon at bay. "These fellows seem to think we stole their car."

"That's ridiculous," Cordelia said. "Did you happen to ask why, if we stole their car, we would have come here in our own? Or point out that if we'd actually been riding in theirs, our butts would be covered in that gunk they left all over the seats?"

"Didn't think to," Wesley replied.

The demon stopped pressing forward for a moment. "You not steal it?"

"We found it," Wesley told him. "Or, to be more accurate, we heard that it had been left here and came to have a look."

"Why?" the demon wanted to know.

"We believe it was used in a crime," Wesley said.

The demon released Wesley's shoulders, but maintained an alert stance, poised to strike if Wesley moved or said the wrong thing. Wesley determined not to do that. He felt as if his back had been flattened and had taken on the imprint of the wall.

"What kind of crime?"

"A drive-by shooting. Could you perhaps get your friends off of my friend?" He pointed to where Gunn wrestled the Roshon on the concrete.

"In a minute," the demon said. "Anybody hurt? In the shooting?"

"No, not in the shooting itself," Wesley replied. "But then, we don't believe anyone was meant to be. It was a distraction, to capture our attention while a friend of ours was kidnapped. We just want our friend back."

The Roshon barked a command, and the demons fighting with Gunn broke free, leaving him alone. Gunn rolled onto his back and lay on the sidewalk, panting heavily. "Thanks," he breathed. "Wasn't sure how long I could keep that up."

"When was your car stolen?" Wesley asked.

"During evening," the Roshon answered. "Or night. While we sleep in our den. We come out, car gone."

"So it wasn't you lot who did the shooting."

The demon laughed, which was hard to differentiate from its speech except for its wicked smile and the tone. "We shoot, people die," it said. "Roshon don't miss."

"You know," Wesley said, trying to dust off his back, "I think perhaps this has all been a big misunderstanding."

"Yeah, maybe," the Roshon answered.

The one Cordelia had perfumed in the eyes struggled to its feet, still whining, one paw draped over its muzzle. "Sorry?" Cordelia offered, putting the little spray bottle back into her purse. "But you *were* all grrr and everything at me."

The injured demon nodded morosely, and its friend helped it back to the car.

The demon speaking to Wesley had a last thought for him. "We let you go, this time. I think you didn't steal car. When I find out who did, somebody die."

"Actually, when you find out who did, I'd like to know. And to ask a few questions of my own before you . . . well, before you do whatever it is you have to do." He handed the demon his card. "I'd appreciate it."

The Roshon took the card and shoved it into a pocket of its baggy pants. "I try," it said. "No promise."

"All I can ask," Wesley said. As he watched, the tall demons folded themselves into their car.

"Nice folks," Cordelia said as they got in. "Stinky, though."

"And absolutely no help to us," Wesley said.

Gunn glanced at the sky. "We better figure out something that will help," he announced. "And soon. Not much time left now."

Wesley followed suit. *Indeed,* he thought. *Not much time at all.*

CHAPTER EIGHTEEN

There were all kinds of theories about time, Fred knew. Time is elastic, not fixed. Time is the fourth dimension. Time is an oval, and everything that's happening now is across the way from everything that happened before. Time is a single point, with everything happening simultaneously: past, present, and future all coexisting in the moment, and only one's perception of events imposing an apparently linear pattern on them.

But she was developing a new theory of her own, and it was this: *When someone with absolutely zero experience picking locks is trying to learn the craft with a completely substandard tool and only one usable hand, under incredible pressure because her very life might be at stake, not to mention the life of someone she thinks is just an amazing person even if he isn't exactly a person, then, for that person, time stands completely still even though for the rest*

*of the world, it races at an accelerated pace. So
even though every minute seems like an hour to me,
the hours until sunrise are rushing past with every
tick of the clock.*

She was pretty sure she understood the basics of
lock-picking. But theory and practice were two
very different things, and her palms were sweating
from the concentration and exertion—*and let's
face it, nervousness*—and that made the tiny hinge
pin hard to hang on to, much less work into the
small keyhole in the lock. She kept trying, though,
slipping it into the hole and fiddling with it, feeling
for the tumblers she knew were in there. When she
got one to fall into place, she heard a definite click
and, if she hadn't been chained to a radiator near
the floor, she might have danced for joy. She knew
that if the room hadn't been so silent, she wouldn't
have heard the click, and after that she had to
remind herself to breathe, so intent was she on
staying quiet and listening for the next one.

Finally it came. This time Fred could feel it, she
was convinced, as it fell in line with the first. She
wondered how many tumblers a lock like this
might have, and when she should start applying
pressure to turn it rather than working on finding
the next one. Time seemed to slow down even
more now that she was making actual progress,
maybe even folding in on itself and running backward. But she did her best to ignore time, knowing

that the main thing was getting herself free, and the pressure of the ticking clock would only hamper that effort if she let herself dwell on it.

Another faint click, another tumbler in line. *This is incredible,* she thought. *It really does work like it's supposed to.* She knew how an internal-combustion engine worked, in theory, but she was pretty sure she couldn't build one with the items found in a half-empty room. *But this lock-picking thing, it happens just the way I've always heard.*

She felt around for one more tumbler, but couldn't seem to locate it. *So maybe there are only three,* she thought. *Handcuff locks probably aren't all that complex in the greater scheme of locks, not like a bank vault's or anything. The point is kind of that the person who's in the cuffs doesn't have a key, or the use of her hands, so picking probably doesn't come up all that often.*

Which meant she had come to the really hard part. She knew that a professional picking a lock would have some kind of tension rod that they would use to turn the lock mechanism to the side while keeping the pick in place, and therefore keeping the tumblers in the proper alignment. But she only had the one little pin to use. When she applied pressure to turn the lock, she ran every risk of having the tumblers slip out of place, and having to start over. The fear was so great that it almost paralyzed her for a moment.

It's a simple lock, Fred reminded herself. She didn't know if they were police handcuffs, or if there were different kinds of handcuffs for different uses, but she guessed they were probably mass-produced, and that any key that opened one set of them would open them all. Which meant there would be nothing especially complicated or difficult about it. All she had to do was try to keep the pin through the tumblers while pressing it the slightest bit to the right. Once the lock caught and started to open, she could finish it with her thumbnail, she believed.

She tried it.

It worked.

It worked! She could barely contain herself, but she knew that this was no time to lose her concentration. She used her thumbnail and the pin, together, and the lock turned. Now she reached a point at which she had to withdraw the pin, and she did, but the lock had turned far enough that the tumblers held their position. She was able to turn it the rest of the way with the pin, and the bracelet around her wrist clicked open.

"Golly," she said out loud. Then she clapped a hand over her own mouth. The room was empty, but she still didn't know what was on the other side of that door—or who. "John" hadn't been back, and she couldn't decide if that meant he was secure in his belief that she wasn't going anywhere, or if

she'd genuinely bothered him and he was just trying to keep his distance. She held the cuff so it
wouldn't swing against the wall and let it dangle,
silently, from the radiator. Then, for the first time
in hours, she stood up.

The big blue that Wes had been chatting with, the
one Cordelia took to be their leader, got in behind
the wheel of the Z-28 and cranked the ignition. But
when the engine roared to life, instead of driving
away, the Roshon backed it up to where she,
Wesley, and Gunn stood on the sidewalk. The front
passenger side window jerked unevenly down, as if
the creature operating it didn't have enough room
to move its arm in smooth circles.

"Car smells," the Roshon in that seat told them.

"Well, I hate to say this, but duh," Cordelia
answered. "You guys know about Scope? Or tooth-
paste, for that matter?"

"No," the demon countered. "Smells bad."

"We pretty much noticed that right off," Gunn
said.

"No," the demon said again. It shook its furry
head like they just weren't getting him.

*Maybe we're not. After all, none of us speak
Lassie.* "Bad like what?" Cordy asked.

The demon behind the wheel killed the motor,
opened its door, and climbed out of the car. "Car
stink like cinnamon," it said.

"That can do wonders," Cordelia agreed. "Just a light sprinkle. You can even use it if you have ants in the kitchen—"

"No, Cordelia," Wesley said, touching her arm. "I believe it's telling us something else."

"Okay, I'll bite," she said, instantly regretting the word choice. "What's with the cinnamon? Some kind of sticky-bun reference?"

"Kedigris," the Roshon said flatly.

"Indeed," Wesley concurred, nodding. "Kedigris demons emit an odor very much like cinnamon. We might not have noticed it because—well, frankly," he addressed the Roshons now, "because the smell of you, umm, fellows, was a bit overpowering to our senses." He turned back to Cordelia and Gunn. "But they would smell it right away, of course."

"Cinnamon," Gunn said, sounding kind of amazed by the whole idea. "I would've killed for some cinnamon smell when I had my head in that trunk."

"So you think it was Kedigris demons who stole your car," Wesley continued.

The Roshon nodded once. "Kedigris. Smells like, anyway."

"It's not possible that someone actually did have some cinnamon in the car? A cup of coffee—or, as Cordelia said, a cinnamon roll?"

"Kedigris," the demon repeated.

Cordelia could practically hear the little wheels

in Wes's head spinning around. He got this expression, when he was thinking—*which he does, a lot*—kind of dreamy-eyed and distant, with a little half-smile as if he enjoyed the very process.

"You and the Kedigris are enemies, aren't you?" he asked the Roshon, who still stood by the car, resting its big Cookie Monster arms on its roof. *Or does that reference date me?* she wondered. *Maybe they're Sully arms. He's blue and furry. At least I didn't go for the obvious big Smurf comparison.* "Rivals, at least."

"Enemies," the Roshon confirmed. "Kedigris bad."

"Very, I'm sure," Wes said. "And now it appears that they've tried to frame you for a crime that they committed."

"Really bad," the Roshon snarled. "Bad bad bad."

"They're bad." Cordelia hoped that maybe this conversational dead end could be avoided. "We're with you on that."

"Maybe they need to be taught a lesson," Gunn offered, catching on.

"Good lesson," the Roshon agreed.

"The best kind of lesson," Gunn said. He made a fist and smacked it against his other palm. "We could help."

"You and Roshon work together?" the demon asked. "Find Kedigris?"

"I think that's a good idea," Wes told it. "We

need to find our friend. You need to punish who-ever took your car and tried to make it look as if you shot at a bunch of innocent civilians. Did I mention the shooting was outside Caritas? The sanctuary?"

"Caritas?" the demon in the passenger seat echoed. "I like singing."

"I'm sure you have a lovely voice," Cordelia said. *Got to make sure I keep away from "How Much Is That Doggie in the Window?" when these guys are there*, she thought. *Not that there's much danger of me picking that one, in the unlikely event I ever accidentally end up onstage again.*

"Elton John," the demon informed her. "'Rocket Man.' Sometimes 'Crocodile Rock' or 'Burn Down the Mission.'"

"I'm just glad you didn't say 'Love Lies Bleed-ing,'" Cordelia said. "That's a little too close to home right now."

"Too hard."

"Then you know Caritas," Wesley said. *Just like him, trying to get the conversation back on track*, Cordy thought. *Which is good, really. On track is important when Fred and Angel are both in danger.* "So you understand what it means that a group of demons fired upon the audience when they stepped outside for a moment."

"Kedigris really bad bad," the Roshon said again.

"Yes, I'm inclined to agree," Wesley said. "If

they're responsible for this, and it looks as if you might be right, they are bad. And we've got to find them. Do you have any idea where to look?"

The Roshon nodded its hyenalike head again. "Sure," it said. "At Kedigris den."

"You know where this den is?" Cordelia asked.

"Know where one is," the Roshon replied. "Right by Caritas. Don't know if it's right one."

"Probably is, if it's right there," Gunn put in. "May not matter, though. We find one, we bust some heads till they tell us what we need to know."

"Exactly," Cordy agreed. "You get us to these cinnamon-stinking Kedigris and we'll . . . uhh . . . do what he said." She shot a glance at Gunn. "Sorry, I just don't think 'busting heads' sounds all that convincing when I say it."

"Girl, you're the only one actually took out one of these guys," Gunn countered, waving a hand at the Roshons.

"People," Wes said in his let's-get-back-to-business voice. "We have a deadline."

"You in big hurry?" the lead Roshon asked them. "We go. Den near Caritas." The demon climbed back in behind the wheel and started up the car again. Wes, Gunn, and Cordelia exchanged glances and then dashed to Cordy's Jeep.

"First one who says 'follow that car' is walking," Cordelia warned.

Gunn and Wes both got in, lips clamped tight.

Cordelia cranked the ignition and pulled out into the street. As soon as she was in place, the Z-28 darted away from the curb, and she had to floor the accelerator to keep up.

"Are we sure this is a good idea?" Gunn asked from the backseat. "You said these Roshons and the Kedigris don't like each other, right?"

"Mortal enemies," Wesley confirmed. "Always have been."

"And none of us smelled any cinnamon in the car. Just that Roshon-musk or whatever."

"That's true," Cordelia observed. "He has a point there, Wes. I'm not sure what the point is, but it's definitely a point."

"My point—"

"No, let me," Cordy cut him off. "The point is, we don't know if they're even telling the truth about the cinnamon, or the Kedigris. We think someone framed the Roshons by stealing their car and using it for the drive-by. But what if they're just framing the Kedigris and getting us to help do their dirty work by turning us loose to"—she glanced over her shoulder at Gunn—"to bust heads?"

"That's a possibility, I suppose," Wesley admitted. "But it seems like a slim one. Frankly, I'm not sure these Roshon demons have the intellectual capacity to come up with such a complex plan."

"Smart enough to get the drop on us," Gunn pointed out. "And maybe smart enough to put us right in the middle of a demon war we don't want anything to do with and don't have time for."

"That's certainly true," Wesley said. "But he said the den is near Caritas. So far, this is the best lead we've had. And if there's a chance of finding Fred and stopping Angel, we have to take it."

"You really think Angel would do that?" Gunn asked. They'd all talked about it already, and Cordelia was certain that Gunn and Wes had covered it before she'd even joined them. She didn't really want to hear all the pros and cons again.

"He'd do it," she declared flatly. Just in case anyone didn't get her message and tried to continue the discussion, she repeated herself. "He'd do it."

They both bought a clue and dropped the topic. A moment later, Wes took a cell phone from his pocket and punched a couple of buttons. "I'm calling Angel," he explained. "To let him know what we've learned."

"Makes sense," Gunn said from the back.

Cordelia concentrated on trying to follow the Roshons, whose NASCAR-style driving made her own look stately and subdued by comparison. L.A.'s dark night streets whipped by, and she found herself seriously hoping that all those black and white cars with TO SERVE AND TO PROTECT stenciled on the sides were safely parked at doughnut shops somewhere far from here.

"Angel, it's me," she heard Wes say. *Like that's*

not the lamest greeting, because how many people could legitimately identify themselves as "me"? "We might have something here. I'll spare you all the details, but we're following some Roshon demons who believe that Kedigris demons are responsible for the drive-by shooting. They know where there's a Kedigris lair, in a building right by Caritas, so that's where we're headed." He listened a moment. "No, I'm not sure. We're just following their car. All right, yes, I'll let you know when we get there."

He put the phone away. "Angel's drawn a blank," he told them. "He's on his way back to Caritas. He says because that's where it all happened, that's got to be the place to start. He's going to cover everything there until he finds her. We're supposed to call him when we find out precisely where this Kedigris lair is."

"Sounds like as good a plan as any," Gunn said.

"Sounds like as good a plan as none," Cordelia corrected. "Which is pretty much what we've been working with all night."

"Sometimes plans are overrated," Gunn said.

"Especially when you can't think of one," Cordy shot back.

"Yeah," Gunn admitted. "Especially then."

Her legs almost failed her, at first. She caught herself on the radiator and supported herself there while her blood remembered how to find its way around her body. Getting free of the handcuffs was only step one, Fred knew. Now she had to get out of this room, if possible, and then out of whatever building she was in, and then find a way to get in touch with Angel, to tell him that she had escaped before he had to face the possibility of sacrificing himself to save her. Any or all of those additional steps might involve running, which would be hard to do on legs that felt, as they did at this moment, like dry, brittle twigs. Her ankle and arm throbbed where John had cut her, and there was blood all over her from her various wounds.

And what if Angel just laughs at me and says, "I was never going to sacrifice myself for you, Fred?" Because that's the right answer, that's what he should say. But would he? She shook her head, hoping to clear away such counterproductive thoughts. She had made good progress; now she just had to work on the rest of it, and thinking along those lines wasn't going to help in the least.

When her legs started to feel a little more functional, she went to the window and pressed her face against the cool glass. No help there. She could tell only that she was a few floors up, too high to jump safely, but beyond that all she could see was a dark alley and a plain brick wall across the way. Nothing to identify where she was. She realized she couldn't even open the thing, because it had been painted shut so many times, it was jammed.

She gave up on that and crossed the hardwood floor to the door, moving on tiptoe, staying as quiet as she could. At the door, she stopped and listened. When she heard nothing, she pressed her ear cautiously against it. Still nothing. For all she could tell, it opened onto some kind of galactic void, and when she passed through she'd be sucked into the vacuum of space, never to return. *But at least there I wouldn't put Angel in danger,* she thought.

Apparently whoever had left her here hadn't expected her to get out of the handcuffs, because the door's only lock, on this side, was set into the doorknob. A key was needed on the outside, but not here. Fred turned the lock with two fingers and then wrapped her hand around the knob.

This was the scary part. She was a prisoner, in here, but as far as she could determine, she was in no immediate danger. But when she went through that door, she might find herself in the middle of her captors. There might be an armed guard with orders to kill her if she tried to escape.

On the other hand, there might be no remaining obstacles between herself and freedom. She had to try.

She turned the knob and opened the door less than an inch, just enough to see through the crack.

Looking out, she saw that the door opened onto a stairway. *Some kind of apartment building, maybe, or an old office building?* The stairs had a smooth wooden banister on white-painted balustrades running alongside them. From here, she could tell that she was on some middle floor—stairs ran up and down from this point. A faded and worn carpet runner was tacked to the middle of the stairs, a couple of inches of wood showing at each side. The walls were covered with a natural wood wainscoting to a height of about five feet, and whitewashed plaster above that. Sconces set into the walls held electric bulbs, illuminating the stairway.

Best of all, there was no one in sight.

She swung the door open all the way and stepped through.

There were three other doors on this level, all closed, all with brass letters on them. The door she had come out had the letter H on it. This wasn't telling her anything useful, she knew. She just had to go down the stairs and out, hoping against hope that there was no one waiting at the bottom for just such an eventuality.

She swallowed and stepped onto the first stair. The runner kept her footstep almost silent. She tried the next one. A little creak, but not too bad. She knew she couldn't take them all so slowly, though—she had to move.

She was about to do just that when she heard a door open and shut, and footsteps sound on the stairs below. Several sets of them. Then voices, more than one. ". . . getting pretty late. I think we're golden," one of them said.

That person—the voice sounded male—was answered by another, saying, "Yeah, but we can't take any chances now."

Fred had heard that voice before. It was John, the guy who had been in the room with her for a while, the one with the remarkable green eyes that had reminded her of Jack's. *Which means they're coming for me. Coming to slice me up some more, no doubt.*

Covered by the noise they made as they tromped up the stairs, Fred spun around. She couldn't go down, and she certainly wasn't going back into the room in which she'd spent the last several, miserable hours of her life. That left only one direction.

She bypassed the floor she'd been on and continued heading up.

CHAPTER NINETEEN

"You're kidding me, right?" Lorne demanded as the imposter tried to commandeer his stage. "I mean, the suit's mine, so you've been into my office. But the rest of it . . . well, it's a good look for you, whoever you are. Unfortunately, it's a look I'm already using!"

"Can you believe this guy?" the phony Lorne demanded of the audience. "What kind of nerve must it take to pretend to be me in my own place? In front of my dearest friends and customers, no less?"

I've got to admit, Lorne thought, *he sounds just like me, and he looks just like me. If I didn't know I was me, I'd have a hard time telling us apart. Which has got to make it hard for everyone else, since they don't have that advantage.*

The fake Host crisscrossed the stage as he

talked, probably relying on the old shell game trick
of making the rubes forget where the pea was by
swapping out the shells faster than the eye could
follow. "Now, I've asked you people to put up with
a lot tonight," he said. "But this—this goes beyond
the ridiculous. For this faker to represent himself
as me, to try to pass himself off to you folks, is just
reprehensible."

"News flash, tall, handsome, and fraudulent,"
Lorne cut in angrily. "You're the one trying to pass."

The fake one raised his hands as if giving up.
"Can you believe it?" he asked the crowd. "Not
only does he have the temerity to claim he's me,
but then he accuses me of not being myself. Who
else would I be?" He suddenly whirled and
pointed a finger at Lorne. "You, sir, are surely a
shape-shifter in disguise!"

There was a murmur of agreement from the
crowd. Given the mood they were in, Lorne knew,
it wouldn't take much to set them off. *And if they
get too involved in trying to undo a nonexistent disguise, they could do some serious damage to my
real face. Which I'm kind of attached to.*

"Don't listen to that phony," Lorne urged the
onlookers. "I've been talking to you all night, wearing these same clothes. You've got to see that."

"Which just proves my point," the other one
said. "How many times have you seen me spend
that many hours in one outfit? I mean, come on.

They'd revoke my clotheshorse license for an infraction like that."

"Give me a break," Lorne said in disgust. "When would I have had time to change?"

"Like I can't do it during a number," the other pointed out. "You've all seen me intro an act in one ensemble, and then greet the next in something totally other. Now he's even casting aspersions on my quick-change capabilities, just to cover for his own inadequacy."

Lorne realized that the imposter was speaking with more eloquence than he was. Flustered by the appearance of the sham Lorne, he could barely stammer out responses to the phony one's charges, while the other one had at least the momentary advantage of surprise. So upset and taken aback was Lorne that he could barely form a complete thought, much less phrase one with any elegance at all. "Now listen," he said furiously. "Get off my stage and take off my face, you fake."

The other Lorne virtually ignored him, concentrating instead on playing to the crowd. "Would the real me ever take to talking like some *Sopranos* extra?" he asked. "If there ever was any doubt as to which one of us was legit, I think it's gone, don't you?"

"Yeah!" someone in the audience answered. "It's gotta be the Skander! Let's get him!"

Well, he's right about one thing, Lorne thought.

The phony me is undoubtedly the Skander. He knew he was exposed, so he decided to go for this stunt. If he can persuade them to try to tackle me, he can escape in the commotion when the protective spell knocks them on their various behinds.

So I can't let him get away with it.

"It is the Skander," Lorne agreed. "But it's him, not me. He's the imposter here."

The audience reacted, but Lorne didn't like the way they sounded. "How do we know that?" someone asked. "Prove it!" another yelled.

Prove it, Lorne thought. *That's the hard part, isn't it?* But something had to be done before the crowd took it upon themselves to work things out.

"I think it's already proven," the false Host said. "I look like me, I sound like me, and I think you know that."

The crowd surged toward the stage, agreement evident in their angry voices. Lorne guessed that he was only seconds away from raw anarchy and rage, mostly directed at him. He'd lost control of the audience, and he was about to suffer their wrath if he didn't do something quick.

"Okay, wait," Lorne shouted, holding his hands up toward them. "Just hold on. I can prove it."

The other one put his hands on his hips and glared at Lorne with mocking distaste. "Oh, you can, can you? I'd love to see how you prove something that isn't true."

"Watch and learn, fraudulent one," Lorne said. He scanned the audience and located Visssclorf, the Shrenli demon. "You, Visssclorf," he said. "I talked to you for a while. I didn't get a chance to read you, but promised to later. I know you have a personal issue facing you—I won't go into what it is, hence the use of the word *personal*. But you know what I mean. And I'd be willing to bet this joker, this counterfeit, over here"—he indicated the alternate Lorne, standing by watching with an expression of disbelief—"has no idea what your issue is, or even that you have an issue. Or what your name is, for that matter, since Skanders and Shrenlis don't tend to socialize."

"Of course I know Visssclorf," the fake Lorne insisted. "How could I not?"

Lorne ignored him, instead picking out Misty from the crowd. "I know your name, which I'm willing to wager this forgery over here doesn't. And I know what you think of Angel's friend Doyle— what did you call him, a hero? He doesn't know any of that, because he spent the night in his true, Skander form instead of talking to each of you like I did."

The other Lorne looked at him, a crestfallen expression washing across his face. The audience fell silent, but Lorne could still sense the barely checked fury that gripped the room. He couldn't blame them—on top of everything else they'd been through, to have someone try to fool them this way would be infuriating. "You didn't really think you could pull off the old bait-and-switch, did you?" he asked. But he knew the Skander almost had, and even though the crowd seemed to be on his side again, their loyalty was tenuous. It wouldn't take much to lose them again.

Pressing his temporary advantage, Lorne raised an accusatory finger toward his opponent, much the same way the other one had pointed at him just a few minutes before. "You don't know that Urf'dil and Mif'tal think Angel is as close to a savior as you'll find in this city! You don't know what Virg blames Angel for! All you know is that you're a fraud and a fake and you're wearing a form that isn't yours. Caritas is a sanctuary, Quort, but not for those who use its safety to hide from their crimes. By hiding, by pretending to be me, you've proven to us that you're involved with Fred's kidnapping." *The big finish! Those* Perry Mason *reruns were paying off after all.*

The sham Lorne backed away from the real one, ruby eyes wide with fear. "Just hold on," he said. "You haven't proved anything."

"You're a fake!" someone called from the floor.

Another voice rang out. "Get the phony!" Then the shouts came all at once, with one thing in common: They wanted blood. Lorne was starting to wonder if there was a way to take the Skander into custody and learn the truth about Fred, or if the mob would simply force him to go outside where they could tear him apart. He'd stirred them up, and now he needed to quiet them or he still wouldn't be any closer to finding her.

"Let's all just calm down, and—," he started to say, but then he stopped in the middle of his sentence. The fake him was undulating, kind of like a still pool of water after a stone has been tossed in. He was changing again, Lorne realized, giving up his handsome, though stolen, form, for something else. *Something nasty.*

When the shape-shifter stopped shifting, he was hideous and frightening looking. He was big and powerful looking, with muscular arms that ended in sharp, steely blades instead of hands or claws. His head was domed and massive, like half a basketball further split by a gaping mouth full of sharp teeth and a flicking, pointed tongue. Short legs gave him a low center of gravity, and a spiked, swishing tail promised danger for anyone who got too close. His yellow suit changed, too, and Lorne realized with some relief that he hadn't actually stolen the backup suit he had in his office but had merely duplicated it. It became a metallic-looking garment that draped across the demon's chest and hung down between his legs like a loincloth.

But the whole thing threw him for a loop, because this guy had actually shape-shifted, which

Skanders can't do. This wasn't a glamour, this was a sea change.

The crowd, which had been edging toward the stage, shrank back. This thing couldn't attack him, or anyone else, inside Caritas. But it could do a lot of property damage if it wanted to, and there would be no way to stop it.

"Listen," he tried, "we don't need to have a problem here. A bigger problem than we already do, I mean. I just want to know where Fred is and how to get her back. You are obviously involved, which means you can help us rescue her. If you don't, there's no way you're getting through this crowd in one piece."

"You don't think so?" Quort said. His voice no longer sounded like Lorne's, or even his own, Skander voice. As he changed shape, Lorne speculated, even his vocal cords must have altered. Now his voice was all clear, booming bass, dripping with menace. *Darth Vader with 'roid rage.* "You want to try me?"

Lorne definitely didn't. He was no coward, but neither was he suicidal. He couldn't really back down, though, and just let the Skander walk away.

"I'll try you," someone called from the floor. Lorne saw Virg, the Kailiff, break away from the crowd and step up onto the stage. Virg, who owed nothing to Angel and, in fact, hated the vampire detective because of his own brother's death.

Kailiffs were tough, no doubt about that. But could this one go up against the Skander alone? Lorne doubted it. *And I have to stop thinking of it as a Skander.* Virg seemed fine with the idea, though, and no one else from the crowd appeared willing to back him up.

"Be my guest, Kailiff," the shape-shifter said. His tail swished twice, fast and terrible with the long spikes at its tip. "Let's go."

"You tried to pin this on me," Virg growled. He closed on Quort, hands closed into gigantic fists, head down so his own spikes would come into play. Lorne backed to the edge of the stage, not wanting to be in the way when these two titans met. "That doesn't fly," Virg continued. "I can take the heat for things I do, but I won't have things I'm not part of put on me. Anyway, I think I know—"

Quort made the first move, cutting off the Kailiff in mid-sentence. He rushed the Kailiff with his sharp-edged arms outthrust and slashing. As soon as they neared each other, the sanctuary spell kicked in. There was a bright flash and a loud boom and a ripple in the air, like a stone cast into a pool. Both Virg and Quort were hurled to the ground by the spell's power, and bystanders scrambled to avoid Quort's vicious arms and tail.

"Oww," Virg complained, rising to his feet and clapping a hand over his haunches. "That hurt."

The not-Skander rose up and circled Virg menacingly. "Not half as much as I'm going to hurt you when we get outside," he warned. "You're not protected by any spell out there, and you're going down."

"No one's taking this outside," Lorne insisted. "Just calm down and let's figure this out like grown-ups."

But instead of giving up, Quort turned on Lorne, teeth snapping, spittle flying from his open maw, bladed arms clanging together like cymbals.

Perfect. Bystander to prey in one easy step.

Half-convinced, in spite of the spell, that the next sensation he felt would be Quort going Ginsu-happy on his innards, Lorne was surprised when, instead, he was touched from behind. Demons were rushing on the stage, crowding past him, putting themselves between him and Quort. He saw red skin, green scales, yellow fur, tentacles and arms, empty hands closed into fists and others clutching bottles or with claws extended.

Half the audience must be up here, he thought, amazed at this turn of events. In his mind's ear, which had always been more developed than his mind's eye, anyway, he heard Gloria Gaynor launching into her signature tune. *I will survive.*

And faced with the size of the crowd, Quort retreated. He moved to the back of the stage, away from Lorne, and from Virg, who was sitting up now, helped by some of the audience members. Quort wavered again, shifting, and when he was finished he'd taken his own shape, pale gray and vciny, with orange eyes in his broad, flat face. The garment had become a silken togalike thing.

"Hold him," Lorne ordered. "You can't hurt him, but you can hang on to him in order to prevent violence. He's got some explaining to do."

The demons who'd crowded onto the stage obeyed, clutching Quort with enough hands and claws to immobilize him. He fixed his orange-eyed stare on Lorne, who found himself repelled by the hatred that seemed to inhabit him. *What have I ever done to earn this kind of animosity?* he wondered.

"You'll get nothing from me, Host," Quort said, pronouncing the title with all the venom he could muster.

Virg faced Quort, fury in his eyes. "We'll see about that," he said. He sounded like he was still angry about Quort trying to blame him for his own crimes, and Lorne was glad it wasn't himself on the receiving end of the Kailiff's animosity. "You're no Skander at all, are you?"

Quort simply stared at him, open hostility in his eyes.

"What is he, then?" Lorne asked.

"It's safe enough," Virg said by way of an answer. "Get in close and take a big whiff."

Lorne wasn't sure of the wisdom of that—Skanders weren't known for their cleanliness, after all, and this one had, he remembered, poured on the Brut earlier in the evening. But since it wasn't a Skander, then . . . suddenly, it dawned on him. He did as the Kailiff suggested, already certain of what he would smell when he got there.

Cinnamon.

"You're a Kedigris," he said. "Not a Skander at all."

Quort shifted again, and the demons clutching him had to tighten their grips to keep hold. When he was done he was taller and leaner, with lavender skin and a hammerlike head. Luminous green eyes on stalks kept watch on the crowd, and his arms had been replaced by tentacles with saucer-sized suckers. As before, his clothes changed with him, becoming loose pants and a kind of tunic.

"Okay," he said, his voice higher now, almost youthful. "I'm a Kedigris. What about it?"

Lorne remembered something Virg had said earlier. "Virg, don't you usually work for Kedigris demons?"

"That's right," someone else said. "Kailiffs and Kedigris go way back."

"Yeah," Virg admitted after a moment's hesitation. "Usually. But I don't know this one."

"Would you?" Lorne asked. "I mean, normally?"

"I know a bunch of 'em, but not all. Usually, a

plan like this one, snatching someone, the Kedigris would just think it up and get some Kailiffs to pull it off. But this time, taking the girl— we didn't hear about it. I mean, any Kailiffs were approached about something like that, I'd have known. It didn't happen. The Kedigris are on their own with this one."

"How can you be so sure?" Lorne asked him.

"We know Angel's bad news," Virg said. "You know I got no love for that vamp. But I wouldn't mess with him like that. Takin' on Angel, that's just stupid. Good way to wake up dead."

"You might have a point there," Lorne agreed. "And the rest of the Kailiffs feel the same way?"

"Absolutely," Virg confirmed. "I mean, how many got better reason than me to dislike him? My brother was stupid to try his luck there. The rest of us aren't that dumb."

"What about it, Quort?" Lorne asked. "Or whatever your name is. Who's in this with you? And where's Fred?"

The Kedigris glared at Lorne, but kept his mouth shut. Around him, the demons holding him muttered, ready to pull him apart with their bare hands if he didn't cooperate. Lorne saw the potential there, and hoped it wouldn't come to that.

"Just hang on to him for a few minutes," he said. He'd had a flash of inspiration he wanted to share with Angel. "I have a phone call to make."

CHAPTER TWENTY

Angel steered with one hand as he fumbled with his cell phone, which had seemed to ring more tonight than in any normal month. He'd really have to thank Frank for the charger cord—and remember to keep his own in the car from now on.

"Angel, it's Lorne," the Host said when Angel answered. "Listen, Fred is here."

"What do you mean, 'there'?" Angel asked.

"In the building," Lorne clarified. "Or very close by."

"I'm already on my way," Angel said, shooting across three lanes of freeway and heading for an off-ramp. Horns blared behind him.

"Sounds like it," Lorne observed. "Try to make it in one piece, studmuffin, okay?"

"How do you know she's there?" Angel asked him.

"Because she was taken by Kedigris demons," Lorne replied.

"That's what Wes thinks too."

"Smart guy, that Wesley."

"But I still am not following you," Angel said. "Why would they keep her so close?"

"Are you paying attention?" Lorne demanded. "Kedigris demons. Mean, evil, crooked as they come. They shape-shift. They bite. They secrete deadly poison. They probably kick small puppies for fun. But they have no teleportation abilities. No portal usage. No dimension-hopping. If it's Kedigris we're looking for, they had to take Fred away by hand. Or tentacle, whatever. Point is, big guy, they had what, a few seconds to spirit her away while we were all distracted by fire and flying bullets? If they'd wandered down the sidewalk with her, or put her into a car, they'd have been seen. Which means they slipped her through the nearest doorway. Not back into Caritas, since we'd have spotted that, too. They could have taken her somewhere else since then, but with the police and firefighters all over the street most of the night, they would have run a risk of being seen. I'm willing to bet they're in one of the suites upstairs, either in this building or one of the neighboring ones."

"Okay, I'm almost there," Angel said. He tucked the phone between his cheek and shoulder, needing both hands to power the car through a tight right turn at high speed. Even so, his tires squealed loudly, and the rear end fishtailed a bit as he straightened out. "I'll see you in a minute."

He raised his head, letting the phone drop to the bench seat without bothering to hit the End button. He had slid into the oncoming traffic lane, and the oncoming traffic at this exact moment was a produce truck that would likely flatten his GTX if they should collide. Angel nudged the wheel, and his car swerved back into his own lane. As he shot past the truck, its driver leaned out the window and shouted a string of words that Angel didn't catch but that could only have been obscenities. *Can't blame the guy,* he thought. *I am driving like an idiot.*

But sunrise was less than an hour away, and he still hadn't found Fred. If Lorne was right, she was close by. Wesley, Gunn, and Cordelia's new Roshon friends seemed to think so too. But if they were wrong, then he'd be wasting that much more time on yet another dead end. And there wouldn't be time to spend on anything else. Either this paid off, or Angel made a one-way trip to Pershing Square.

He knew it was the wrong decision to make, knew it with every fiber of his being. He'd lived for hundreds of years, and in that time had saved uncounted lives. He had killed, too—too many years spent as a ruthless villain, roaming Earth, taking blood whenever he pleased. He was still trying to make up for that, he knew, and he'd never be able to. Every life was precious, and saving another person's—a hundred people's—couldn't bring back one that had been cut short.

No, he still had a lot of work to do, a lot of wrongs to try to make right. He wasn't ready to leave the planet, to shuffle off his immortal coil. *But it's Fred.* A true innocent, someone who had never hurt a flea. Someone whose brilliance could make incalculable contributions to the world one day, offsetting even the good that Angel might still do. And who knew how badly she'd been hurt already?

As he pulled up and parked illegally in front of Caritas, Angel knew his mind was made up. If this didn't pan out, he was going to the park. He would see the sun again, after all. *One last time.*

Lorne must have been waiting near the door, because he came out as soon as Angel climbed out of his car. "Thank goodness you're here, Angel," he said, sounding a little breathless.

Lorne pointed to Caritas. The club was downstairs from street level, in a building of eight stories. All the buildings on the block were as tall—big, for Los Angeles, but these had been built with earthquakes in mind and were fully stress-tested. They had been put here to make a point, which was that the threat of earthquakes didn't have to mean the city couldn't expand up when it had to, instead of always out, swallowing more and more land. The demonstration hadn't worked— while some developers did indeed build taller buildings, the city still sprawled across the land-scape like a cancer.

"We were right there," Lorne said, explaining himself. "When Fred was grabbed. So like I told you, whoever took her wouldn't have been able to haul her down the street without us seeing. There are only so many hiding places inside Caritas, and I've checked all of those. So that leaves us with two possibilities."

"Which are?" Angel asked.

"The Kedigris are working together with some other demons who do have teleportation powers," Lorne said. He waved at the two buildings, both the same height and apparently the same age, con-structed of brown stone like urban buildings every-where. They reminded Angel of New York City buildings, or even older ones he'd seen in the capi-tals of Europe, Prague and Budapest and Paris. "Or they simply took her through one of the nearby doorways. Above Caritas and in the build-ing next door, they're all offices. Hardly anyone around overnight, and by morning, when people started coming back in, they'd be gone. Between the two, there must be sixty suites she could be in."

How do we narrow it down more?" Angel wanted to know. "That's not good enough."

Before Lorne could answer, two vehicles roared down the street and pulled to the curb behind Angel's GTX. The first was a dark blue Z-28 that Angel thought looked very much like the car that had opened fire on the crowd outside Caritas, hours before. Behind it was Cordelia's black Jeep. When they stopped, Roshon demons emerged from the blue car, and Cordy, Wesley, and Gunn climbed down from the Jeep.

"I think your answer just arrived," Lorne said.

Cordelia rushed to Angel and wrapped her arms around him, giving him a squeeze. Gunn clapped him on the shoulder. "Ready to kick some butt?" he asked.

"As soon as we figure out whose, and where," Angel replied.

"Point the way," Wesley said to one of the furry blue Roshon demons. *They look like big Smurfs,* Angel observed offhandedly.

"Wes made a new friend," Cordelia explained. Angel had heard it already, from Wes, but he let her talk. "He says the Kedigris demons have a lair right around here."

"He thinks they have Fred there?" Angel asked.

"He didn't know anything about the Fred situation," she replied. "But we figured if we knocked them around a little, they'd tell us what we want to know."

Angel nodded and addressed the Roshon standing beside Wesley. "You and the Kedigris are enemies, right?"

"Right," the Roshon demon said.

"So if you know about this lair, why haven't you attacked it already?"

"Lair new," the Roshon answered. "One week, maybe two. Not important, not a mess of Kedigris. Just some."

"Which makes sense," Wesley pointed out. "If this had been a major Kedigris headquarters, Lorne would certainly have known about it."

"I'd like to think so," Lorne agreed, straightening his rumpled suit.

"But if it's brand-new, and there are only a handful of Kedigris here, it might have gone unnoticed. Long enough, at least, to put this plan into operation. They could have watched Caritas, known when we were all inside, and gone into action. From there it would have been easy enough to set the fire, bring in the shooters, and grab Fred. With the additional benefit that if we were able to trace the car, we'd blame their mortal enemies, the Roshons. Being shape-shifters, the Kedigris who did the shooting were disguised as Roshons, not realizing that we would be too busy ducking to get a clear look at them, anyway."

"Do you know which apartment?" Angel asked. "Or even which building?"

"Think that one," the Roshon said, indicating the one next to Caritas.

Angel checked with Lorne. "Offices, right?"

"Right. Low rent. High turnover. Nothing in the way of extras, just four walls and a window if you're lucky."

"We smash Kedigris now?" the Roshon wanted to know.

"Not just yet," Angel said.

"But Angel, the time . . . ," Wesley put in.

"I know," Angel assured him. He hadn't forgotten the urgency of the situation. "But if we just invade the place, they might kill Fred. They've been slicing her up, just to make a point. And they might have already seen us here. We need to move fast, but smart." He ushered everyone toward the stairwell that led down to Caritas. "We need to know more," he said. "Where's that Kedigris?"

Inside the club, the customers, now less anxious to hurry away since something interesting had taken place, had bound the Kedigris with electrical cords and linens from the kitchen. His tentacles were pinned to his sides, but his eye stalks still waggled on his oddly shaped head when Angel and the others approached him.

"I understand you're involved in the kidnapping of my friend," Angel said. His tone was calm and quiet. He'd save threatening for later—but not very much later.

The Kedigris just stared at him with his four green eyes.

"Well?" Angel demanded. "You pretty much have two choices: You can talk right now, or I can take you outside and you can die right now. I don't have time for any more options than that."

"I have nothing to say to you," the Kedigris said coldly. "You have hunted my kind for too long. You have slaughtered us without mercy. You will kill me, too, if you get the chance. If not now, then later. Maybe instead, this is the day you die."

"I've killed some Kedigris in my time," Angel admitted.

"Because they're evil!" Cordelia interjected.

"There's that," Angel agreed, still addressing the Kedigris. "And you seem to have a knack for getting involved in activities that threaten innocent people. I look out for innocent people, so that puts me in conflict with you."

"We get by, however we can," the Kedigris said. He didn't sound defensive or remorseful. He was just stating a fact. "People do the same. Everyone does."

"Some people do," Angel said. "We call them criminals. Most people make the effort to obey the laws, to look out for others, to live in society by the rules that keep everybody safe. Those who go outside the rules, I hunt down. Just like I hunt down Kedigris who prey on others."

"Kedigris are the mobsters of our community," a Brachen demon told Angel. Beneath her blue spikes she was quite attractive, he noticed. "With the help of Kailiffs, they rob, they murder, they pillage."

"But Virg, there," Lorne added, pointing to the Kailiff, "he helped us out with this one. He says this time the Kedigris were acting on their own, without involving Kailiffs."

"Kedigris, Roshons," Angel said wearily. "The two groups must account for eighty percent of the demon-against-demon crimes and violence in the city." He looked at Wesley's Roshon pal. "Not to mention a significant proportion of demon-against-human crimes. If you guys would just cut it out and learn to live peacefully, we'd all be better off."

"Or we stomp Kedigris," the Roshon said. "And be happy."

"We'll stomp some Kedigris," Angel said. "But first, I go in alone. I just need to know where I'm going."

"Oh . . . my . . . God . . ."

Angel looked at Cordelia. She was staring at the Kedigris. Her face had gone white, and as Angel watched, her eyes closed and her brow furrowed as if she were in pain.

"Cord?"

"He's the one," she said softly. "Or one like him, anyway. A Kedigris."

"What one?" Angel asked her.

She opened her eyes, blinked a couple of times, and rubbed her temples with her fingertips. "I had this vision," she said. "Back at the hotel. It wasn't helpful in the least, or so I thought at the time, anyway. I just saw people in trouble, all over the world. You'd be amazed at how many people's lives just suck at any given moment. But in one vision, I saw a demon with pale purple skin. It was threatening someone, but I couldn't see the victim, just the demon. There was something else about it, too, that I couldn't remember until just now. This is the demon—it was a Kedigris, I'm sure of it."

"Threatening Fred?" Angel asked. "What's the something else you remembered?"

"There was a door with a letter on it," she said. "I didn't think it was important, at the time. It could have been any demon, anywhere. But I remember the letter now. It was the letter H."

"Suite H." Angel squeezed Cordelia's hand. "Good job, Cordy. I'm going to go get Fred."

CHAPTER TWENTY-ONE

Fred took the stairs up as quietly as she could manage in her weakened state, knowing that the guys climbing up below her were making enough noise to mask small sounds and that speed was the most important thing just now. They were making no effort, as far as she could discern, to be quiet or discreet. Their feet landed heavily on the wooden steps, and they talked and laughed at full volume. She wondered if maybe the rest of the building was unoccupied—that would account for the fact that she heard no noises while she was handcuffed in that one room, and for the lack of concern these guys had for being discovered by neighbors now.

But when she reached the top, she was momentarily stumped. There were several doors, as there had been on the other levels. If there were people behind those doors, though, how would they react to someone banging on their door in the middle of the night? Or simply trying the knobs, hoping one of them was unlocked? In a minute or so, the guys downstairs would discover that she'd gotten away, and then she'd need someplace to hide, and quick. And what if everyone in the building was in league with them? Wouldn't she just be replacing one bad situation with another? Maybe worse? *I should have just stayed put and waited for Angel*, she thought. *He'll be here. He always comes through.*

Sound traveled well enough up the curving stairway for Fred to know when the men below had stopped their ascent and stood at the doorway to the room she'd escaped from. She estimated it had taken her about fifty seconds to climb the five flights of stairs to the top. It would certainly take less than that, from the time they opened the door, to determine that she was gone—there was no place in that room where she might have been able to hide, and only the one door to go through. So within a minute—two, tops—chances were there would be someone on this flight looking for her.

"Gone!" she heard the voice—definitely the man she'd exchanged a few words with, who called himself John—drift up from below. The tone was a mix of disbelief and rage. "Find her!" came next, and she knew the minute or two she had thought she had was being abbreviated.

She looked more carefully at the doors. Most of

them had the brass letters on them, but a couple—
she'd noticed this on the story below, as well—
were missing the letters. On one of the letter-less
doors, she could make out a faint faded spot where
a v had once been. The other door with no letter
had no such spot, and when she looked more
closely at it, there wasn't even a tiny hole where a
nail had held the letter on.

That's my door, then, she decided. No time to
second-guess herself. She rushed to it and gripped
the knob. It turned. She pulled the door open,
hoping she wasn't walking into a trap.

Another staircase rose up beyond the door, no
wider than the doorway and illuminated only by
the light that fell in from the hall. She pulled the
door shut behind her, as silently as she was able,
and went up the stairs three at a time. Another
door waited at the top, and if that was locked, then
she had just sealed herself in a dark, narrow death
trap.

When she reached the top, hearing commotion
below as the men shouted to each other and
stomped around the staircase, she felt for the
doorknob. There wasn't one. She felt a rush of
panic. Her cheeks flushed, her heart zoomed, and
she couldn't seem to catch her breath. Blindly, she
pawed at the door. It had looked like a door from
below, when a small bit of light glowed from the
sconce outside.

At last, her fingers touched a hook-and-eye latch. She managed to slip the hook free of the eye, and the door fell open a bit. Fred shoved it the rest of the way. Outside, she saw sky. She stepped out.

She found herself on a flat roof, covered with grainy roofing sheets. Air-conditioning units rose up here and there, and strange vents and pipes pointed toward the starry sky. She looked about quickly for something she could prop against the door to hold it closed, since she couldn't relatch it. A side panel of one of the air conditioners was hanging off, she noticed, held in place only by one screw that had worked itself mostly out. She went to it and turned the screw with her fingers, ignoring the way it bit into her skin. Then the panel was free, and she ran back to the door with it. She pushed the door into place and leaned the panel up against it. There was no way to wedge it so that the door wouldn't open, but at least if they just glanced up from below they wouldn't know that she'd gone through.

Now, though, she couldn't hear where they were or what they were doing. Looking for her, of that she had no doubt. But how close? How much time did she have? No clue. When they got here, though, it wouldn't take them long to find her. She could hunker down behind one of the air-conditioning units, but that wouldn't fool them for long. She had bought herself a few minutes, that was all.

• • •

Angel went into the office building next to the building that housed Caritas. A quick glance around told him that the units started at *A* through *C* on the ground floor. So H would be on three. He headed up the stairs, swift and silent, ready for action. Hearing some kind of disturbance upstairs, he sacrificed silence for more speed. He couldn't tell what had happened, but whatever it was couldn't be good for Fred.

As he reached the second floor, he saw two men coming down from above. At least, first glance, he thought they were men. But they fixed him with glowing green eyes. "Angel," one said, sounding surprised.

"Where's Fred?" Angel demanded.

The one who had spoken answered, even as he started to change. "We have no idea," he said. "But when we find her, you're both dead."

The transformation took only a second as the two came down the last couple of steps. Before they had looked like human men; now they were Kedigris demons. They approached Angel with reaching tentacles and gnashing teeth. As the one in Caritas had complained, though, he had killed Kedigris before and would have no problem doing so again.

Just have to watch out for those suckers, he thought. When a Kedigris was able to wrap its tentacles around an opponent and latch on with its suckers, small barbed hooks emerged from the center of the sucker and dug into the enemy's flesh. Poison traveled through a tiny vein in the barb. Paralysis was almost immediate; death came soon after.

Anticipating Kedigris, though, Angel had brought a Guatemalan machete with him from the car. As the Kedigris reached his level and charged him, he whipped it out from beneath his long coat and slashed upward at the nearest tentacle. The demon hissed and whipped his tentacle out of the way. Angel reversed course, slicing down, and this time caught a tip of a tentacle. It fell to the floor with a wet, meaty *thump*. The Kedigris it had belonged to screamed in pain.

Angel hadn't wanted that—he didn't know what was going on upstairs, and the idea that they had somehow misplaced Fred gave him hope. But he had hoped this fight could be kept quiet so he'd at least have the drop on whoever remained above. *So much for that plan.* He feinted with the machete, and when the wounded Kedigris reacted by withdrawing its tentacles, Angel slashed toward the other demon.

The Kedigris tentacles were more agile than he remembered, though. The demon stepped back, his tentacle dodging Angel's flashing blade, and then curled and darted forward, surrounding Angel's arm.

It caught him, coiled like a snake from the wrist up to his shoulder. The sword was useless now—he couldn't break free of the demon's grip, and couldn't use the machete at all. He let it fall to the floor.

Fortunately, he'd worn his leather duster. He felt the demon's suckers prodding at it, the barbed hooks trying to work their way into his flesh, but they were only biting at the leather. He still had a shirt on underneath that, and the hooks weren't reaching his skin.

Small comfort, really, he realized. Because the Kedigris still had hold of him, and the power in their tentacles was immense. The other tentacle snaked toward him, and there was still one more demon to go. A smell like cinnamon hung heavy in the air now.

He batted at the second tentacle with his left hand, and kicked at the Kedigris's torso. But he couldn't quite reach it, and the tentacle managed to evade his swings even as it worked nearer to him. *It's like trying to swat a snake,* he thought, *only the snake has had three triple-shot espressos and you're half-asleep.*

The second Kedigris, the one he'd already wounded, came forward more cautiously, but he seemed to be working his way around Angel to grab him from behind. Which, since the first one held him fast, was probably going to work, Angel realized. He had to come up with something, and it had to be soon.

Maybe they won't come up here, Fred told herself. *Maybe they don't know about the stairs to the roof, or they'll just glance up and see that the door is closed and assume that if it's closed, it must be latched from the inside. Maybe when they don't see me right off they'll figure I went down, not up, like any smart person would do, and they need to be looking for me on the streets and not on the rooftops.*

And maybe wishing won't make it so, and maybe caves are better than roofs because if you fall, at least you're already on the ground. She had a lot of maybes there, she knew, and not much certainty. The only certainty she could really come up with was that when they caught her—and they would catch her—they would kill her. No more waiting for Angel, no more offering her up for trade. She would have made herself into too much of a problem, and they would just finish her right there, right then.

She was crouched behind an air-conditioning unit, watching the door carefully. The unit was a big sheet metal box with ducts and pipes and grates, silent now. She had glanced inside the one she'd taken the panel off, wondering if there was enough open space in one for her to hide, but there wasn't. She thought it was possible, given time, that she'd be able to dismantle one enough to slip down into the ductwork and escape from the rooftop that way. But she'd need a screwdriver, at the very least—or time to fashion one from the steel at hand—and probably hours, to work. And if she had hours, certainly there were better ways down. A fire escape, maybe—she'd determined that there were none from this building, but seve-ral buildings adjoined and it was possible that one of the others had one. She hadn't gone looking yet because she figured she had only seconds until they came, and felt more comfortable hiding instead of standing and walking from roof to roof—or, worse yet, being caught near the edge of one.

So she hid, and she waited. And she was right, as it turned out—she had only been waiting for about a minute when the door jiggled and the sheet metal panel she'd propped against it fell with a sound like a rifle shot. The door flew open, and three men came through: the one called John, and two others she didn't recognize. They all had those bright green eyes, though. Which meant Jack was one of them, whatever they were. She had thought she'd met a nice guy in Caritas, and instead she'd just met some kind of evil demon who had been looking to use her to hurt Angel. *There are some nights it just doesn't pay to leave home.*

Most of them, actually.

She held her breath as they stepped out onto the roof. She watched from around the corner of the

289

unit, staying low, knowing that if she showed her head over the top they'd be far more likely to spot her. But the roofline was so busy with wires and ducts and big metal boxes, the outline of a quarter of a head would not call much attention to itself.

She hoped.

"She's here somewhere," John said. "That door didn't get propped by itself."

"Maybe she's already down," another one suggested.

"Only if she fell," John suggested. "We made sure the fire escapes were worthless when we moved in here. She tries to use one, she'll drop like a rock."

That's good to know, Fred thought. *Or is it? There are fire escapes, but the word "escape" doesn't really apply, in that case.*

"If she fell, we'd better not let Angel find out," the third guy said. "A dead girl doesn't do us much good as a hostage."

"We need her back," John agreed. "Alive is best. Spread out."

The way he said that reminded Fred of Moe, from the Three Stooges. Gunn loved those guys. She found out she could tolerate them, in small doses. The idea that the green-eyed fiend who was looking for her, hoping to use her to lure Angel into a death trap, could be Moe made her giggle nervously. *Better name for him than John, anyway.*

She let out only the tiniest squeak before shoving her knuckle between her teeth to silence herself, and she drew her head back so she was completely hidden by the metal box.

"What was that?" Moe demanded sharply.

You couldn't possibly have heard that, Fred thought. *It was the wind, a noise from the street, a bird . . .*

Footsteps crunched on the tarpaper roofing material. She huddled against the air conditioner, desperately willing herself invisible, squeezing her eyes shut as if that would make it so. A couple of moments later, the footsteps stopped. Fred didn't want to, but she opened her eyes.

One of them stood a dozen feet away, looking right at her. *Larry,* she decided. He looked enough like the other guy, Moe or John or whatever, to be his brother. *And like Jack,* she realized. They were all of a type.

"Got her," he said. Moe and the third guy, who could only be Curly, came to where he was.

"You're a troublemaker," Moe said. "I didn't think you would be. I thought you'd be cooperative, but look at you." His form started to shimmer as he talked, like she was looking at him through heat waves. Then she realized he was changing. All three of them were. Bodies elongating, arms slimming and stretching out, those green eyes protruded and extending on the ends of stalks. Their

291

heads changed shape, spreading at the tops and narrowing at the chins until they assumed a kind of *T* shape.

So they were demons all along, Fred realized with a gulp of horror. She had suspected it, but the confirmation made it worse. *It just figures, doesn't it?*

CHAPTER TWENTY-TWO

Angel's right arm was beginning to go numb, but he was guessing it was simply because of the Kedigris's tight coils. He hadn't felt the jab of any of its barbs piercing his skin yet, and he still managed to fend off its other tentacle with his left hand.

The other one was behind him now, though, and he couldn't dodge tentacles he couldn't see. Which meant that the time to do something about this had definitely come, and if he couldn't, then the whole night's efforts had been for nothing. The demons needn't have bothered kidnapping Fred at all; they only needed to sic two good fighters on Angel and he'd fold like a lightweight.

But I'm no lightweight, the vampire thought. He grabbed hold of the tentacle that held his right arm with his left hand. He had avoided that because he knew the creature would be able to snag his left with its other tentacle if he did it, but he decided there was no other choice, and hoped that it wouldn't be an issue long enough for the Kedigris to paralyze him. Once he had the fleshy limb in his grasp, he leaned toward the Kedigris briefly. The demon corrected his own balance to compensate for Angel's move, and as soon as he did, Angel lurched in the other direction, tugging with his left hand and his immobilized right arm.

The demon's other tentacle had just settled on Angel's left hand, and one of its suckers clamped down on the skin there when Angel's sudden motion yanked the thing off-balance, falling toward Angel. The vampire lashed out with one booted foot that slammed into the onrushing Kedigris, breaking an eye stalk and driving into the demon's skull. The Kedigris's legs folded at the knees and it went down, its tentacles losing their grip at the same time.

Angel spun around, knowing that the immediate threat now was from behind. The wounded Kedigris had been just about to clamp its suckers down on Angel's neck when the sudden flurry of action had interrupted its attack. Angel was able to dodge so the tentacles missed his neck, but one of them whipped across the front of his shirt, tearing it open. Angel slapped it aside. It struck back, whipping across Angel's face. The vampire blinked from the sudden sting and tried to catch the flailing limb. He missed, and the tentacle landed on his chest again, a sucker fastening itself there like a massive suction cup. Angel felt one of the barbs prick him. His left hand already felt numb from the barb he'd taken there. This one was much nearer his heart. He wondered how much time he'd have before the paralysis was total.

He grabbed on to the tentacle that was shooting poison into him and held it as he hurled himself to the floor. The Kedigris fell forward, too, losing his footing as Angel pulled on it. Angel had a reason for hitting the floor, though—that was where he'd left the machete. He scrabbled about with his right hand until he found it, then closed his fist around its handle. Rising to a kneeling position, he sliced up with the blade, severing the tentacle seven or eight inches from his chest. Disconnected from its owner, the end that stuck to him lost its grip after a second and fell away.

Now the Kedigris had two sliced-up tentacles, and it didn't seem very happy about it. It backed away from Angel, but Angel pursued, weaving a net of flashing steel in front of him with the machete. Every time the Kedigris raised a defensive tentacle, Angel slashed toward it. Finally, the Kedigris backed against a wall. It could go no farther. Angel expected it to plead for its life, or maybe to utter some defiant phrase. But it didn't— it just glared at Angel with those strange green eyes and waited for the end.

Angel obliged it. When that was done, he finished off the other one, the one he had stunned but which was starting to recover already.

When he started up the stairs again, Angel realized with concern that his left arm had gone completely numb.

Since they didn't actually have her surrounded, Fred pushed herself to her feet and started to slowly back away from the freaky-looking creatures. The one she now thought of as Moe laughed, showing his pointy little teeth as he did so. "You could just make this easy on all of us," he said, his voice deeper than it had been when he'd looked human. "You're not getting away, so why make me work harder than we have to, and make me angry at you? Anything that happens to you now is just your own fault."

"I didn't like you when you looked like a regular guy," Fred replied, continuing to put distance between herself and them. "If you think I'm just going to go quietly with you looking like a reject from some evil squid movie, you're just crazy. Not that there's anything wrong with that—I guess I've been a little bit crazy myself, from time to time. But not stupid crazy, not the kind that would look at you and say, 'Oh, sure, you look trustworthy, let's go back downstairs so you can lock me up again.'"

She felt something across the back of her ankle as she stepped backward, and glanced down to see that it was a guywire extending from a tall vent. She stepped gingerly over it, knowing that the demons needed only the slightest advantage and they'd be on her. As it was, they kept coming toward her as she retreated.

"I was just trying to save a little effort," Moe said calmly. "You can't blame me for that, can you? I don't really like heights, if you want to know the truth. I'd be much happier if we all just went back inside and talked about this like civilized beings."

"Don't count on it," Fred snapped, not believing a word of his entreaty. She whirled around and ran, high-stepping over low-lying cables and pipes, dodging the big A/C boxes. She could hear the scuffling footsteps that meant her pursuers were running too, and she already knew there was nowhere to go, that the fire escapes from up here were gone or sabotaged in some way. But she couldn't just let them take her. She couldn't let them use her against Angel again.

She reached a stone rise that marked the end of the building she had started out in, and even though the next building adjoined it, there was a moment of psychological terror at going from the familiar to the unknown. She stepped over the low wall and onto the next building. Hazarding a glance behind her, she saw that the demons were making steady progress toward her, even closing the gap a little.

Still, she kept running, thankful for the clear night that illuminated her way so well. The moon was low on the horizon, almost set, but she could still see the various obstacles, limned against the grayish backdrop of the tarpaper.

She passed onto the roof of yet another building, running a similar obstacle course here. But when she reached the low wall at the edge of this one, there was nowhere else to go.

Except down.

Eight stories. She looked down, felt a wave of vertigo, and clutched the edge of the low wall. Behind her, the demons came nearer. *I'm good at math,* she thought. *And the math here all points to only one option. If they take me back, they'll use me to get Angel to commit suicide. Or they'll kill me. Maybe both.*

But if I die before Angel can commit suicide, then he won't have to worry about giving up his life for mine. He'll never even have to answer the question. He'll be free to go on doing what he does best, helping people. And I . . . I can't even help myself, not really.

Angel has to live. Well, not live, but . . . continue. Which means I have to go over the side.

She hesitated there, looking back at Moe, Larry,

and Curly. They had stopped, about a dozen feet from her. They had, she guessed, figured out what she had in mind.

"Don't do it," Moe said. "Why bother? It won't save Angel. My way, at least you save yourself."

"Maybe Angel doesn't need saving," a voice said from behind the demons.

Angel had made his way to the roof after finding the empty suite H, redolent of human blood, and encountering no more Kedigris resistance on his climb up. Emerging from the door, he had spotted the demons chasing a bloodied Fred across the rooftops. He'd suspected they wanted to take her alive, so he'd hung back, not wanting to advertise his own presence until he absolutely had to. Alerting them to his proximity might have made them panic and kill Fred, and he didn't want that.

But when she stood at the edge of the roof ready to throw herself over to save him—he guessed—he knew he had to speak out. He'd closed the distance as much as he was able, and then he announced himself.

Fred let out a loud gasp, and the three Kedigris spun around as if they were mounted on the same lazy Susan. Angel didn't even give them a moment to react before he lunged toward them, machete out. He slammed into the nearest one, slashing with the sword's keen edge. Vampire and demon both went down in a pile, but he managed to sever the thing's tentacle near the shoulder. A fine mist of Kedigris blood, cinnamon-scented and hot, sprayed into his face as the demon writhed and screamed below him. He raised the blade and drove it into the demon's chest, and the Kedigris fell still.

A tentacle lashed out toward him from one of the remaining two demons, and Angel twisted his body, letting it land on his already paralyzed left arm. As soon as the sucker clamped down, Angel sliced with the sword. The demon wailed and drew back what was left of its tentacle.

Angel glanced over at Fred, still standing by the wall. "Get away from the edge, Fred," he warned.

She looked as paralyzed as he was beginning to feel, but when she saw the third Kedigris start toward her, she obeyed. *And keep away from the demon*, Angel wanted to add, but it looked as if she had already figured that part out. She made a roundabout loop, away from the building's edge and away from the demon. When he made a grab for her, she threw herself down flat against the roof and wrapped her arms tightly around a pipe.

Angel knew he had to wrap this fight up before the poison spread any further, or before the Kedigris decided to poison her. Totally paralyzed, he'd be no good to Fred, himself, or anybody else. They'd be able to simply leave him on the rooftop until the sun finished him off. The Kedigris was keeping its distance now, though, wary of the machete Angel wielded.

So Angel didn't bother trying to close with it. Instead, he hurled the machete straight for the creature's breast. It flew end over end but straightened out and sailed true, driving itself deep into the Kedigris's heart. Its tentacles flailed for a moment as it collapsed, and then stopped.

The last Kedigris was almost to Fred. "Come to me, Fred," the creature pleaded. "I'll take care of you."

"Don't do it, Fred," Angel warned her.

"I have . . . no intention of . . . doing it," Fred managed, still clutching the pipe with what appeared to be every ounce of strength she had. Even if the demon got its tentacles around her, Angel felt certain it would have a hard time prying her loose from her anchor. "He . . . cut me! I think he's the boss one," she continued. "He talks like it, anyway."

"Face it, Kedigris, your plan's a bust," Angel said.

"His name's . . . Moe," Fred announced.

"No, it—Moe?" the Kedigris said, sounding surprised.

"Where you're going, names don't matter," Angel assured the demon. He closed on it. Its tentacles bobbed as if it stood in heavy surf, and its eyes rotated swiftly on their stalks, like it expected attacks from every side. *Or reinforcements,* Angel realized. *It's not getting either one, though. Just me.*

The vampire made his move.

"You're walking funny, Angel," Fred said as they descended the staircase inside the building. "Did you get hurt?"

"Paralyzing agent in their tentacles," Angel explained. "Took some in my left arm, and my chest. It's spreading."

"Oh, no!" Worry clouded her pretty face. "Is there an antidote?"

Angel tossed her a smile he hoped was carefree, but he wasn't sure that the left side of his face was still working, so it might have been more like scary. "I sure hope so."

"I'll figure one out if I have to," she said. "It's the least I can do. Thank you, Angel. I mean, I knew you'd come for me, but I didn't want to just sit around and expect to be rescued, you know? I figured if there was something I could do for myself, then I should go for it."

"You did the right thing," Angel assured her. "You were perfect."

She looked at him, face beaming now. She was small, he understood, but her bravery was without limits. *I thought I had to keep her safe. I was stupid. All I have to do for Fred is what I've been doing—let her know she's in a place where she's appreciated and accepted. I got her out of her cave, I brought her here, now she just needs to know that here is a good place to be. She can do the rest.*

"I hope you're not sorry you came out with us," he said.

"I am, a little. Okay, a lot. I mean, I feel safe in the hotel, you know? But the world's full of not very nice creatures, just like Pylea was."

"There are good ones too," Angel said, trying to find persuasive words. He knew it would be hard to prove it to her, after what she'd been through tonight. "We should try it again, soon. I promise a more relaxing evening than this one turned out to be."

She shared a tiny glimmer of a smile. "Okay, if you promise."

By the time they'd reached the ground floor, Fred had put an arm around Angel's ribs and was helping him walk. Outside, a group waited for them—Cordelia, Wesley and Gunn, Lorne, a bunch of those fuzzy blue Roshon demons, and some of the audience he remembered seeing in the club. That had just been earlier tonight—*last night, now*, he realized, since the sun was almost up—but it seemed like months ago.

"Angel's been poisoned by one of those things!" Fred shouted. "He needs an antidote!"

"Kedigris goop?" one of the Roshons asked. "Hang on." The demon walked toward a blue car parked nearby.

"A few more Kedigris came around," Lorne told Angel. "The Roshons sure seem to enjoy whaling on them."

"It's an acquired taste," Angel replied, attempting another smile. "I'm getting to be fond of it myself."

"They're disappointed, actually, that there weren't more," Wesley added. "I don't imagine you left them any in there?"

Angel shook his head.

"He was like a one-man demon-whomping machine," Fred said enthusiastically. "You should have seen him! He killed all three Stooges!" She let go of Angel to demonstrate his Kedigris-whomping technique, and Angel stumbled as his left leg gave out beneath him.

"Don't let go," he said weakly. Fred gave a little squeak and grabbed him again, exerting all the strength she had to hold him up. Wes and Gunn dashed forward and helped support him.

"Sorry," she said, her voice tiny.

The Roshon returned with a capped flask. He unscrewed the lid and handed it to Angel, putting it carefully in his right hand. "You drink," the demon said. "All."

Angel took a whiff. It smelled like rotgut, but

worse—much worse, since the Roshon who had given it to him was kind of on the pungent side himself, and this stuff completely masked the smell of him. But Angel knew he needed to counteract the poison—and then get inside someplace, quickly, before the sun rose. *Not a lot of options,* he thought. He tilted his head back and poured the stuff down his throat, trying not to taste it. When some splashed against his tongue, he almost gagged on it, but he kept it down. "Man," he said, handing back the empty flask. "I've had some bad drinks in my time, but nothing like that."

"Angel, you live on pig's blood," Cordelia pointed out. "How bad can it be?"

"You don't want to know," he wheezed. He felt a warm flush, though, spreading from his throat and belly. He hoped that meant it was working, and not just that he was going to die drunk, victim of a Roshon's practical joke. He tried to lift his left arm and to his surprise was able to elevate it a couple of inches. He closed the fingers of his left hand slowly and with great effort. "Stuff works fast," he said.

"Good thing," Cordelia told him. "Because that half-paralyzed face thing? Doesn't work on you. Mona Lisa you're not."

As the crowd in front of Caritas dispersed—customers heading home to get some needed rest, Roshon demons to go plot the next night's action against their Kedigris foes—Lorne ushered Angel and crew inside. The sun's first rays were just lightening the eastern sky, and Caritas was dark and inviting.

Which is really kind of the whole point of the place, Angel realized. *It's the safe place.*

Not the only one. Not by a long shot. Safety can be wherever friends and family are.

Just one of the best.

JEFF MARIOTTE

Jeff Mariotte is the author of several Angel novels, including *Haunted* and *Stranger to the Sun*, as well as, with Nancy Holder, the Buffy/Angel crossover trilogy Unseen and the Angel novel *Endangered Species*. He's published several other books, and more comic books than he has time to count, including the multiple-award-nominated horror/Western series Desperados. With his wife, Maryelizabeth Hart, and partner, Terry Gilman, he co-owns Mysterious Galaxy, a bookstore specializing in science fiction, fantasy, mystery, and horror. He lives in San Diego, California, with his family and pets, in a home filled with books, music, toys, and other examples of American pop culture. More about him can be gleaned from www.jeffmariotte.com.

**As many as one in three
Americans with HIV...
DO NOT KNOW IT.**

**More than half of those
who will get HIV this year...
ARE UNDER 25.**

**HIV is preventable.
You can help fight AIDS.
Get informed. Get the facts.**

**www.knowhivaids.org
1-866-344-KNOW**

When I was six months old, I dropped from the sky—the lone survivor of a deadly Japanese plane crash. The newspapers named me Heaven. I was adopted by a wealthy family in Tokyo, pampered, and protected. For nineteen years, I thought I was lucky.
I'm learning how wrong I was.

I've lost the person I love most.
I've begun to uncover the truth about my family.
Now I'm being hunted. I must fight back, or die.
The old Heaven is gone.

I AM SAMURAI GIRL.

Aaron Corbet isn't a bad kid—he's just a little different.

On the eve of his eighteenth birthday, Aaron is
dreaming of a darkly violent landscape. He can hear
the sounds of weapons clanging, the screams of the
stricken, and another sound that he cannot quite
decipher. But as he gazes upward to the sky, he
suddenly understands. It is the sound of great wings
beating the air unmercifully as hundreds of armored
warriors descend on the battlefield.

The flapping of angels' wings.

Orphaned since birth, Aaron is suddenly discovering
newfound—and sometimes supernatural—talents. But
not until he is approached by two men does he learn
the truth about his destiny—and his own role as a
liaison between angels, mortals, and Powers both
good and evil—some of whom are bent on his own
destruction....

the
fallen

a new series by Thomas E. Sniegoski

Book One available March 2003

From Simon Pulse

Published by Simon & Schuster

. . . A GIRL BORN
WITHOUT THE FEAR GENE

FEARLESS™

A SERIES BY
FRANCINE PASCAL

PUBLISHED BY SIMON & SCHUSTER